Miracle
on
Mall Drive

PAOLINA MILANA

Cover Design by 100Covers.com
Interior Design by FormattedBooks.com

First paperback edition November 2020.

ISBN 978-1-7354364-1-8 (Paperback)
ISBN 978-1-7354364-8-7 (Ebook)

www.madnesstomagic.com/books

This book is dedicated to those in my life who have helped me learn such incredible lessons about courage, judgement, compassion, connections, understanding, forgiveness, and love.

"If you look for it, I've got a sneaky feeling you'll find that love actually is all around."

—*Love Actually*

ACKNOWLEDGEMENTS

This story has been asking to be told for decades. And the characters in these pages finally banded together, a choir of voices in my head, refusing to be ignored until I wrote them down. Throughout the whole creative process, I had my doubts. *What in the world was I doing writing this Christmas Eve story?* One day on a hike in the canyon near my Californian home, a place where I talk to God, I asked Him if this story was what I was meant to be doing. On my drive home, His answer came to me on a license plate belonging to a car that nudged itself in front of mine. It said: XMAS EVE. You may think that was coincidental—or even a bit crazy. But I know it's not. It's the magic that happens to me—and to all of us—when we take time to listen and to see and to read the signs that life and the powerful forces from beyond give to us.

This book would not be what it is without a team of powerful forces right here on Earth that came to help: Author and mentor Jennie Nash, along with her Author Accelerator editors Michelle Hazen and Sheila Athens; Samantha Clements who served as pied piper in helping to align this story's ensemble of characters; and to Kendra Muntz who went above and beyond in her editing, asking the right questions, filling in the gaps, and adding such richness and depth to this story that I am forever grateful.

CHAPTER ONE

BETTY & LEO

Old School, New School

It took a minute for Betty to realize the car came to a stop. She looked up from her vintage Dooney & Bourke handbag, and stared out the window, still mindlessly playing with the wispy strings on her bag's fraying red handles. It had seen better days; then again, so had she.

The morning sun just broke through the darkness. Ghostlike halos outlined the skeletons of dormant oaks and maples that dotted the parking lot. Throngs of bundled-up shoppers—some cheerily chatting, others impatiently hopping around to stay warm—stood in lines that wrapped around the mall's main entrance. Braving the icy wind gusts of yet another Chicago winter, it seemed as if everyone for miles around had decided *this* was the place to be on the last shopping day before Christmas—weather and wait time be damned.

The Uber driver's expressive eyes tried connecting with hers in the rearview mirror. "I gotta say, Christmas Eve crowds scare me. Why anybody with half a brain would come within a hundred feet of this here Maplefield Mall today when you got Amazon delivering right to your door—I just don't get it. Look at 'em… They're all crazy!"

Betty's eyes met his with a twinkle. "Well, I'm perhaps the craziest one of them all." She gathered up her bag and coat, opened her door, and stepped out. "For the past forty years, I've been the mall Manager here, and *this* is my favorite day of the year. It's so full of miracles. I still believe."

"Merry Christmas!" the driver grinned.

He waved as he drove away, his license plate UBERJOE gradually becoming unreadable in the distance. Pulling out her phone, she tapped on the screen to give him a very generous tip and review: "Five stars for you, Joe."

She straightened the multicolored tweed jacket of her favorite Chanel suit and stopped to breathe in the scents of Christmas anticipation—sweet cinnamon spiced with seasonal pines. She swore she could smell a hint of snow in the air, too, but perhaps that was just wishful thinking. She desperately wanted this Christmas to be a white one. After all, it was going to be the last holiday season she worked here at this magical mall.

"Spoiler alert, folks," a booming baritone voice called out to the crowd. "It's Christmas Eve. December 24. The day before Christmas. I know, I know: *HUGE* surprise."

Betty rolled her eyes. She knew that voice all too well. Every time she heard it, she somehow expected it to be coming from something other than the walking stick of a man who had been by her side—at least professionally—for nearly her entire career. No matter the season, she found his silver head of hair and carefully groomed matching beard oddly comforting. It was silly of her, but his appearance made Betty feel as if she had her own private Santa Claus all year round—even if this Santa might be a skinnier, slightly less jolly version. She quickly made her way to Leo who stood holding two Venti cups from Starbucks. She gave him a mocking look of disapproval.

"What?" Leo blinked his crystal blue eyes, feigning innocence. "Every year has the same number of days in it, and yet, every year, the last-minute pileup on Christmas Eve gets worse."

"Well, what about leap years?" Betty said and then laughed. "Oh, never mind. Merry Christmas to you, Leo, and please tell me that one of those coffees is for me."

Leo bowed, as if she were his queen and he her loyal subject, and handed her a cup. "One peppermint mocha for m'lady. And please don't tell me this is some surprise to you, too. I've been bringing you these holiday drink concoctions for decades, almost since the first day we met."

"Yes, you have. Have I ever thanked you?" Betty laughed again and took a sip. Just one taste of her special, minty chocolate beverage automatically conjured visions of twinkling lights and sleighs.

"Never."

"As the mall's General Counsel, you should remind me to do that. Would you please?"

"I'll have my legal team check into the statute of limitations on gratitude in my spare time." Leo arched one eyebrow and turned up the right corner of his lip in response. Pivoting, he followed her to the building's entrance.

Fumbling with her keys, Betty nodded to Elmer, the young security guard, who stood behind the glass doors she was trying to unlock. He quickly moved forward with his own jangling keys and opened the door for her. With a look of gratitude, slipping her keys back into her bag, she heard Leo slurp his coffee and give out a sigh of his own. His familiar habit always made her smile.

"Enjoying your drink, Leo?"

"You know it. Those frou-frou drinks can't hold a candle to old school mud."

She already knew his cup contained straight-up black coffee. Leo never touched the fancy handcrafted stuff. He was a basic black coffee kind of guy, and it was one of the many reasons she appreciated him.

The pair squeezed through the narrow entryway, careful not to swing the door open any further than need be, lest some seasonal shopper would attempt to get a jump on the crowds and slip through the door along with them. Once across the threshold, Elmer locked the doors behind them. A soft, low groan emitted from the disappointed crowds still waiting in the chilly weather outside.

Betty chuckled as they made it to the quiet safety of the massive, empty mall. "Thank you, Elmer. With all those keys on your ring, you always make me feel as if I'm being granted entry through the Pearly Gates."

Betty couldn't remember exactly when Elmer started working at the mall, but she knew it was more than just a few years ago. She had grown fond of his boyish charm, and he repeatedly impressed her with his work ethic. He was the kind of young man who, without a doubt, made his mom proud. Elmer reported for duty day after day, year after year, but Betty still didn't know him well enough to determine if he worked for the paycheck or for the girls. He had made it into college, that much she remembered him saying recently. He sure did love to strut around and show off his uniform, that much she could see, but beyond that, she knew little else about him. Betty smiled at the young man, wishing she could see his emerald green eyes more often, but the mirrored aviators he wore both day and night were part of his whole fashion statement, and it was one she didn't feel the need to disrupt.

"Just doing my job, Ms. Bryant. And nobody would mistake *me* for a saint," Elmer chuckled respectfully, lowering his head and peering over the top of his glasses. "Merry Christmas to you, and also to you, Mr. Sawyer."

Betty and Leo made their way across the main lobby which was festively decorated in a Winter Wonderland theme. Betty loved it, and she couldn't help but smile as she surveyed the snow-blanketed pathways leading to ice castles, gingerbread cottages, elf workshops, and, of course, Santa's golden chair where he and the elves would hear the wishes of so many awestruck children. Silver and ruby ornaments, glittering garlands, and shiny bows laced a forest full of spruce, pine, and fir trees. Large and small, the trees looked so real. Even the snow, created by a flocking effect, still fooled her into believing it had freshly fallen from the sky.

Several mall workers were rearranging and putting the final touches on this winter scene before the mall opened to the masses. As if playing scales on a piano, each staffer called out to them with "Good Morning!" and "Merry Christmas!" as they walked by. Betty nodded, smiled, and waved in response.

What would happen to all of them when they shut down the mall?

Betty didn't want to think about it, especially not today. It was Christmas Eve, and this was one she wanted to remember with nothing but smiles and good cheer, even if her heart was breaking.

She shook off any trace of melancholy, sipped her peppermint drink, and playfully chastised Leo: "You know I'm from the same 'old' school as you. Although I prefer the word 'seasoned.' I'm still hoping for a miracle, Leo. One day, you'll surprise both of us by trying one of these other-than-old-school coffee flavors. They're really quite yummy. I bet they'd do wonders to soften the Scrooge in you."

"Scrooge? Me?" Leo flashed his crooked smile.

Betty widened her already big brown eyes and playfully fluttered her lashes. When Leo looked at her in that way, she felt like a little kid again—ready for anything. No matter what the weather—rain or shine—and no matter the circumstances —feast or famine—Leo brought a fairy-tale kind of joy to her day. What would her days be like without him?

Turning her attention back to business, she stepped onto the escalator with Leo close behind her. As they slowly ascended to the second-floor executive offices, Betty surveyed her surroundings, taking it all in for what she feared might be the last time. A look of longing swept over Betty's face as she dwelled on the future of the mall and her own professional fate.

Betty's thoughts came to an abrupt halt as she felt an unexpected jolt in the middle of the escalator ride, causing her to lose her footing and fall back into Leo's tall frame.

"Betty, you okay?" Leo asked, balancing himself—and his coffee—with one hand gripped onto the rail and his other hand supporting Betty's bent elbow, making sure she remained upright. The two exchanged the briefest of glances, sharing more than one emotion without speaking a single word.

Betty momentarily lost herself in his eyes, wishing she could tell him what she felt for him. But that would be strictly unprofessional. She shook her head, steadied herself, and then held up her mocha, smiling as she joked, "Phew. Not a drop spilled."

As they distanced themselves and took their first steps up the now-disabled escalator, a high-pitched, sing-song voice rang out: "I am *sooooo* sorry."

"Nothing to be sorry about, Ms. Timbers," Leo said, using his soothing voice. "It's not as if you stopped the blasted thing on purpose."

With an iPad and stylus pen in hand, the childlike voice continued, "Oh, but that's just it. I *did* stop it on purpose. As soon as I realized it had been accidentally left running all night."

On the landing, Betty stopped with a quizzical look as her gaze set on the young woman she knew was here to facilitate the mall's closing. And if, by some miracle, they did manage to keep the place open, she figured she was looking at her successor. Color-blocked from head to toe, the 25-year old's exterior projected a level of "Girl Boss" confidence today's professional millennials wielded like a medieval suit of armor. Betty knew this attitude well, thinking back to when she was so young and felt so much in charge. "Darci, why would you stop the escalator, especially while we were on it?"

"The mall doesn't open for another thirty minutes," Darci replied, glancing at her rose gold Apple Watch. "Escalators are one of our biggest energy zappers."

"You've got to be kidding..." Leo scoffed.

Darci's eyes widened. "No, I'm not. Our average unit has a 7.5 horsepower motor and runs 16 hours each day, seven days a week. That's 10,000 kilowatt-hours of electricity in a year. Do you realize how much that adds up to in terms of our budget?"

Betty suppressed the urge to burst out laughing at the earnestness before her. Darci was so young, so ambitious. She was smart for sure but in all her book learning and data-driven analytics, she somehow missed the chapter on common sense.

"I understand. Tell me, Darci, had Leo and I rolled head-over-heels down the escalator when it stopped, aside from the dry-cleaning bill to get peppermint mocha out of my suit, what other costs might we have incurred?"

Darci nervously shifted her weight from one foot to the other, tapping her stylus against her hip. She was just as aware as Betty of the newly minted crack in her armor. "I didn't realize you and Leo—or anybody—was on it, Ms. Bryant. I'm sorry." The apology didn't sound terribly sincere, but it was an effort nonetheless.

Leo shook his head, this time raising both eyebrows. He knew he should officially do something about Darci. After all, this wasn't the first time her short-sightedness had put people in harm's way and the mall in jeopardy. But given that she was hand-picked to work here by the real estate tycoon who owned this and many other shopping centers, he knew his efforts would be futile.

"No harm done," Betty said, a touch of benevolence in her smile. She had crossed swords with Darci before.

Repositioning her winter coat on her arm, Betty took a deep breath and led the way down the corridor as Leo and Darci trailed behind.

"Mr. Wiggins called to say he's flying in from Dallas this afternoon," Darci said. She hesitated, expecting a reaction. When she didn't get one, she continued. "He said he'd be here in time to wish you bon voyage."

"You mean, he'll get here in time to give her a kick out the door no matter what his General Counsel advises," Leo mumbled under his breath but loud enough for everyone to hear.

Betty chimed in, robotically responding, "Oh. Yes, Darci, how thoughtful." She turned the corner, finally arriving at the office that she had called home for so very long. Standing in the doorway, she took another sip of her mocha to subdue the sigh that threatened to spill out from her chest. Rows and rows of stacked moving boxes leaned up against one wall like giant-sized Jenga blocks, just waiting to fall. All of her years of overseeing the mall were now filed away, her memories packed up and seemingly littering the floor. The antique desk's richly polished mahogany top peeked out from the mound of beautifully wrapped gifts that sat atop it, all of them patiently waiting to be opened.

"What's this?" Betty took a few steps closer to admire a potted cactus sitting on her desk. She hung up her coat on the free-standing wooden rack in the corner, all the while keeping her eyes on the mystery plant. It seemed a bit out of place growing in a red-and-white candy-cane-striped planter. Do a cactus and Christmas candy belong together?

"That's a Christmas cactus," Darci answered her unspoken question.

"Really? I don't think I've ever heard of it." Betty's eyes twinkled. "So lovely. Thank you, Darci."

"Oh, no, it's not from me. I saw it earlier sitting on your desk and Googled it. It said it's only supposed to bloom on Christmas Day." Darci shrugged.

"Hmmm. I don't see a card…" Betty said upon further investigation. "You didn't see who left it?"

Darci shook her head. "I'm afraid not."

"Leo?"

"Not me. I gave the gift of coffee."

Betty set her bag on the chair, bending down ever so slightly so as not to drop it. Given its aging state, she knew its days were numbered. It was then that she saw *him,* nestled into the folds of the cactus, peeking out between its shiny leaves.

"Oh, too funny! Elf on the Shelf." She said, feeling the joy flow up through her from her belly. "Here you are again." She turned with a grin to eye Darci and Leo. "And *still* no one is taking responsibility for your daily spying on me this entire month?" She bent down to whisper in the elf's ear, "Has there been any 'undesirable behavior' reported back to the big boss? Can you tell me who's on the naughty list and who's on the nice list this year?"

Darci lowered her head, avoiding Betty's glare.

CHAPTER TWO

PASTOR MAX & KARINA

The More Things Change...

"**T**OO MUCH VOLUME, PEOPLE!" Pastor Max yelled with a smile, trying very hard to slightly lower the near-deafening decibel level of the fifty excited foster kids currently under his care. Being trapped in a giant bus for a three-hour road trip resulted in every one of them becoming a bit spastic, squirming all about to get out of their seats, exit the bus, and race one another into the mall. Shaking his head at the futility of his attempts to silence them while loosening the white collar that never quite comfortably rested against his black skin, he wondered again what had possessed him so many years back to take up the ministry. And on top of that, he took on organizing the annual outing for needy kids to go to the mall. Surely, it had been easier for him to quiet down a bunch of motor mouths—a term he called people who went on and on about nothing, just like the guys he met during the three years he spent in prison for stealing cars.

Carjacking was his ticket to becoming a gang member during his younger years. Growing up without a family or home to call his own, Max mistakenly believed that joining the gang would give him a sense of belonging to a group of people who would care for him and always have his back. Boy, had he been wrong.

When a "simple" car theft accidentally included snatching a baby in a car seat sleeping in the back, he immediately pulled over and turned himself in to the police. At that moment, he realized he was on a very wrong path, both literally and figuratively. That was the last time he ever saw his gang— his "family"— and the first and last time he saw the inside of a police car. After a holding cell, a court case, and, ultimately, a prison sentence, he did time for grand theft auto and attempted kidnapping.

Pastor Max saw so much of his younger self in these kids on the bus: From the too-cool-for-school bullies who only acted out because they themselves were getting abused at home, to the shy and quiet wallflowers who blended in and hoped to disappear, their wounds silently festering inside, until one day they snapped, destroying themselves and anyone else who got in their way. Definitely opposite ends of the spectrum, but at every kid's core, no matter how they behaved, he believed the common denominator to turning their lives around was simple: Love. At the end of the day, love is what they needed—just like what he needed and eventually got when he was their age.

As Pastor Max made his way down the center aisle from the front of the bus to the back, he set out his ground rules for what he expected of these kids while at the mall. Doing his best impression of a drill sergeant addressing new cadets, emphasizing certain words for effect, he shouted out:

"Repeat after me: I EARNED my seat on this bus."

The teens, ranging in age from 13 to 17 and from all backgrounds and ethnicities, responded weakly, "I earned—"

"Oh, no…" Pastor Max stopped them before they even started. "That's all ya got? I heard you talking louder to each other when you were trying to whisper. This ain't gonna do at all. Maybe you all don't think you EARNED this day of FREE gifts and a great lunch and lots of treats and shopping for the people on your holiday lists…?"

The grumblings grew louder as the kids objected.

"Okay, then, let me hear you this time. I EARNED my seat on this bus."

In a thunderous response so loud Pastor Max couldn't help but smile, the kids shouted back in unison.

"I EARNED my seat on this bus," they cheered.

"Again," Pastor Max said as he raised his hands facing palms-up to the heavens, almost as if conducting an orchestra and calling for a crescendo. "That's it…. Repeat after me: I AM worthy."

"I AM worthy," they echoed.

Pastor Max now spun around doing his own kind of dance from where he stood in the very center of the bus.

"I AM grateful."

No child remained seated. As they repeated the words, Pastor Max looked at everyone's smiles and continued.

"Okay, now, last one, and this one's SO IMPORTANT. Listen to the whole thing, alright? You ready now?"

"I AM a GUEST of the mall today, and I WILL be a MODEL for all others who see, hear, and interact with me."

Suddenly, instead of the thunderous affirmational response, a high-pitched voice pierced the air, screaming the words, "BACK OFF!"

Pastor Max sighed and dropped his arms, recognizing the voice and its ever-present sharpness of tone. It was Karina. His most challenging problem to solve.

At once, the entire busload of kids turned toward the back of the bus, jockeying for the best view of what was no doubt a fight.

"I said, back off or somebody's gonna get hurt." Karina's warning boomeranged from ear to ear and brought everyone on the bus to attention.

Although Karina was Max's problem child, if he was truly honest with himself, she also was his favorite. She had such potential. She was so smart and so caring…well, when nobody was looking.

At only 14 years old, Karina had already lived a life that few could imagine, let alone one that anyone would wish on their worst enemy. Since birth, she had endured terrible abuse at the hands of both her parents. They both ended up in prison—and she in foster care—but periodically, her parents would be released, and Karina returned to live with them. Heavy bruises and broken bones led to hospital visit after hospital visit until the court finally terminated her parents' legal rights when Karina was 8 years old. Though the decision to remove her from the cruelty of her parents likely saved her life, it also introduced a whole new set of obstacles: Karina's countless placements in different foster homes escalated her bad behavior, and, perhaps worst of all, developed a sense of hopelessness. Max knew her backstory and was concerned for her future. Losing a sense of belonging and faith in what was good and possible in life were feelings that Max understood far too well.

Had it not been for some random stranger from the Legal Aid office who took on his case pro bono, and, by the grace of God, got him a reduced sentence and placement in a minimum-security facility, who knows where Max would be today? Max frequently remembered how scared he was throughout it all and how surprised he was that this man, this *lawyer,* who didn't know him from the man in the moon wanted to help him for no foreseeable reason. Back then, he couldn't believe that anyone did anything with zero expectations of getting something back in return. Yet, somehow, that's what this angel-lawyer did. While he could never repay the debt in full, Max could offer the lawyer—and himself— one thing: The promise of turning his own life around. Helping kids like Karina was part of his promise.

In a flash, Max maneuvered his linebacker-like frame down the aisle. Acting like Moses, he managed to part the sea of kids who were now standing in his way to get a better look at the fight breaking out in the back of the bus. From what he could see, no real punches were thrown yet. He was far less concerned about Karina being able to handle herself than the well-being of poor Randy, a younger boy who was cowering underneath the last row of seats.

Max struggled to keep himself from laughing out loud at the sight. Karina was tall, loved trendy fashion, and acted older than she really was. She adored her long, painted fingernails and flashy, hoop earrings. In what Max thought was her attempt to stay connected to her heritage, she purposely incorporated a certain Mexican-style flair into her clothes and appearance.

Randy, on the other hand, was more akin to an 8-year-old boy's mental and emotional state. Physically, however, he seemed to inhabit a body belonging to an 18-year-old man. Growing up, Randy was labeled "white trash," partially due to a woman finding him in an actual trash can when he was a toddler. He wasn't really a bad kid, although that may have been an assumption based on Max's love of the movie *Boy's Town*, along with his belief that there were no such thing as a "bad kid."

How he wished Father Flannigan could be with him now.

"THAT'S ENOUGH. Karina. Randy. *Enough*." Max's tattooed-covered arms pulled Randy out from where he hid under the seat, while his backside kept Karina at bay. As he struggled with the two troublemakers, he looked up and suddenly became aware of all the other kids on the bus. They were still crowding, taking sides, and shouting in support of their preferred contender.

Max bellowed, turning his head toward them: "SIT DOWN AND BE QUIET ALL OF YOU RIGHT NOW!"

At that very moment, Karina's head accidentally knocked into Max's nose. Her golden earring got caught in his loosened collar, and they both fell back onto Randy. Like a stack of pancakes piled one on top of the other, all three of them were now wedged behind the last row of seats.

The entire bus became silent. Every person's eyes grew wide.

Pastor Max couldn't hold it in any longer. He erupted in laughter. Karina covered her mouth at first in shock, but then began giggling herself. Then Randy followed, snorting with glee. Seconds later, everyone on the bus dissolved into peals of laughter.

"Am I too late to join in on the fun?" Leo's baritone voice put an end to the hilarity, not to mention absurdity, of the situation. All eyes were now on the slender, silver-haired stranger who had silently stepped onto the bus during the commotion. There was an abrupt silence as everyone turned to stare at him.

Karina scrambled to pull herself up, aided by Pastor Max's gentle push. He then righted himself as quickly as he could. Once standing, Pastor Max reached down to yank Randy free, a task that didn't prove so easy.

"Seems like you could use a hand." Leo suppressed his own chuckles at the sight of such an entanglement. As he took a few more steps down the bus's aisle, the children silently slid back into their seats. When he reached Max, he nearly had an encounter himself with Randy, who at that very moment, popped up from the floor with the force of a cork shooting free from a shaken champagne bottle. Leo dodged and managed to stand firm as the boy steadied himself.

"There you go." Max sighed in relief. "Now take a seat. You, too, Karina."

Max then turned to Leo and shrugged. "Kids…"

It was then that Leo noticed a tiny trickle of blood dripping from Max's nose. He reached into his back pocket, pulled out a white handkerchief, and handed it to Max. "Kids…yes. The more things change…"

"…the more they're exactly as they should be." Max finished the sentence while wiping his nose. "Man, it's good to see you my friend."

"You, too," said Leo, as the two men heartily turned their initial handshake into a bear hug. "You look like you have your hands full, as usual."

"I'm sort of grateful you could only handle one busload of kids this year," Max joked.

"There's always a silver lining to every dark cloud. Although I do wish the mall had a bigger budget to help more kids. Who knows about next year…" Leo's voice trailed off.

"Pastor Max, I gotta pee." A random voice shouted out, giving rise to others' rumblings.

"Right," Max shouted back. "Everybody, this is Leo. He's a good friend of mine, and he helped make this trip possible for all of you. Let's give him a round of applause."

The kids clapped, hooted, and hollered.

"Grab your stuff, and let's get ready…"

Leo nudged Max with his elbow, whispering, "Please don't say 'to rumble.'"

Max chortled and whispered back, "We already sorta did that, didn't you notice?"

The kids, oblivious to the interchange, yelled, "…for some Christmas magic." They clearly memorized Pastor Max's affirmations—even if they'd probably never admit out loud that they actually liked the familiar, corny phrases. With minimal pushing and shoving, the energetic group made their way off the bus.

"Form a line once you get outside and wait for me," Pastor Max called out. He directed his attention to Karina and Randy. "You two are lucky that Leo is here to remind me of second chances. We'll discuss what happened here later. Now go."

"The more things change…" Leo repeated the phrase. Karina and Randy scampered off the bus, feigning a friendly glare at one another before escaping to fresher, yet more frigid, air.

"…the more they're different." And Max again finished the sentence with a sigh.

As Leo turned to follow the kids outside, Pastor Max held back for a moment, reflecting. He had learned the hard way that there'd always be questions to answer, obstacles to hurdle, challenges to overcome, and problems to solve. But he always found a way to rise.

While he was in prison, Max worked as one of the Brownies—a label given to inmates who worked in the kitchen and wore brown uniforms. He quickly rose in rank to become the top cook, partly due to his love of food and the joy it brought to others, but also due to his determination to learn a trade, get out of jail, and never come back. Max worked extremely hard to keep his nose clean by steering clear of any hint of trouble. He spent most of his time attending classes and trying to improve himself, earning the title of The Programmer and a reputation as the "go-to book-nerd" and "guy with all the answers." Although, truth be told, he never felt as if he had the answers to much of anything. One thing he knew for sure, however, was that he was given a second chance in life and there was no way he was going to blow it.

That's when Leo came in—his legal-eagle and guardian angel. This then-stranger took on Max's case and ended up rooting for him so much that Max had no choice but to believe in himself, too. They became close friends and have been ever since.

All these years later, Max was pleased that he had made something of himself. Leo's faith in him was worth it. He was worth it. Now the leader of a congregation in one of Chicago's roughest neighborhoods, Pastor Max provided alternative occupational training and education opportunities for thousands of people, both young and old alike. Max was most proud of his Open Kitchen restaurant concept. By combining the kitchen and book-smart skills he learned in prison—both how to cook and how to operate a business—Max created a safe eatery where ex-convicts literally ran the place: Food prep, menu selection, restaurant décor, customer service, bookkeeping, marketing, and more. Plus, at the end of every evening, the excess food was handed out for free to anyone who was hungry and needed a home-cooked meal. It was Max's way of paying it forward and making good on Leo's investment in his life.

Much to his surprise, Open Kitchen had taken off. Reservations were now required and depending on the time of year, the wait list to snag a table was longer than a week. He didn't know if it was due to the taste of his dishes or if it was simply people's curiosity to see ex-cons. Then again, maybe it all was just the newness of the restaurant acting as the trendy "flavor of the month," so to speak. Quite frankly, Max really didn't care about the "why." Whatever the reason, business was booming, and the media kept sharing positive stories and reviews, not just about Open Kitchen, but about the people and the purpose. So, while Max was constantly aware that his success could all go away tomorrow, he also was aware that all anyone ever had was the present moment, and, for right now, it was great—and he was grateful.

Leo's voice bellowed from outside: "Max, you coming?"

Max snapped into action, strolled to the front of the bus, and shook his head free of his thoughts—all except one: Why, lately, did he find himself wishing it would all go away? And why could he not get out of his head the big ticket offer he had received a few weeks ago to sell the restaurant? Especially since the offer came from a guy he knew would bulldoze the whole place and erase everything he had built?

CHAPTER THREE

IAN & HOLLY

Unscripted, Unstuck

"For the last time, NO!" Carter Reins snapped as he stomped through the television studio's newsroom, side-swiping desks and disrupting the handful of reporters typing away on their laptops. They rolled their eyes and returned to their work, as they witnessed similar rants from the Big Boss before.

As if still in his "terrible twos," Carter continued to repeat the word "no," almost in sing-song fashion. He should have already outgrown this behavior, given he was nearing retirement. Trailing behind Carter was a reporter half his age, Ian McConnell, whose flailing arms and sweat-stained collared shirt communicated his frustration. Like the classic Tom and Jerry cartoon, the duo were as much cat-and-mouse adversaries as they were codependent, love-hate pals.

"No, no, no, no, no, and no," huffed Carter. "Shall I sing it to the tune of 'Santa Claus Is Coming to Town'? Will you hear me then?" He paused abruptly to take off his jumbo thick-rimmed glasses, an homage to Harry Caray who everyone knew was his favorite baseball sportscaster from his childhood. In the process of Carter's sudden halt, Ian nearly collided with his boss's backside and stopped just short. Unfortunately, when Carter turned around to face him, Ian couldn't hop back fast enough to escape bumping into Carter's oversized belly.

"Carter, please just listen to the whole story before you shoot it down." Ian ran his fingers through his thinning hair. He thought it ironic that his five-o'clock shadow seemed always at the ready to emerge by noon, and he wished the same were true for what used to be his thick mane of mossy brown hair. For every bit of stubble that grew on his chin, he seemed to lose at least twenty hairs from up top. "Grass doesn't grow on busy streets" he tried to remind himself, not that it actually helped his balding. He was only 32, but he felt twice that age and, sometimes, even older. He thought that by now, his life would have gotten easier. The exact opposite was turning out to be true. And no matter how hard he tried to make things work the way he wanted them to, life had other ideas. Just like Carter did now.

Carter yanked on the bottom of his slightly rumpled shirt, pulling out a corner that was struggling to stay tucked into his waistband. He breathed heavily onto the lens of his spectacles until a layer of fog coated them. As he slowly wiped the glasses with his shirt, he let out an annoyed grunt. "Fine. Get to it. I'm listening…"

Ian knew he had just seconds to speak, so he inhaled deeply and began. "Christmas Miracles. Peace on Earth. Goodwill to Men. Carter, that's what it's supposed to be about. But shopping always brings out the worst in peop—"

"No. Now go away." Carter turned his back again to Ian and resumed marching toward his office.

Ian felt his shoulders sag as he lowered his head in momentary defeat, hearing the sound of his boss slamming his office door. The entire newsroom of staffers continued with their duties as if nothing had transpired; this battle between the two played out daily in some form or fashion.

"Damn it." Ian swore louder than he intended. For three years he'd been slaving away, covering the simplest stories at Chicago's WACK-TV: Little League, the Police Blotter, and Neighborhood Council meetings along with school lunch programs and promoting celebrities he'd never even heard of, let alone admired. He did not become a journalistic reporter just to waste away doing this nonsense.

A voice suddenly piped up from behind. "For what it's worth, I think it's a great idea."

Ian turned around. All he could see was an unchaperoned video camera sitting on the desk from where the voice seemed to originate.

He looked around, puzzled. "Come again?" he said.

Slowly rising from underneath the table just behind the video camera, a bandana-covered head emerged. The bandana was covered in pink unicorns dancing atop a black background. Holly, the cherub-faced intern with blonde pigtail braids that made her look as if she still belonged in grammar school, rose to her feet. Lifting a power cord to eye level, she shook the snakelike coil as if it were alive.

"Power cord. We're gonna need it." She winked.

"What are you talking about?" Ian knew of Holly's bold reputation. Her childlike wonder and unwavering fearlessness were evenly matched with her creative storytelling and wicked technology skills. He knew without a doubt that this station—and probably many others—would offer her a job before even graduating from Columbia College where, he had heard, she was studying on a full-ride scholarship.

"Oh, Ian, trust me, I get what you want to do and why," she smirked. "I, too, would be bailing if I were stuck like you."

"Stuck? I'm not stuck."

"Huh, really? Well, okay. If you don't want to…"

"Want to what, exactly?" Ian was as annoyed as he was intrigued.

"Come on, now. We both know. You're sick of sticking to the script, sitting on the sidelines, proclaiming the 'good news' like you're some sort of trumpeting Gabriel. You want to do stories that get people riled. The ones where you gotta pick a side. The kind that go viral. You're sick of vanilla. You don't care who's nice. You want to expose the naughty people on Santa's list." She folded her arms, power cord still held in her hands. "Am I right?"

"Uh, not exactly," Ian shrugged, feeling a little sheepish.

"Oh, no? Okay." Holly flung the power cord over her shoulder and grabbed the video camera. "Never mind then."

Ian felt a spark ignite inside his chest. She was right—he *hated* vanilla—but he didn't want to admit it to her face. "No. Wait. Okay. Yes. Sort of."

"Well, which is it?"

Ian swallowed and nodded. "Yes," he said, not quite fully committed.

"Awesome." Holly fist-pumped the air. "So, what are we waiting for? It's Christmas Eve! One good old-fashioned last-minute shopping brawl at the mall is all we need. Hey, that's what we could call it—Brawl at the Mall."

"Great, Holly, except what about Carter?"

She smirked and quoted her favorite book's title, "*Well-Behaved Women Seldom Make History.* That's MY motto, but, hey, if you gotta get Daddy's permission to chase a story…"

Ian's ire rose at Holly's words. "I don't need anybo—"

"Besides, once Carter sees the ratings it'll bring in, he'll be taking all the credit. You know it. And then you'll be able to write your own ticket. You'll finally get yourself out of community outreach stories and into hardcore news. Isn't that what you've always wanted?"

He slowly nodded. "What's in it for you?"

"I need it for my reel," Holly whispered. "It's the only way I'm gonna get noticed by anybody that really matters."

Ian looked toward Carter's closed office door. A beat later, he turned to Holly. "I'll drive."

CHAPTER FOUR

HARRY & MR. WIGGINS

Excess Baggage

The airplane smelled of corn chips, burnt coffee, and the perspiration of passengers exhausted from their travels. The overhead speaker blared out: "Ladies and gentlemen, this is your Captain speaking."

From his window seat, 1A, Mr. Wiggins peered over the edge of his Dallas Morning News. Only his caterpillar-like, grey eyebrows and the very top of his black eyes were visible to others still settling into their first-class seats. The plane's speakers surrounded every word the Captain said with a muffling of white noise, making him quite difficult to hear. His message came across sounding more like this: "—dies –n –gentl— —is your Capt——ing."

"Here with us, again, Mr. Wiggins. Something to drink?" asked the flight attendant.

Mr. Wiggins raised his hand like a stop sign with his palm facing outward to silence the interfering conversation. "Shh...I'm trying to listen," he said, rudely shooing the man away.

Harry sat in aisle seat 1C, just to the right of Mr. Wiggins. Apologetically, Harry gave the flight attendant a conciliatory gesture and an almost embarrassed grin. While he was tempted, he stopped short of asking for something to drink himself, despite being parched. He knew better than to ignore his boss's cues.

"On beh— of the —tire crew, —wa— to welco— you to Fli— 1— bound for Chicago. —flight time —day *should* be 1—— –n– 48 min——, –n– we— be fly— —— av—age alt—— of 30,—— feet."

"What did he say? What about 'should'?" Mr. Wiggins now turned, searching for the flight attendant he had just dismissed. "Such incompetence. You know, Harry, how much I pride myself on punctuality and performance, there's nothing more important. Other than profit, of course."

Harry stared straight ahead and nodded once, not in agreement, but out of habit.

As a low grumble of frustration grew among the passengers, with a couple of voices shouting out, "Can't hear," and "Repeat, please," the loudspeaker went silent.

Mr. Wiggins rolled his eyes, irritated. "Where is that stewardess? I still can't get used to men as order takers in planes."

Harry cringed in response.

Just a moment later, the Captain was back on. "Sorry about that, folks. I think we're good now. Just wanted you to know that there is a chance of up to an inch of accumulation on the ground from what the weather computers are now telling us. So, this may just end up being a white Christmas after all. We'll keep you updated throughout our flight. For now, just sit back, relax, and if there's anything our inflight crew can do to make you more comfortable, let us know."

Mr. Wiggins turned to his direct report, Harry, and more loudly than was necessary, offered what would be another of his many critiques: "Such inefficiency, eh, Harry?"

Harry nodded without really agreeing. He looked at his phone. A picture of his wife, Emily, was smiling back at him. Emily was the one who grounded him. Whenever he looked at her pixie-cut blonde hair, her soulful hazel eyes, and those dimples, he could forget all about his worries. He'd known from the day he met her in high school that they were meant to be together. He promised he'd always take care of her, in sickness and health.

The flight attendant circled back and stopped in the aisle next to Harry. His golden name badge read *Corey*. "Sir, we need you to turn off all electronic devices for takeoff. Thank you."

Harry lightly kissed his fingertips, pressed them to her picture, and then powered down.

The flight attendant turned his attention to Mr. Wiggins. "Ready for that drink now?" he asked. "What can I get you?"

Mr. Wiggins ignored him, turning his gaze out the window. The attendant, sighing quietly under his breath, turned to Harry.

"Can I get you anything?"

"A water, please?" Harry replied. "Do I have time to go to the restroom?"

"Yes, but hurry. And I'll have the water for you by the time you come back."

Harry unbuckled his seat belt, rose to his feet, and in barely a few steps, found himself in front of the bathroom door at the very head of the plane. He entered the tiny silo and secured the door behind him. The lights overhead blinked a few times until they stabilized, but they didn't afford much light at all. Harry stood, staring at himself in the mirror. He barely recognized his own face. He peered into his bloodshot eyes. They actually weren't as bad as he thought they'd be, so he supposed that he must be getting used to these 16-hour workdays. His wife was right, though. His face was looking "gaunt"—her word not his.

He slapped his own cheeks and pinched them. He had seen someone in a movie do it once to regain some color. It wasn't working. He tried to smile. He had heard that it took fewer muscles in the body to smile than it did to frown. It should have been easy, but he couldn't make the corners of his mouth stay up. He even tried to use his pointer fingers to manually push his lips into position, but he couldn't stay smiling. How had he gotten here? And now he was going to be responsible for another human life? He wasn't old enough to be a dad. He wasn't ready. Not yet.

The flight attendant knocked on the outside of the door. "Sir, we really need you to take your seat."

Harry jumped at the interruption into his thoughts. "Yes, right away," he called back. *Oh, man,* he thought. He could just imagine what Old

Malcom Wiggins would say the second he returned to his seat. He was absolutely sure he was in for some rude lecture about time and delays and waste. Harry washed his hands and exited the bathroom. He shut the door behind him and noticed all of the passengers in first class glaring at him.

"Apologies everyone. Nature calls and all that…"

Mr. Wiggins shook his head in disappointment. Harry was used to his boss's constant disapproval.

Harry slid back into his seat and buckled himself in.

Mr. Wiggins managed to glare at him without even turning his head to look in Harry's direction. "You couldn't wait? You thought it best to make the rest of us wait on you?"

"No, sir."

Harry didn't bother to look him in the eye. He feared the old man would be able to detect how he really felt about him. It definitely wasn't favorable. When he took this job, Harry never intended to work for Mr. Wiggins longer than a couple of years.

After graduating from the Illinois Institute of Technology with a degree in Civil Engineering, Harry dreamed of designing and building skyscrapers. He loved construction and found great satisfaction in working with his hands to create something out of nothing. He thought he'd be able to grow in his passion and pursue a career in construction as a member of Malcom Wiggins's Property Investors Group, but he thought wrong. Now, nearly a decade later, he basically was Malcom Wiggins's official baggage carrier, both literally and figuratively, doing little more than project managing, budgeting, shuffling contracts, and spearheading wrecking crews. Lately, almost every project he touched related to destroying somebody else's property that, he was sure, they had worked so hard to build. He now knew that Malcolm Wiggins's operation had the reputation of demolishing good things and turning them into nothing.

Harry hated that they were on a plane—again—to ruin thousands of more lives by shutting down the largest shopping mall in the Wiggins's playbook. Right before Christmas. It was more lucrative to close it than to keep it up and running. At least that's what Wiggins insisted.

"When we land, I expect the car will be waiting to take us directly to Maplefield Mall," Malcom said out loud to no one in particular. He was used to speaking and having someone listen, whether they wanted to or not.

"Actually, Mr. Wiggins, I planned to meet you there, remember? My wife is so close to her due date, and I've been gone for so long. I'd like to see her as soon as I'm in her same zip code, if that's possible."

"Your wife's having a baby?" Mr. Wiggins applauded in mock celebration and with maximum sarcasm. "Wow, such anticipation. I'm surprised anybody is still working. I know—we should just stop everything until the baby's born, and you and your little family are all safe at home together."

"No, sir, I didn't think—" Harry gritted his teeth.

"That's right. You didn't," snapped Mr. Wiggins. "As planned, we'll go together directly to the mall without any stops along the way. When our work is done, then you'll be dismissed."

Harry feared that word "dismissed." He couldn't afford to be without a job, especially not now with Emily about to deliver their first baby. Mr. Wiggins always seemed to use that word "dismissed" as some sort of veiled threat or, at best, a not-so-subtle reminder that Wiggins held such power over his fate. For some inexplicable reason, it always worked, like an anchor dragging him further underwater. Harry needed the paycheck. Too many people depended on him and, if he were really honest, he no longer had faith that he could cut it doing anything else.

Harry was supposed to have been home with Emily nearly a week ago. However, as he was told time and again by the old man, Malcom expected Harry to be at his beck and call. As a result, Emily had been pretty much on her own throughout this entire pregnancy. In a weird way, it almost felt as if Mr. Wiggins didn't want Harry to have any interactions with his pregnant wife at all. Harry couldn't quite figure it all out—or even if there was something to figure out—but Harry stopped trying to understand the man or his motives years ago. He just didn't care.

The loudspeaker interrupted again with another announcement. "Folks, this is your Captain speaking again. We're getting some reports of rough weather ahead. It would appear that our 'snow flurries' are quickly turning into something more. We'll keep you updated as we continue on our way."

Mr. Wiggins reached out his arm and it hovered over Harry's lap, grabbing the flight attendant's pant leg as he passed by. "I have an important meeting to get to. It's unacceptable to be delayed."

The flight attendant looked down at Mr. Wiggins's hand that entrapped his leg. Then with his best poker face in position, he looked first at Mr. Wiggins and then, bemused, over at Harry.

Harry bravely reached over and, with a little effort, unhinged his boss's offending hand.

"I'm so sorry," Harry half-whispered, his tired eyes looking upward, pleading. "We just want to land."

"Nothing for *you* to apologize for." The flight attendant gave Harry a nod, having read the power dynamic between the two businessmen.

"Now see here—" Mr. Wiggins huffed and puffed. "I..."

"Thanks for all your help," Harry interjected, cutting his boss off before anything might escalate. "My wife's about to have our first baby. I just really want to get home."

The flight attendant softened, taking pity on Harry and what was clearly his "excess baggage." He then directed his attention squarely on Mr. Wiggins, and in an overly playful manner chided him. "Sir, I do hope you know how lucky you are to have someone like this young man at your side." He looked at Harry again, "What's your name?"

"Harry."

The flight attendant grinned. "Well, Harry, soon to be Papa Harry, it is good to meet you. I'm Corey. And congratulations. I'll send over something to help you celebrate as soon as we're cruising." Corey then spun on his heel and disappeared.

Mr. Wiggins huffed in annoyance, turning his attention back to the newspaper.

Harry shut his eyes, exhaling. Emily and the baby: If he just stayed focused on what mattered most to him, he could weather yet another of his boss's frigid storms.

CHAPTER FIVE

DAMIAN & ISABELLE

Black Sheep and Bad Influences

The couple seated in 2A and 2C, directly behind Harry and Mr. Wiggins, weren't actually a couple at all, but they both couldn't help but eavesdrop on the commotion in the row in front of them.

Isabelle's paperback novel, *Of Love and Shadows,* hid her face well enough, except for her well-groomed eyebrows, long lashes, and saucer-sized brown eyes peeking through a few wayward chestnut curls hanging down over her forehead. As a child, she hated what she considered her "monochromatic looks," always wishing for her sister's blonde hair and blue eyes girl-next-door vibe. Now approaching her mid-thirties—or as the media kept calling it, "middle age"—she had learned to embrace who she was, no apologies and no regrets. Although, if she were honest with herself, she still wished for that special someone to magically appear and sweep her off her feet; hence, her love of novels that told tales of passion and ecstasy especially during times of uncertainty and fear, just like the book she now held loosely in her hands. Or, apparently too loosely, as it suddenly tumbled into the lap of the man with the spiky gelled hair—black on bottom with blonde tips up top, and in need of a color touch-up—who was seated to her right.

"Oh, I am so sorry." Isabelle absent-mindedly reached over to retrieve her fallen fiction novel as the man reacted with a little bop of his body upward from the surprise. It was then that Isabelle realized she was about to inappropriately grab her book from the stranger's crotch and quickly withdrew her hand without the book, her cheeks immediately turning red from her near faux pau.

They both watched as the book fell in between the man's legs and onto the floor, somewhere out of sight.

Isabelle scrunched up her face and shrugged her shoulders to her ears, apologetically, just as the man threw back his head and laughed out loud. The wireless Bose headphones he was wearing, one ear on and one ear off, slipped back, popped off his neck, and nearly toppled over the back of his seat and into the row behind them. He caught them with his right hand just in time, still laughing through the whole ordeal.

"Well if you wanted to get to know me, all you had to do was say, 'hello,'" he said as he rested his headphones in his lap and extended his hand to Isabelle. "I'm Damian."

Suddenly finding herself a bit unnerved, Isabelle started to give him her hand and then pulled back. "I wasn't trying to get to know you," she stammered to the man that she guessed must have been about her same age. "My book fell. That's all."

"Uh-huh," Damian dropped his hand and shifted his body over to the side to make more room between them. "I didn't mean…I mean, it was a joke. Here, let me get it."

He reached down with his right hand, fumbling for the book. In doing so, he gave Isabelle an overhead view of his coiffed crown. She found herself mesmerized by the tiny daggers atop his head and reached out her right hand to touch them.

Suddenly Damian's spikes jetted upward, poking Isabelle's palm as he flung back his head from the search-and-rescue mission below, unaware of her touch. He looked over to Isabelle. "Sorry, I can't get it. It keeps sliding back. Maybe we can ask the pilot to slam on the brakes, so your book gets a good shove toward the front?"

Isabelle's eyes widened as her forehead wrinkled just a bit. She wondered: *Was he kidding again?* She opened her mouth to object.

"Man, I need to work on some new material. Lame joke." Damian flashed a mischievously inviting smile, or so Isabelle thought. He unbuckled his seatbelt and started to stand, tossing his headphones onto his seat.

Now, very embarrassed, Isabelle stammered, "Oh, listen, that's okay. I can get my book when we land, after everybody is up and out of their seats."

Damian tossed a wry smile at her as he slid past her. "What? You'd rather lose the very thing that stops you from talking to other people and risk it being trashed by spilled drinks, dirty footprints, or worse…being abducted by one of these misguided and literary-starved souls?" He unfolded his torso and stretched his extremely long legs as he stood in the aisle.

Isabelle unbuckled her seatbelt and rose to meet him. "Wow! I can't decide if you're funny or if you're kind of dark."

Damian looked her in the eye as if it was the first time that he actually saw her. Nervously, he said, "Maybe I'm a bit of both. Although if you asked my family, they'd definitely say I've gone rogue. My family even calls me 'The Black Sheep,' but when I was old enough to read, I learned my birth certificate didn't agree."

Suddenly stopping himself from continuing, Damian shook his head and widened his eyes. "I'll stop rambling now."

"No, no," Isabelle jumped in without really meaning to. "I like your ramblings." She extended her hand to him. "I'm Isabelle."

While she expected they would just shake on it, Damian lifted her hand to his lips and gave it a gentle kiss. "It's a pleasure to officially make your acquaintance, Isabelle. Consider me, at your service."

Stunned, it took a minute for Isabelle to find her voice. "I'm Isabelle, um, like I said. Um…Except for my sister. She calls me 'Izzy the bad influence.'"

The voices in Isabelle's head began their rapid inquisition: *Oh my God. What IS your problem? Why in the world would you say what you just said to this perfect stranger? And why aren't you taking back your hand already?*

Isabelle collected herself, averting her eyes from his, and pulling her hand out of his grasp. She suddenly found the ceiling and overhead compartments of the first-class cabin so very interesting. She heard Damian laugh, and forced herself to look back at him.

He was grinning. "Well then, we black sheep and bad influences need to stick together. Isabelle, I'm going in," he said, as if about to embark on some impossible mission.

With that, Damian exaggerated his movements, pouncing like a predator down to the floor, practically shoving his head underneath his seat. "Ah-ha, I see it." He looked up to Isabelle with an encouraging smile. Extending his right arm underneath his seat, he suddenly gave out a little yelp and pretended he was being swallowed up by a creature that lurked beneath. "Oh no! It's got me. Help me, bad influence Isabelle."

Isabelle covered her mouth with her hand, trying to suppress her giggles.

"Got it," Damian lifted up the book and sprang back to his feet. His eyes flashed a look of excitement as he connected with hers. He slowly delivered the book back to her but as she reached out to take it, he pulled it back. "*Of Love and Shadows*." He read the title out loud. "That sounds deep."

Isabelle's cheeks turned pink. She tried to pluck her book out from his grasp, but Damian kept it from her, holding it just beyond her reach. He turned slightly without really taking his eyes off the book's cover and, with the other hand, lifted his headphones up from his chair. He then seated himself before investigating the book further, using his thumb to skim the pages.

"Interesting cover. Interesting title. What's it about?"

She hadn't expected the question, but then she hadn't expected any of this. She sat back down, turned to face him, and swiftly grabbed both her book and his headphones from his hands.

Resting them both in her own lap, she retorted, "Okay, so tell me: What does a black sheep listen to in order to keep from being bothered by others while flying?"

"'In Hell I'll Be in Good Company,'" Damian matter-of-factly responded.

"Excuse me?"

"The song I was listening to," he explained, then started to softly sing its lyrics. "...*hell's bells, miss-spells, knocks me on my knees...*"

Isabelle found herself mesmerized by his voice. And his lips.

"My favorite bluegrass and classic folk band, The Dead South. *Such a great song*," Damian offered. "But not *at all* great at keeping me from being 'bothered' by others while flying."

Isabelle opened her mouth. She was about to apologize, but Damian stopped her and said with a wink, "I'm *actually* thanking my lucky stars about that."

VI & VERN

Black and White

"**Y**ou'll catch your death of a cold!" *How many times did she have to tell him?* Vi thought, as she shouted at her husband, Vern, from the open front door of their rusty-colored brick bungalow. She battled a bit with the gaudy Christmas wreath that hung on the outside. She tolerated it, but in truth, she hated it. It was the only decoration she would allow during the winter season because she felt obligated to display her neighbors' annual holiday gift. God forbid she was perceived as anything less than grateful. She knew people in the neighborhood already gossiped about her and her husband. She could imagine how they judged her. That said, she was certain that nothing they thought or said about her was any worse than the things she thought and said about herself ever since *it* happened. *It* weighed on *her* heart every day.

Why did they have to give her a wreath of this size? She thought. It made it so difficult to properly close the door without smashing the fresh evergreens, glittery pinecones, and scarlet ribbons that adorned it, or without her long hair catching it and getting all tangled up.

As much as she disliked vanity, Vi admitted that she loved her thick locks. She considered her hair to be her crowning glory and was so grateful it had yet to thin out. At nearly 70 years old, she felt blessed that she had not lost a single strand of hair from her youth—and that her rich cocoa color had transformed into a beautiful silvery sheen that made strangers stop to ask for her hairdresser's name and number. Her reply to such a request was always the same: *God Almighty at Heaven's Gate*, she would say. After all, she had nothing to do with it, nor did any overpaid stylist. She still cut her own hair, as well as Vern's, just as she used to cut their daughter Grace's hair, too.

Vi shook her head as if to clear away any memories and ducked back indoors. A few moments later, she emerged again, this time with a long, dark grey, slightly pilled winter coat in hand. She held it over the front concrete stoop and shook it out to get her husband's, attention. "Vern, come get your coat."

Oh, how she wished he had his hearing aids turned up. She hesitated to walk the coat out to him in the driveway; her legs were no longer as stable as they once were. She feared that the inch or so of snow that already blanketed the ground might cause her to slip and fall, and then where would she be? And who would take care of Vern? And when did snow make it into the forecast for Christmas Eve? It hadn't been forecasted on the Weather Channel last night. The jumbo-sized flakes falling from the sky should have brightened her spirits; there was a time when they would have. However, Christmas Eve hadn't brought her any joy for *several* years now. "Vern!" she called out once again, her exasperation seeping through more than she would have liked.

He hadn't always been this way. Or had he? Did Vern ever really listen to what she had to say? Surely, he did half a century ago when they were first married. And throughout all these years, if it hadn't been for her making all of the decisions that mattered—the house, the finances, Grace's education—where would he be? Lost. That's where.

But ever since Grace passed away, Vern hadn't been the same. While they were together, they weren't really there together.

Vi knew she could be a bit overbearing. Sometimes, she could even be downright controlling. But it wasn't because she was some narcissist who had to have *her own* way. Was it? No, she shook her head free from any doubt. She just wanted to protect the people she loved. She wanted what was best for them, and, sometimes, they didn't know what that was. Especially Grace.

Oh, how headstrong that girl could be! Ever since she popped out into this world a full three weeks before her due date, Grace was always trying to get ahead of herself—and everybody else, she felt, was holding her back. As her mother, it was her duty to teach Grace right from wrong. She wanted to guide Grace onto a path that would lead to the life she wanted for her only daughter: A good husband, children, a family of her own. Was that too much to ask?

Vi looked out at Vern, tinkering again with that old Volvo. He refused to give it up. A part of her was glad that he wouldn't get rid of it. It made her feel as if Vern valued what he had and wasn't the kind of person to just throw things—or people—away. Vi never meant to throw Grace away. She couldn't have known what would happen in the future when she finally put her foot down and demanded that Grace get the help she needed.

All she ever wanted for Grace's life was what she had always wanted for her own with Vern: A happy home filled with memories of her children. Somehow, she didn't have either, and, at least with Grace, it was too late to even hope for anything more.

As for Vern, she wasn't sure.

"Vern!" She yelled out to him once more.

Vern pretended not to hear her or her sharp tone. He knew it drove his wife of 52 years crazy when he didn't immediately respond to whatever orders she was dolling out, but he didn't care. He knew he could always blame it on his hearing aids. Thank God for that. At the age of 75, he had earned the right to listen or not, respond or not, and dress himself just as he felt was appropriate for whatever the weather. Or…even…not. Nothing much mattered anymore.

The car's engine idled as he lifted the driver's side windshield wiper. Almost as if caressing the window, he brushed away the accumulated snow.

He was surprised how quickly it was coming down, though now that he thought about it, he didn't recall it was even coming. He hadn't heard it on the forecast last night.

Vern made his way around all sides of his beloved beige vintage Volvo wagon. He knew it looked a little like a refrigerator on wheels. But once again, he didn't care. This vehicle could pretty much outlive anything—which is the reason he kept it. He bought it brand spanking new as a gift to himself for his 50th birthday. He remembered Grace had just turned 25 a couple of months earlier. At the time, he wished he had known that it would be the year she finally left the nest, moved out on her own, and started a life that he and Vi could no longer monitor nor control.

He stared at the puffs of smoke burping out of the exhaust pipe. The car's heater was warming up the interior. For as old as this baby was, she still ran well and could outrun slowpokes at any stoplight. He did wonder a little whether the old girl was polluting the air, but as he breathed in deeply, he could smell nothing other than the snow. Snow had a smell to it, or as Grace used to say when she was little, "*Aroma*, Daddy. Smells are bad. Aromas are good." Black and white. That's how she saw the world. That's what they taught her to see.

"Vern." Suddenly Vi was standing at his side, snapping him back to the world around him. "I've been calling you. Didn't you hear me? Turn up your hearing aids." She pointed to her ears and pumped a thumbs-up motion in the air.

Vern turned to look at the love of his life. Some called her bossy, but her take-charge personality was one of the things that still attracted him to her. They had endured so much together, especially with Grace. Anybody living as many years as they had, he supposed, probably endured similar heartaches, trials, and even occasional triumphs. What made him think they were so different? Oh, that's right, he thought to himself. Their only child chose to end her life on Christmas Eve. And it was all their fault.

CHAPTER SEVEN

PICKPOCKET & RAINBOW

Fur and Feathers

In her office at the mall, Betty's Elf on the Shelf still sat beneath the Christmas cactus atop her desk. The pile of unopened gifts wishing her *Bon Voyage* or *Happy Retirement* surrounded the little creature, his eyes staring straight ahead. Betty sat in her chair, unable to take her own eyes off of the elf's tiny face. His knowing grin seemed as if it would crack open to let out a Santa-worthy "Ho-Ho-Ho" at any moment.

"Okay, my special scout," Betty said, leaning closer and keeping her voice low. "Santa himself supposedly sent you here to make sure I'm not misbehaving, eh?" She paused just a moment, not really expecting a response, but wishing for something, even if she didn't know what. "Do you think you could ask him a question for me?" Betty's eyes filled with unwanted tears. "I've never been on his naughty list, always doing what's right. This mall is my Santa's workshop. These people are my elves, my family. What happens when this all goes away? Who will I be if I'm no longer 'Betty Bryant of Maplefield Mall'? Work has been my entire life." She wiped away her tears. "At least Santa has Mrs. Claus. What do I have?

Maybe you could ask Santa to send me a sign that everything's going to be alright?"

Interrupting her one-on-one with the elf, loud shouting and stomping feet just outside her door commanded her attention. Betty stood up, breathed in deeply, and put on her happy face, ready to confront whatever this might be.

A deep voice called out, "Pickpocket! Come here, boy."

Another voice, much higher and much more panicked, followed. "If anything happens to Rainbow…"

"Hey, your dumb bird started it." A loud whistle echoed in the air. "Pickpocket, Daddy loves you."

"I'll have you know my Moluccan Cockatoo is *extremely* intelligent. Her IQ probably rivals your own."

"Oh, right. This coming from the woman who names an all-white bird 'Rainbow'—what are you, color blind? And who brings a bird to a mall?"

"Who brings a dog to the mall on Christmas Eve? Aren't pit bulls banned from being pets because of their fighting and aggressive temperaments?"

"Shows what you know. He's an American Staffordshire Terrier. He's got papers. And pit bulls aren't the problem. Their owners are."

"Clearly!" The feminine voice scoffed.

The voices continued sparring outside Betty's office. With a nod of her head and her usual take-charge resolve, Betty stepped out from behind her desk, intending to walk out into the noisy fray, when all of a sudden a giant, 50-pound muscular dog bounded through her door with, of all things, a white, tropical bird riding on his back.

Though startled, Betty couldn't help but laugh. She never saw such a site. A bird riding a dog like a cowboy rides a horse! How absurd. The pair paraded around her desk, with the dog sniffing at her hands and brushing up against her skirt, legs, feet, desk, and finally stopped on the Christmas cactus.

Elf on the Shelf kept staring straight ahead, even when a big, wet, pinkish tongue licked him from his base all the way to the top of his pointy elf hat. And when the snowy feathered friend hopped off of the dog's back and onto the desktop to screech into his ear, the elf still didn't flinch. Nor did Betty who forgot all about whatever the future had in store, delighting in this rare moment that she was convinced could only happen inside of her magical mall.

The caramel-colored dog finally spoke, greeting her with a throaty, "Woof!" causing the bird to take to the air, then land again on the desk, hopping and flapping its wings as if performing some sort of hip-hop dance style known only to cockatoos.

Betty's eyes widened as she watched in awe. She always thought this place was a bit of a zoo. A dog and a bird on Christmas Eve, particularly this one, was definitely a good sign—wasn't it?—maybe even the one she had desperately asked for.

The stampede of footsteps finally reached her, and with the two owners very out of breath, these equally mismatched souls scrambled into her office.

"Pardon the interruption, ma'am," the man said, quickly running to his dog. "Pickpocket, you naughty boy."

Betty grinned. "I'm guessing they belong to you?"

"Rainbow is mine," said the woman, still trying to catch her breath.

Betty watched in amusement as the pet owners called out names, each one of them extending leashes and harnesses in an attempt to rein in their respective animal. Then, as if in protest, the snow-white bird hopped onto the back of Betty's chair, flapped her wings, raised her crest, and seemed to scream in joy.

The young woman, who was now trying to coax the bird into her arms, wore an Ivy Park camo print bomber jacket that Betty knew well. Every day she passed by this jacket from Beyonce's clothing line displayed in the Nordstrom store window. She loved the magenta, black, and pink camouflage design and had often thought to herself...*if only I were younger and, well, hipper...* She mused. What she couldn't quite figure out now, purely from a fashion perspective, was how Rainbow's owner would have thought to complement her extremely high-ticketed jacket with a quite peculiar shade of moss-green, knock-off, velour pants? Hmmm. She hoped it was an attempt at combining Christmas colors.

Betty couldn't help but think of how much the man resembled Harry Potter all grown up. She watched, trying not to laugh, as each time the man moved within arm's reach of Pickpocket, the playful pooch would hop backwards, circle the desk, hide underneath it, and then bound back toward his keeper. It appeared as if the dog was playing some sort of game. *Oh, so close that time!* Betty thought to herself, as once again, the two just missed connecting.

Darci burst into the office, nearly stumbling backward as she happened upon the scene. "Betty!" she started to say, and then her eyes took in the fur and feathered duo. "What in the world…?"

All eyes turned to Darci, but only for a moment. As if hearing a voice from beyond commanding them to "come," both the dog and the bird made one final turn around Betty's desk and then together made a run for it out the door. On his way out, Pickpocket pushed his snout as far as he could toward Betty's Christmas cactus and caught Elf on the Shelf by the arm. The poor elf was along for the ride before he even knew what was happening.

The woman with the snazzy jacket and bizarrely mismatched pants seemed ready to swoon, her left hand brushing aside a stray black curl that kept poking her in the eye. Shaking her head as if in defeat, she turned to Betty, "I am SO sorry! This isn't how my bird usually behaves. I'm Andrea." She held out her right hand, the bird's empty harness still in her grasp.

"Quite an introduction, Andrea!" Betty reached out her own hand. "I'm Betty Bryant. What a beautiful bird you have!"

Andrea grinned, slightly sheepish. "Thank you. Rainbow's been with me for six years now. And it's not *An-Dree-Uh*. It's *On-Drey-A*."

The man, exasperated, interrupted. "Ha! Of *course* it is. I'm Hank, ma'am," he said while extending his own hand to her. "Pickpocket's eleven years old, and he isn't usually like that. I think that bird of *On-Drey-A's* is a bad influence." He dragged out the woman's name, dousing it with sarcasm.

"Me?" huffed Andrea. "I think it's you who's the bad influence!"

Betty stepped forward, positioning herself between them. "No harm done," she said cheerfully. "And don't you think that instead of chatting with me, you two might want to go after them? Sooner rather than later?"

"Of course," the embarrassed-looking odd couple both said in sync.

"And maybe rescue my Elf on the Shelf while you're at it?"

"Right away!" They harmonized again. Betty couldn't help but giggle when the duo exited her office in a hasty attempt to retrieve their respective pets.

"What *was* that?" Darci exclaimed. "A dog. And a bird. Here in the mall?"

"On Christmas Eve, nonetheless." Betty giggled. "I have absolutely no idea." Betty walked around her desk to sit back in her chair. "But Elf on the Shelf is certainly in for quite an adventure!"

Darci laughed. It was a hearty kind of laugh, a genuine one from her belly. Betty seldom saw the young woman relax and be herself. It was a nice moment, but she realized that she might have been staring at Darci a second longer than she should have, as Darci met her gaze. Suddenly self-conscious, the millennial cleared her throat and addressed the business that she originally came to talk to Betty about in the first place.

"We have a problem, Betty," she stammered. "Santa is missing."

CHAPTER EIGHT

EMILY & THE DRONE

Unexpected Gifts

Lying on her back on the exam table in her doctor's office, Emily shut her eyes as she nervously listened to the voice on the other end of her cell phone. Her dimples showed, despite the lack of a smile, and with her pixie-cut blonde hair, she looked more like a child herself than an expectant mother. Frustrated, she let out a very loud, "WHAT?" She would have leapt to her feet if she could even see where they were. Her Santa-sized belly prohibited viewing anything in its path: Toes, stairs, doggie poop on the sidewalk… That last one was her least favorite.

Now, 39 weeks into her pregnancy, she couldn't wait for her first baby to be delivered, though right now, all she wanted delivered was her husband's Christmas gift. Preferably *before* Christmas Day!

Emily over-enunciated her words into the phone, "'Gua-ran-te-ed de-liv-er-y.' *That's* what you said." Her voice started to quiver. "You said that that drone was '*guaranteed* delivery' by Christmas Eve. Today is Christmas Eve…day." Emily tried to hold back her tears, but it was no use. Tiny trickles of salty water began to fall down the sides of her scrunched face as she paused to listen to the shop owner on the other end of the phone.

Her exasperation grew. "No, I can't come to the mall to pick it up. No, it doesn't help if you're open late."

The door opened just a crack, then, with a tiny knock, Dr. Sarah Grey walked into the examining room. The woman towered at nearly six feet tall; her slender figure made her appear even taller than she was. Her jet-black, corkscrew ringlets framed her makeup-free face, softening the wrinkles of her 50-something years with their own kind of halo effect. She didn't look up, her eyes fixated on the chart in her hands. "We're almost at the finish line, Emily," she joyfully proclaimed, as she shut the door behind her. Dr. Grey looked up and noticed that Emily was on the phone, crying.

Emily tried to smile at her doctor but continued her mission into the phone. "Mr. Abdullah, I know you're sorry. I'm sorry that your delivery guy got into an accident. I hope he'll be okay."

Dr. Grey furrowed her brows and drew closer to Emily.

Emily wiped away tears. "What's that? Oh. Thank you for the offer. Giving me the drone for free is very kind."

Another pause as Emily half-listened and half-zoned out. "Yes, we could use the money. But it's not about the money…" Her voice trailed off.

Gesturing to Emily to hang up, Dr. Grey patted her on the forearm. After handing Emily a tissue from the box on the counter, she took a seat on the little, navy swivel stool beside the examining table.

"Okay. I understand. Yes. Merry Christmas to you, too." Emily pushed the disconnect button on her phone. Using the tissue, she wiped her tears and then fluttered it in the air toward Dr. Grey, making it look a bit like she was waving a white flag in surrender. "Thank you for this, Dr. Grey."

"You're welcome. Now, I must ask, what was *that* about?"

Emily took one gasp of a breath. "Harry comes home today. Finally. Tomorrow's Christmas. And his present can't be delivered, so now he won't have anything from me under the tree." Emily's trickle of tears turned into a waterfall.

"Hey, hey, now," Dr. Grey stood, placing her right hand on Emily's baby bump. In the most soothing of voices, she whispered, "He's not going to care about some toy being there on Christmas Day, Sweetie."

"It's not a toy," Emily wailed. "It's the Parrot Bebop 2 Quadcopter with Skycontroller 2 and Cockpit FPV Glasses. And *I* care."

Dr. Grey wrapped her left arm around Emily's shoulders, resting her chin on the top of her head and giving her a motherly hug.

"Okay, now," Dr. Grey cooed. "In all these months together, this is the first time I've seen you get emotional like most of my pregnant patients do. I'm relieved, actually. I was starting to worry that you were super-human or something. What you're feeling is absolutely normal. Your hormones are heightening your emotions." She then paused and took a step back to look Emily in the eye. "Is this really just about your husband's Christmas gift?"

Emily pouted, sniffling. She lowered her head, twisting the tissue in her hands.

"So, what's going on in that head and heart of yours?" Dr. Grey continued. "When it gets this close to your due date, a lot of women get a bit freaked out, understandably, especially when it's your first baby." Dr. Grey tried to lighten the mood, mimicking different voices with every question: "*What was I thinking? Is this really happening? I can't have a baby. What do I know about being a mom?*" She patted Emily's hands. "So many doubts and fears bubble up to the surface. I've heard them all, and all of them are justified. But you know what? Rarely, if ever, are any of them worth granting credence. So come on, tell me. What's really causing those tears?"

Emily raised her head, her eyes still filled with tears ready to spill down her cheeks. She opened her mouth and sobbed, "I told you. It's the Parrot Bebop 2 Quadcopter with Skycontroller 2 and Cockpit FPV Glasses that my Harry won't find under the tree on Christmas morning."

Dr. Grey hid the impulse to chuckle. "Okay, okay," she tried to soothe Emily, leaning over so as to look directly into her eyes. "Just breathe. You're growing another human being in there. You've got so much going on inside. All this outside stuff… Even Harry's drone… Sure, it's important, no question. But, Emily, it's not nearly as important as you and your baby, right? Everything is going to be okay. You'll see."

Emily sniffled, nodded, and dabbed at her tears with the now twisted rope of tissue. "Okay," she whimpered.

"Now, let's talk about that baby. Any contractions, swelling, headaches?" Dr. Grey began gathering her tools for a pelvic exam.

Emily shook her head no.

"Good. I'll take a look inside, but I think this baby is going to bake a little bit longer. If I were a betting kind of gal, I'd say her first Christmas will have to wait until next year."

Emily started weeping again. "No baby for Christmas, either…?" All she could think about was Harry's Christmas presents, or lack thereof. No drone. No baby even. She thought that for sure she could give him one of those gifts. And she had saved for quite a while to buy him that drone. It was supposed to be the expensive, "guaranteed" one.

The truth was, Harry was such a big kid—at least he used to be. It was one of the things Emily had loved most about him from the moment they met. When she saw how excited Harry got this past summer when he tried out their neighbor's drone, Emily knew that she would get Harry his own drone for Christmas. Now, she couldn't believe that there was a real possibility that she wouldn't be able to deliver something to make him smile with joy. Of course, the baby was the ultimate gift, a real "now you're a grown-up" kind of present. But she hoped that this drone would help Harry relive a little bit of what it felt like to be a kid…before *he* actually *had* a kid to parent.

She breathed in the calming eucalyptus scent of the examination room and started to think more logically, pushing away the disappointment that her plan had gone awry. Plans could change, after all. Maybe she *could* make it to the mall, pick up the drone, have it wrapped somewhere there, and be back home before Harry's plane even landed.

"Dr. Grey, if everything looks okay, can I assume that for these next few days there aren't any restrictions on anything? Like, I can still go about my day as usual?" Emily asked as nonchalantly as she could, trying to hide her excitement at the possibility of still getting that drone—and the fact that there wasn't really anything "nonchalant" about the question she posed.

Dr. Grey threw back her head and laughed. "If you're asking me if you can head on over to the mall to get that drone for your husband, I'd say, short of any Act of God that might befall us, I don't see any reason why you shouldn't. As a matter of fact, maybe even treat yourself to a mani-pedi with the money you get back from our good friend, what was his name? Mr. Abdullah…? And *that* seems worth the inconvenience to me."

Emily felt her face light up. Now there were no more tears, just a big grin and a squeal as she wiggled her unpolished toes and tried to get a glimpse of them over her big belly. "I can't see them, but my toes are doing a happy dance!"

Dr. Grey confirmed with another laugh, "Yes, indeed they are!"

CHAPTER NINE

HOLLY & IAN
Rogue Trip

"Move!" Ian's patience for navigating the beast-sized WACK-TV news van during a snowstorm was wearing thin. The beige Volvo wagon in front of him that was barely moving only contributed to his growing road rage.

"Look at that thing," Ian gestured to Holly who was chilling in the passenger seat. "It's a refrigerator on wheels," he quipped. "But I know it can actually go faster than that!" Ian accelerated, stopping just short of kissing bumpers.

"You know it's not cool to tailgate," Holly reprimanded.

"Sweet baby Jesus, man. Step on the gas already." Ian slapped both of his hands on the steering wheel, gesturing in frustration. He turned to Holly, "Is it *cool* for him to drive so slowly? He's more of a danger out here in this weather than somebody driving too fast."

"You need to chill," Holly said, hiking her Dr. Martens black combat-booted feet up onto the news van's dashboard. "With a car that old, you know it's got some hard of hearing, slow-moving senior citizen at the wheel. Give him a break. He probably should have given up his right to drive long ago." She then thought about it a second. "You know, *that* oughta be a story. 'Grandad Danger: When and why it's time to hand over a driver's license.'"

Ian dramatically gasped, giving her a look that oozed critique.

"What?" Holly shot back. "Everybody reports on teen drivers and how dangerous they are behind the wheel. I'd bet we'd find that old people are just as bad, maybe worse."

Ian just shook his head, tooting the news van's horn, but the Volvo wagon kept its pace, as if completely oblivious to the 5,000 pounds of metal riding its bumper.

Holly raised her voice, "For the love of Pete, change lanes if you can't handle it. Or here's an idea…you know…just enjoy the ride."

"Enjoy the ride?" Ian scoffed as he looked around outside. The snow had accumulated quickly. About six inches of the white stuff already coated the road. Vehicles left and right housed weary drivers and passengers, some just staring straight ahead, others trying to defog their windows, and, yet, others in a battle to keep backseat siblings from poking one another. He dramatically gestured, sweeping his right arm to all the drama visible to them. "Like everyone else?"

"Oh, right. I forgot. Your generation's all about judgement." Holly leaned forward and turned on the radio.

"Oh, that's rich. This coming from Ms. 'Grandad Danger,'" Ian promptly reached out his right hand to switch off the music.

"And denial," Holly turned her head to stare out her window.

The moment the word left her mouth, she realized just how hypocritical her accusations were. Denial. Judgement. How many not-so-kind thoughts did she keep secret? Even innocent ones, like something as simple as just how much she actually loved the trail of red taillights when they were in a single file on the road, those little puffs of smoke pooping out the back ends of cars. Or how much she loved watching all the big, fluffy flakes land one-by-one on the rooftops and windshields? She learned in kindergarten that each snowflake was unique; "No two alike," she remembered the teacher saying. Ever since then, she would imagine individual flakes falling and grabbing onto one another as they gathered on light poles, trees, grass, moving vehicles… She could almost hear them saying, "I got you. Hang on."

It was dangerous to let others see the inside of you, Holly thought. *The more others know, the more they can use against you, to hurt you.*

Ian interrupted her reverie. "That's what's wrong with your generation. You think you know it all, you're owed it all, you've got it all figured out…" He twisted his neck back and forth, raising his hand to massage his tense muscles. "Get your feet off the dash."

Holly snorted. "*And* you just continue to prove my point." She kept her feet where they were, repositioning them even further apart from one another on the instrument panel.

Ian shook his head at the hot shot seated to his right. "I should never have taken you with me."

"Ha! *You* didn't take me anywhere. This was *my* idea."

Ian blew out an exasperated breath. With one swift turn of the van's steering wheel to the left, he maneuvered his way into the fast lane, despite the fact there was nothing fast about it. Vehicles behind him honked their horns, some even swerved.

"Oh, please," Ian dismissed the reactions, emphasizing his words so those behind him could read his lips from the news van's oversized rearview mirror.

"Nice move," Holly nodded in a clear mocking manner. "Very *Fast and The Furious.*"

As they passed the sputtering Volvo wagon on their right-hand side, Holly and the old man driving exchanged glances. Holly didn't know why, but she felt compelled to smile and wave. The old man looked so sad. Vern acknowledged Holly with the slightest of nods, and what almost looked like the start of a smile, but then he turned his head back to the front and returned his eyes to the road ahead. Holly turned her own attention back to the front windshield.

Ian's cell phone rang through the news van's Bluetooth audio system. One ring. Two rings. Three…

"You might want to get that," Holly snapped at Ian.

"Why?"

"My guess is that it's Carter. I want to hear you tell him this was *your* idea. Right before he probably fires you."

"I will!" Ian scanned the steering wheel's controls and hit the button to pick up the call on speakerphone.

Carter's roaring voice bounced off the inside walls of the van, "WHO IN ALL THAT'S HOLY DO YOU THINK YOU ARE?"

Ian rolled his eyes. "Carter, calm down. You sound a little bit like your head is gonna explode." He looked over at Holly, her eyes wide and jaw fully open.

"Are you nuts?" she mouthed to him.

Ian whispered to her, "You said to take the call."

"Yeah, but I didn't say you should say something stupid that actually might get you fired."

"Explode?" Carter's voice interrupted the interchange. It sounded a little muffled, as if he had either put the phone down or cradled it against his shoulder.

Ian and Holly turned to one another and at exactly the same time said, "He's probably counting to ten." They both chuckled, as they both experienced many of Carter's anger-management "counting to ten" episodes before he let loose on someone or something.

Ian turned his attention to the brake lights ahead, momentarily taking his hands off the wheel and waving his balled-up fists in the air. Trying to regain his center, Ian placed his hands at ten-and-two on the wheel and continued to poke at Carter. "Breathe, Carter. Breathe. This won't be as much fun for you if you're turning blue and about to pass out."

Holly covered her ears with her hands, lowered her eyes to the floor, and shook her head, trying not to howl with laughter. Ian turned his head to her and took note. The longer Carter stayed silent, the more Ian began to worry.

"Carter?" Ian's voice sounded a lot less confident and much more wary than just moments ago.

Click. Carter had hung up on them. It caused the dial tone to sound across the speakers, as if someone in an ER operating room just flatlined.

"You are *so* dead." Holly lifted her head, lowered her hands, and turned to meet Ian's eyes. An impish grin overtook her entire face. "Didn't know you had it in you."

Holly and Ian both erupted in laughter.

Ian hit the button to hang up the phone call, and the van became silent. Slowly shifting from laughter to a nervous quiver, he squeaked, "Me neither."

"He'll call back," Ian choked a little, trying to speak while laughing. "He will. Always does. You'll see."

Seconds later, the phone rang.

Ian let out a sigh of relief but caught it just in time to turn it into a whole-hearted, "Ha—See? Told ya so…"

Ian picked up and started, "Carter, listen. We've been in this van surrounded by snails for, what, like at least a couple hours…"

"Hello? Is this Ian McConnell?" It wasn't Carter on the line.

"Hello. Yes. This is Ian. Who's this?"

"Ian, this is Doctor Haywood, Vince's doctor."

Ian was silent, his face showing he was at a loss for words.

"Hello? Did I lose you? Are you there, Ian?"

Holly flicked both her hands toward Ian, mouthing the words, "Say something."

Ian looked out the frosty window.

Holly watched him bend his neck from left to right to left again. Whatever this call was, she suddenly felt so uncomfortable being in the van and listening to what, clearly, Ian didn't want to hear.

Slamming his right fist onto the steering wheel, Ian focused his eyes back onto the road ahead, and responded, "Yes. I'm here. Is everything alright, Doc?"

Holly tried to make herself disappear, turning her own gaze out her passenger side window, as if giving Ian some privacy. She couldn't help but think about how the voice on the other end of the line sounded so Mr. Roger's-esque, but the look on Ian's face registered something quite the opposite, as if the doctor was evil Darth Vader telling Ian he was his father.

Dr. Haywood chuckled, "Everything will be alright, as soon as you get here. What's your ETA? Vince can't wait to see you."

"My ETA?" Ian stalled, searching for something to say. "Right, Doc… ya see…I'm in the news van on my way to Maplefield Mall for a story."

"Did you forget?" Dr. Haywood asked. "You know your brother has been talking for weeks now about you coming to spend time with him over the holidays. I know you won't disappoint him. Not at Christmas." A tone of warning laced the doctor's voice.

Ian saw out of the corner of his eye that Holly's head was shaking back and forth in disapproval. "No, no, of course not. I was on my way, but this traffic with the snow…"

"Yes," Dr. Haywood's voice sounded so full of possibility. "Vince is so excited; all the residents are thrilled about the unexpected snow. Vince said that you told him you'd make snow angels together if it snowed on Christmas Eve."

Ian shut his eyes for a moment and said nearly under his breath, "I did. I told Vince a lot of things."

"You should see what Vince made for you in Arts & Crafts."

As he momentarily took both hands off the wheel to run them through his thinning hair, Ian blurted out, "Can't wait, Doc." He repositioned his hands back on the wheel. "Tell Vince I've got a surprise for him, too." Straining to peer out the window at the coming highway exit signs, he added, "I'm not far. Tell Vince I'm on my way."

Holly straightened up in her seat. She knew she had just eavesdropped on a private conversation, but what else could she have done? It was on speakerphone, after all.

"Splendid! He'll be so happy," Dr. Haywood sang out.

"See you soon, Doc," Ian hit the disconnect button.

Silence surrounded them. Holly didn't know what to say. This is exactly the kind of thing she worked so hard to keep others from knowing about her. And now to find out that Ian has secrets she never would have imagined. She felt such empathy for this guy, knowing exactly how exposed he must be feeling right now. Knowing someone else's weak spots made you vulnerable. But what Ian didn't know about her was that she'd never use this secret information to hurt him. She knew what it felt like to have someone else expose you. No way would she do it to anyone else. She figured she'd break the silence by keeping their conversation strictly about business.

Holly cleared her throat and glanced over to Ian. "Guess Carter's not gonna call?"

Ian chuckled, seemingly grateful for her response—and for her not asking any questions. He inhaled and exhaled deeply, then checked his mirrors, turned on his blinker, and started inching his way toward the next highway exit.

Holly looked in the direction the van was headed, then turned back to look at him. He reminded her of a puckered, half-filled helium balloon struggling to keep itself airborne.

Ian rigidly sat upright, staring straight ahead, his eyes shifting ever so slightly to the right to survey the expression on Holly's face.

Exhausted, Ian dribbled out: "My younger brother, Vince, my only sibling, he's in the hospital. They call him a 'resident.' I guess cuz he's lived there after our parents died when he was in his 20s. It's a place called Alexander's. Sounds like it oughta be a bar, until you add the rest of it: Alexander's Behavioral Health Center. 'Resident,' that's exactly what they call him—but he's really a patient in their psych ward. Man, he's been there for like ten years."

Holly stayed silent for a moment longer than she had intended.

Ian rambled on. "He's not a danger or anything. He's just a little, well…" Ian struggled with his words, finally opting to not finish his thought.

More silence.

Finally, Holly spoke, keeping her voice casual, feigning a bit of disinterest, "What's his diagnosis?" She never would have guessed that Ian was dealing with something like this.

After a few more awkward seconds, Ian responded, "Paranoid schizophrenic." He over-enunciated the words, almost wincing as he said them. "God, how I hate saying those words." His hands gripped the steering wheel so hard his knuckles had turned white.

Holly took her feet off the dashboard, planting them firmly on the floor beneath her seat. She leaned forward and asked, "So, like, he hears voices and sees things that aren't really there?"

"That's part of it, yes, when he's off his meds…" Ian trailed off.

Holly slowly nodded her head, then met Ian's drooping eyes as he shrugged.

She cleared her throat. "You know there's a Jewel near the exit we just passed."

He gave her a quizzical look. "So…?"

"So…I used to live out this way. That's how come I know. It's your typical Jewel— groceries, salad bar, deli counter—so we can get something to eat. I'm starved. Aren't you?" She continued to ramble. "They have a couple of aisles with some Christmassy stuff. You know. And little gifts and things."

Ian raised an eyebrow at her.

She continued, "You said you had a surprise for him. Your brother. You can't show up empty handed. And I think Carter will really fire you if you give your brother something you lift from inside this van."

Ian swallowed a lump in his throat. She knew that probably the last thing he needed was to completely dissolve into a puddle in front of an intern. He already disclosed way more to her than he ever meant to. At least, if Holly were in his shoes right now, he knew that's how she'd be feeling.

Glancing in his mirrors to see the traffic pattern, Ian set his sights on the next exit and exclaimed, "Christmas Eve shopping. At a grocery store. Here we come. Heaven help us. You may just get your 'brawl' a little earlier than 'at the mall,' courtesy of your colleague."

Colleague not "intern"; Holly liked the sound of it.

"We *will* have to come up with another name for our segment," Holly joked. "What's another word that rhymes with 'mall'? 'Brawl at the—?' or 'Brawl in the aisle of alcohol…?'"

"That's awful," Ian howled. "You should stick to visuals. I'm the wordsmith."

Holly nodded, "Deal."

She thought about exposing her own secrets. She wanted to tell him that he and his brother weren't alone. But she decided her story could wait for another day.

CHAPTER TEN

DR. HAYWOOD & VINCE

All I Want for Christmas

After his call with Ian, Dr. Haywood pocketed his cell phone. As he pushed away from his weathered desk and rose from the captain's chair, his old bones creaked. Taking a moment to steady himself, he eased his way over to the credenza. He paused at the slightly off-kilter mirror that hung just above, with its artistic kaleidoscope of buttons encircling its frame, and Vincent's signature boldly scrawled in the bottom right corner of his masterpiece. He examined his own still-chiseled face and winked. "Not bad for an old fart." His bony fingers traced the edges of his treasured, hodge-podge artwork. "Ah, Vincent," he said wistfully. His own hazel eyes with their hooded lids looked back at him. "It's show time, Haywood. Look alive, now."

Easing open one of the credenza's drawers, Dr. Haywood pulled out his crushed-velvet Santa hat. Adjusting it atop his salt-and-pepper-haired head, he suddenly sprang to life. Like Frosty the Snowman with his magical top hat, Dr. Haywood exited his office and sashayed his way down the festively decorated halls of Alexander's Behavioral Health Center. Any bit of pain he may have felt, he left behind, purposely swinging his white lab coat behind him as if it were a superhero cape. He took up a lot of space. Not his body, per se, as he was still rather tall and solidly built, but his very presence filled a room with energy, making him seem so much larger than life.

He passed a floor-to-ceiling windowed room and saw a handful of residents swaying and shaking their hips, bobbing their heads and having fun dancing to their own beat. He could barely make out the tune. *What was that song that was playing?* He cocked his ear, trying to place it. Doubling back to the door with the sign that read, "Art and Movement Therapy," Dr. Haywood opened it wide and stepped inside.

There were jingle bells ringing, piano keys tickling, drums beating, horns blaring…all of the sounds that instinctively made his feet want to move. The jolly sounds soared out into the hallway, filling his heart with pleasure and pushing away any possible worries of how the holiday might play out—especially for those who were left alone on Christmas Eve each and every year, like Vincent. *Maybe this year would be different,* he hoped.

"Ah! I love this song!" Dr. Haywood sang out. "*All I want for Christmas, is you…*" He belted out the only line he actually knew, and though his singing was completely out of tune, he still delighted every person in the room. He then twirled himself about, weaving in between and all around the other dancers. "Keep it up! You all look so fine. It's like *Dancing with the Stars* in here!"

Dressed in a variety of clothes from fancy holiday attire, to a mishmash of Christmas pajamas and lived-in sweats, each resident moved to their own interpretive rhythm of the music. They reveled in Dr. Haywood's merriment, pointing to him and howling in laughter.

Dr. Haywood winked and nodded to the therapist in charge of the group. "Merry Christmas, Annie! Great job!" Almost in unison, she and the entire group responded with their own wishes.

"Merry Christmas, Doctor Haywood!" voices sang out. "Hope Santa's good to you!" "Have you been naughty or nice?"

Dr. Haywood threw back his head, heartily shouting his own version of a "Ho-Ho-Ho!" followed by, "Always nice…sometimes naughty! As it should be!"

As quickly as he had entered the room, Dr. Haywood waved goodbye and exited. He continued to dance down the hallway, humming to himself, greeting staff and patients he encountered along his path. It seemed as if everyone was in a happy holiday mood. How could they not be when nearly every square inch of space—from the walls to the desks to the center nurses' station—was festively decorated to celebrate the season?

Every square inch, that is, except for Vincent's room. As Dr. Haywood approached, he noticed that while every other doorway was decorated with evergreen garland and bright lights, Vincent's was void of any holiday cheer. Quietly, Dr. Haywood peeked in, making sure he wouldn't be seen. It broke his heart to see Vincent sitting quietly on the pristine bed he'd carefully made earlier in the day. His bent knees curled up to his chin, making him look so small, so uncomfortable, and more like a child than a full-grown man about to turn 30. His eyes stared straight ahead, fixated on some spot on the wall. Low to the floor, with half-railings on either side, the bed upon which Vincent sat was pushed up against one of the steel-blue-painted concrete walls. To his left, a flat-screen TV hung just above a six-drawer, white wooden dresser. A plain, brown cardboard box no bigger than the size of a shoebox sat on top of the dresser, tied up with a single red ribbon. To his right sat a solitary club chair, its brown and white pattern hiding its wear and tear, and always at the ready for guests who never came. High above, the room's only window was sealed shut and outlined with a string of multicolored Christmas lights that flickered on and off—the only holiday decoration in the entire room.

Dr. Haywood set his jaw, determined to make Vincent smile, whether or not Ian made good on his promise. Backing up a good six feet or so, and taking three deep breaths to get his blood pumping, Dr. Haywood raced to make his entrance, sliding to a stop directly in front of Vincent's doorway, pretending to hold a microphone in one hand about to belt out a tune.

Vincent's coal-colored eyes blinked and registered the interruption. His lips curled upward into a smile. Even his jet-black hair, parted neatly on the side and slicked back with perhaps just a little too much gel, stood at attention. Finally, he broke free from his stony expression unable to hold in his laughter. "Ha-ha!" He gleefully raised his hands in applause. "*Risky Business!* You look just like Tom Cruise! But you still have your pants on."

Dr. Haywood snorted. "Vincent, that's exactly what I was going for. And I even got to keep my pants on. You are *so* good at this game." He entered the room, walked over to the dresser and tapped his finger on top of the ribboned box. "You ready for your brother's visit?"

"Is Ian here?"

"Not yet. But I just talked to him on the phone, and he's on his way."

"He forgot again, didn't he?" Vincent's expression failed to mask his disappointment.

Dr. Haywood closed the distance between them in two steps. "Scoot over," he said. Vincent complied, making room for his doctor—and friend—to sit beside him. "Did you hear what the kitchen is cooking up for Christmas Eve dinner?"

"Nope. Don't want to know. I'm going home with Ian."

Dr. Haywood noticed Vincent's overnight bag peeking out from beneath the foot of his bed. He felt himself become clouded with concern. He knew what was probably coming—another disappointment. Vincent had spent over a decade here. Not once had his brother, his only living relative, taken him out for an overnight visit.

"Ian's a pretty busy guy, Vince," Dr. Haywood tried to lay some groundwork, just in case. "Especially today and tomorrow with his job at the TV station. He's out there right now chasing stories. And did you see the snow outside?"

"Yup. Snow's good. Ian and me, we're going to make snow angels."

Dr. Haywood nodded. "That sounds like fun. I might even join you."

"You're never too busy to play, Doctor Haywood." Vince smiled, almost shyly.

Putting his arm around Vincent, Dr. Haywood proclaimed, "Never, and certainly not when it comes to you."

Vincent leaned his head on Dr. Haywood's shoulder but only for a moment. He then perked up, sniffing the air, comically mimicking a dog that had just picked up a scent of something worth chasing after.

He lifted his head up to face Dr. Haywood. "You think maybe they need a taste-tester in the kitchen?" He stood, robotically walking backwards, bouncing his eyebrows up and down, and licking his lips in exaggerated jest as he made his way toward the door.

Dr. Haywood howled. "Michael Jackson moonwalk. We need to get you one of those bedazzled gloves." He then sprang to his feet, clicked his heels together, and saluted Vincent in grand military fashion. "And I like your idea to serve as taste-testers. I'm up for the job. Reporting for duty, sir."

The pair marched and moonwalked their way out the door.

Vincent stopped abruptly. "Wait. I forgot my bag," he said as he raced back to his room to pull the bag out from underneath his bed.

"We'll have to stop at the nurse's station and make sure they pack up enough meds to last for your visit," Dr. Haywood cheerily reminded Vincent, knowing full-well just how much Vince hated to talk about his medications. He needed to make sure that Vince completely understood that leaving the hospital building in no way meant he could stop taking his meds.

Vincent scooped up the ribbon-bound box from his dresser on his way out. "Can't forget Ian's gift." He turned back around and continued to moonwalk towards the exit doors.

Dr. Haywood followed, not bothering to bring up the meds again. The probability of Ian taking his brother overnight was pretty much next to none. Why bother upsetting Vince for no reason?

"Lead the way. Somebody has to make sure Santa's cookies are safe for consumption."

CHAPTER ELEVEN

LEO & BETTY

The Poly-Filled Santa

Crammed into one of the mall's unused storage closets, Leo stood dramatically pouting in the center of the much-too-small room as Betty tugged at his jacket, trying to force him out of it. "I don't even like cookies," he argued. "Or milk."

Betty snickered, undeterred from her task. "You think I don't know that after all the years we've worked together? I know you don't want to do it, but you're all we've got right now with our real Santa taking a snow day, so, please, Leo, think of all those kids out there waiting for the party to start—and hold still while we get you into this Santa suit!"

Betty's back was to Darci, but Leo could see that the girl was blushing. He guessed it must be a sight to see with Betty essentially stripping him of his clothes, from his first outer layer to now unbuttoning his dress shirt.

He stifled a laugh at the thought of his genius. The smartest thing Leo did when asked to take on the role of Santa was to do absolutely nothing. He would have agreed to play the part—if it made Betty happy—and could have easily undressed himself and put on the costume; but the more he objected, the more he realized Betty was going to take matters into her own hands. And he liked being in her hands.

Poor Darci, though. Every time he caught her eye, she averted her gaze and turned six shades of pink. *Oh, well,* he thought. *Serves her right for playing a part in the demise of this place and all Betty had worked to build. She and that boss of hers had no idea what they had in Betty.* As far as he was concerned, Betty was one-of-a-kind and irreplaceable.

He looked down at the top of Betty's curly hair as she worked her way around him. She always made him feel like a giddy schoolboy. His inner child just wanted to come out and play whenever he was around her. Betty made him feel young, alive, and as if anything and everything was possible. From observing the way others responded to her, Leo knew that he wasn't alone. Maybe those big brown eyes of hers had something to do with it. Rich, like the color of one of her coveted caramel coffee concoctions, her eyes had the power to hypnotize him if he stared too long. He often had to catch himself. How he loved to just look at her. And the only way he was guaranteed to banter with her everyday was to stand beside her as General Counsel. Betty had devoted her whole life to her career. She regularly said she didn't have time for both her job and a family of her own. But how he wished she felt for him the way he felt for her. It's true, he never told her his feelings, and he never asked her what she thought of him. But taking a chance at love meant risking the sure thing of working with her side-by-side, day-by-day, colleague-to-colleague. If that's the only relationship he could have with her, he'd take it.

Betty suddenly started fanning herself, taking her hands off of Leo's buttons. "Goodness, it's hot in here."

Leo let out a "Ho-Ho-Ho" followed by a real belly laugh causing Betty to look up at him looking down at her.

"And, what, exactly, do you find so funny?" Betty came to her feet. Perspiration pasted a few ringlets of her hair around her reddening face. Either she was really warm or really annoyed.

Leo figured it was a little bit of both. As much as he himself was annoyed at playing dress-up, he was mostly amused and enjoying having Betty's hands on him in places he hadn't imagined they'd be when they'd met outside the mall earlier that day. *What that woman wouldn't do for this job of hers.* He looked over at Darci whose embarrassed face was now bright red, perfectly matching the gorgeously plush, velvet Santa suit she held in her arms. With both hands, she lifted it higher to cover her face.

As Betty returned to helping Leo dress, he gently grasped both her hands and moved them aside. "Good Lord, woman, before Darci here reports us both to HR, let me do it."

Betty stepped aside, not really sure what to do with her hands now that they had been relieved of their duties. She lifted them to wipe away the wisps of hair sticking to the sides of her face. "Need I remind you that you *are* HR."

Darci peeked out from behind the costume, clearly still embarrassed but intrigued at the dynamics between her boss and the man even she could tell was her match.

Leo continued undressing himself. "I'm HR only by default," he reminded Betty. "And only because that bastard who owns this place is too cheap and self-centered—"

"Everybody decent?" Pastor Max's voice called out from the other side of the door, accompanied by three forceful knocks, putting an end to Leo's commentary.

Darci retreated back behind the costume again, as Betty took charge, "Alright, that's enough of that. Let's just try to enjoy Christmas Eve, shall we?"

Leo blew out the rest of his hot air and shouted, "Come on in, Max."

The door swung open but taking more than a few steps into the room was a challenge for Pastor Max with so many people already crowded into the space. Pastor Max chuckled as he poked his head in and surveyed the surroundings. "Define 'in.'"

"Is that as far as you can go?" Betty asked.

"No worries," Pastor Max said, nodding, "You don't need me. And I gotta get back to my kids. I left them with a timed challenge. Can't wait to see what they've come up with. Here's all you need." He pulled two bags of Poly-Fil fiber out from behind him. Lifting the bags of white, fluffy filling material, he presented them to everyone, then shoved them through the door and into the room. In his best announcer voice, he read aloud from the back of the last package, "Made from recycled materials. Superior resiliency. Smooth consistency. Washable. Will not bunch." Max looked up at everyone, "Now *that* is super important. You don't want your belly to be all lumpy, Leo. Not a good look at all!" He continued to read. "And, last but not least, it's hypoallergenic. I didn't even know this mall had a fabric store, or how many different kinds of Santa-belly-stuffing there is to choose from. The clerk at the store said this should do the trick. Nothing but the finest to transform our Scrooge into Santa." Pastor Max erupted in laughter, almost immediately realizing he was laughing alone. He stopped, suddenly. "What? What did I miss?"

"Nothing. You just keep laughing, Max." Leo stood, arms akimbo trying to look professional, despite wearing just his white undershirt and dress slacks. "Though you're dangerously close to making my naughty list."

Betty cocked her head, giving Max a silent reprimand. She grabbed a bag of Poly-Fil, then joked with Leo. "If only you came with your own padding. You know, all the other Santa's we hire bring their own."

"News flash," Leo barked. "I'm not one of your Santa's." He then thought about it for a moment. "Hey, wait a minute. Now that I'm thinking about it, what does this gig pay?"

Suddenly Darci poked her head out from behind the suit. "Oh, we haven't got it in the budget to pay another Santa. We already paid the Santa who called in sick."

Betty, Leo, and Max all laughed out loud. Darci joined in moments later, but from the quizzical look on her face, she wasn't exactly sure what it was everybody found so funny.

Leo collected himself, "I was kidding…I didn't mean—"

Betty cut him off. "Thank you, Darci. Good to know." In her own frustration, Betty tore open one of the bags of filling. She reached inside with her right hand and pulled out a wad. She contemplated her next move. With a nod of her head, she decided to just do what needed to be done.

She took a deep breath and handed the bag of filling to Leo. "Make yourself useful," she commanded. She then straightened her back, grabbed

66

the front of his undershirt with her left hand, and began packing the inside of his shirt with the filling she held in her right hand.

There was no denying it, thought Leo. No matter how hard Betty tried to mask it, everyone knew just how uncomfortable she felt. By the same token, Leo couldn't help smiling in satisfaction, enjoying her discomfort.

As his eyes met with Betty's, his grin just got bigger, and her cheeks became a deeper shade of pink. "I could get used to this. Couldn't you, Betty?" Leo whispered, winking at her.

Betty rolled her eyes, trying to maintain her professionalism, despite her clear embarrassment.

Max came to the rescue, still standing just outside the door. "I've always said you needed somebody to help fatten you up, Leo!" He chuckled at the sight of his friend stuffed to the brim with fluff. "Not sure this is exactly what I meant, but I wouldn't miss this for the world."

"Didn't you say you needed to get back to your kids? I'm pretty sure you're breaking some law by leaving them to their own devices." Leo chastised in jest.

"That's my cue," Pastor Max saluted. "I know when I'm no longer wanted. See you all at the party."

As Max closed the door behind him, Leo inhaled deeply and filled his cheeks with air, holding his breath until they were two reddish bulbs; he looked like a chipmunk with a face full of nuts, hoarding them for the winter.

Betty crinkled her face and furrowed her brow, a visible question mark at the sight of his inflated cheeks. "What *on earth* are you doing?"

Leo exhaled and then recited a line from the "'Twas The Night Before Christmas" poem: "'His cheeks were like roses, his nose like a cherry!' Betty, I'm just getting into character."

"We have makeup for that," Darci offered up, still ill-at-ease but trying to join the fun. It was obvious she wasn't quite as used to comfortable camaraderie as the others. Still, her comment made them all laugh, albeit, probably for different reasons.

CHAPTER TWELVE

EMILY & THE ELF

Plans Change

Emily judged her reflection in one of the mall's store front windows. "Dear Lord, I'm huge," she exclaimed more loudly than she had intended. Tiny head, tiny feet, and in-between, she carried a Santa-would-be-proud-sized belly. She shook her head and shut her eyes at the sight. She turned away to waddle through the crowd of last-minute shoppers at Maplefield Mall, taking it all in. Her eyes sparkled, reflecting the Winter Wonderland scenes, the glittering lights, and the pure energy of her surroundings. Emily loved absolutely everything about Christmas, and she couldn't wait to share the miracle of the season with her own little miracle.

She rested her hands on her big belly, hugging her baby unconsciously. "Soon, Sweetie. Soon." In a surprise response, the baby kicked, causing her to catch her breath. "Oooo!" She braced herself with one hand against one of the store's front windows and breathed in methodically.

For just one moment, she thought, *Oh, no. Is this it? Was this what the start of contractions felt like? No. It couldn't be. Too early. Doctor Grey said her baby still needed to "bake." She said so.*

With a little too much effort, Emily dismissed her concerns and the twinge of pain subsided. She straightened up, dropped both hands to her sides, and filled her lungs with cinnamon-scented air. She paused in front of the store another few seconds and shut her eyes. Then, suddenly, she felt something else touch her; something wet and cold. She quickly opened her eyes and looked down.

There, poking her hand with his nose, stood a rather large, caramel-colored dog with a big white bird riding on his back. "What?" It was not at all what she'd expected. "Well, hello there!" Emily scratched under the dog's chin.

"Hello," the bird replied in its own high-pitched, screechy voice.

Emily playfully inquired, "Well, who are the two of you? Aren't you a mis-matched pair?" The dog nuzzled her again, enjoying the attention, as the bird sat placidly atop the mount it had chosen.

Continuing to scratch the dog's ears, Emily realized that the canine had something in his mouth. He nudged at her hand, almost as if he wanted her to have what he was carrying. Emily carefully lowered herself to the ground, a harder feat than ever with her baby bump. Bending at the waist was no longer an easy task, rather more of an act of faith. She hoped that once she eventually did get down, she'd be able to rise back up.

Once she was at eye level with her new furry friend and his feathered companion, she identified what was in the dog's mouth.

"Is that an Elf on the Shelf?" she said.

The bird screeched and flapped its wings. The dog released the little elf into Emily's open hand. It was slightly wet with slobber. The dog stepped back and stared at her. Emily didn't know what to make of it. Then, the dog nodded his head, licked her briefly on the nose, and barked, "WOOF!"

Emily giggled, and just as soon as she attempted to stand up, she stopped and looked over her shoulder at the commotion stirring behind her. A man and a woman just turned the corner and were racing towards her. Even from this distance, she could see that the woman's eyes were filled with tears as she cried out, "Momma's not happy, Rainbow…"

Seconds later, the man reached the woman's side. Emily heard him say, "I'll get your bird, Andrea. Please, don't cry. I hate to see anybody cry. I'll get Rainbow. I will!"

Immediately, Emily turned back to the dog and bird, but they had already fled the scene. As the woman and man rushed past her, she heard the man huff back to the dog, "Pickpocket, you're gonna be in the doghouse if you don't come back here right now!"

And then, just like that, the fur and feathers she'd met just moments earlier, and the people who followed, disappeared out of sight.

"Huh. So, who do *you* belong to?" Emily now contemplated the Elf on the Shelf she released from the dog's grip. She assumed that it must belong to one of the pets' owners, but it was too late to call out to them. The chase was on, and they all were well beyond where she currently stood.

"Okay, Mr. Elf on the Shelf," she addressed the little flop of red and green flannel that was lazily sprawled across the palm of her hand. "Looks like you're with me for now."

Holding the felt creature in her hand, she looked up at the giant, obnoxiously glaring neon sign before her that screamed GAMES & GADGETS GALORE.

"Oh, Elf, look, it's my first stop," she said to her new sidekick. "This is excellent. So now, we introduce ourselves to Mr. Abdullah and get Harry's drone for *free*." From the doorway, she could see mobs of people inside collected in a semicircle. To her dismay, they surrounded a bewildered-looking employee, gesturing in not the most holiday spirited kind of way. Emily took note of the security guard in his mirrored shades, monitoring the crowd from his position behind the counter. She could tell he was young, but he did strike quite a fierce pose in his uniform and seemed to be keeping the crowd civil.

That said, maybe now wasn't *quite* the best time to expect any kind of above-and-beyond customer service. She hesitated at the thought of entering the store and, fortunately, another store's sign down the way captured her attention: WindEE City Nail Salon.

Emily's eyes ping-ponged between the two signs and vastly different shops. Almost immediately, she made a decision.

"Change of plans," she triumphantly called out to no one who was actually listening. "First stop, mani-pedi."

She looked down at the elf. "What do you think? Paint my toes holly green in honor of the season?" Though he didn't give a verbal response, she decided to hear it anyway. "Yes, I agree, Elf on the Shelf, a nice holly shade of green sounds lovely." She hiked up her shoulders and nearly squealed out loud. She couldn't remember the last time she treated herself to a mani-pedi. "Oh, maybe they can do green with little red dots for decoration so that my toes look like they have holly berries on them. Doesn't that sound festive, little elf?"

Elf on the Shelf seemed excited as Emily focused on his little face and walked to her first destination of the nail salon. Unfortunately, she completely missed glancing at the flat-screen TV monitor hanging in the window of one of the other stores along the way. Had she stopped to briefly watch the news broadcast, she would have seen the destruction already caused by the unexpected snowstorm raging outside. She also would have heard the warnings about the dangerous weather conditions, the call for businesses to close up shop early, and the request for Chicagoans to not venture outdoors and stay safe inside their own homes.

CHAPTER THIRTEEN

HARRY & DAMIAN

Unpacking a Punch

The echoing airport announcements about flight delays and cancellations due to the unexpected snowstorm had people scurrying about, trying to find a route to their destinations before Christmas Day. Harry could barely hear himself above all the noise as he shouted into his cell phone.

Plugging his other ear with the palm of his hand, he repeated himself, "Hoping you can hear me, Emily. There's been a change of plans. We just landed at O'Hare and it's a complete zoo here at the airport. I wish I could come straight home to you first, but Wiggins isn't budging on going directly to Maplefield Mall. I'm sorry I'm not there with you. Wish you were here now. Em, call me when you get this…I miss you, Babe. I can't wait to see you. Call me if you need me. I love you and our baby."

Harry hung up and slipped his phone into the back pocket of his pants. He hoped his message was clear enough for his wife to hear. The fact that she didn't picked up had him just *slightly* worried. He let his mind wander to the possibility that she already was in labor. Without him. *She would have called him…Right?*

He got a grip. *Nope. Couldn't be. She would have left me a message.* Nevertheless, he wished she were around to take his call; he hated not actually being able to speak to her.

"Stop dragging your feet, Harry!"

He needed to hear her soothing voice instead of the voice Harry had been subjected to for hours now—that of Mr. Wiggins. He didn't know how much more of that condescending sound he could take. He watched as his impatient boss walked purposefully ahead of him, careful to keep his distance, lest anybody think he was associating with the hired help. In preparation for the blast of frigid air certain to hit them the second they ventured outside the airport doors, Mr. Wiggins already donned his long, black cashmere overcoat and was wrapping his matching scarf around his neck. He walked at such a fast clip.

Easy to do, thought Harry, *when unencumbered by any baggage.*

Unlike Harry, who trailed behind, not because he was "dragging his feet"—quite the contrary. Harry was tasked with dragging not only his own shoulder bag, but also the duffel belonging to his boss. The more he actually thought about it, however, he wasn't exactly "dragging" anything. That would have made things much easier, but it wasn't allowed per Mr. Wiggins's rule. It was made perfectly clear to him when they deplaned that he was to show the utmost care for Malcom's beloved Fendi mink fur duffel carry-on suitcase, imported from Italy to the tune of just under $10,000. Harry just shook his head at that fact. How he and Emily and the baby on its way could use that money. Ten. Thousand. Dollars. The bag didn't even come with rollers.

"Harry!" Mr. Wiggins stood just inside the sliding exit doors. He waited for Harry to reach him, not out of courtesy, mind you, but because he expected Harry to brave the winter weather outside to flag down the limo *before* he would even think of stepping foot into the cold.

Harry quickened his step while trying to pull on his own insulated, hooded parka. Emily gave the beast of a thing to him last Christmas. She was all about practicality, his girl. He knew his coat wasn't as fancy as Mr. Wiggins's, but he bet it was a heck of a lot warmer. For sure, it was cheaper.

Harry couldn't quite get his right arm into the sleeve of his coat. After battling it for a few seconds, he decided he needed to show it who was boss. So, he just balled up his fist, mustering all of his pent-up anger, and gave it his best push, hoping he'd finally be able to get his arm and sleeve to work together.

Unfortunately, Harry neglected to secure his perimeter, so to speak, and when he pushed his fist through the other end of his parka's sleeve, loaded with intention and focus, he accidently punched another traveler's jaw.

"Watch out! Damian!" Isabelle stood near them, waiting at baggage claim for her luggage when she happened to look up from her phone just in time to see the impending collision. By the time she shouted, it was too late. Damian got clocked right before her eyes, ironically, by the nicer of the two men sitting in front of them on the plane ride from Dallas here to Chicago.

As Damian's head snapped back from the force of the punch, Harry nearly fell over with his follow-through. Harry's wobble caused his cell phone to pop out of his pocket and skid across the floor, stopping under a row of chairs in a dark corner of the room—and nobody seemed to notice. Both men stayed standing, causing Isabelle to let out a huge sigh of relief. Not everyone, however, felt as she did.

"Harry! What are you doing?" Mr. Wiggins shouted. "Come on, man!"

It took a moment, but in that moment, Harry had no idea what had just happened. *Did I really just punch a stranger in the face? Could this trip get any worse?*

Absent-mindedly dropping Mr. Wiggins's $10,000 bag onto the dirty airport floor, along with his own, he turned to the spikey haired guy his hand just hit: "Oh, man, I am so, so sorry!" Looking over his shoulder at Wiggins's approaching outrage, Harry ignored him and turned back to Damian. "It was an accident. I am so sorry. I was just trying to get my coat on and—"

"Holy moly, Batman!" Damian interrupted Harry's mea-culpa moment. "You really decked me!"

Isabelle watched as Damian exaggerated the shaking of his head looking like a wet dog shaking itself dry. Damian erupted into laughter, and Isabelle couldn't help but smile herself at him. She took hold of her roller bag from the conveyor belt and quickly made her way to where they all stood.

"You pack one powerful punch, Kemosabe." Damian faced his mortified and unintending assailant. "You work out? Boxing? Tell me you work out. Otherwise, I'm hanging up my gloves."

Mr. Wiggins inched a little bit closer, cleared his throat, and gestured to Harry to pick up his precious cargo. Harry pretended not to see or understand what his boss wanted. *He could pick up his own damn bag!*

"No," Harry replied. "I have no time to work out." Harry shook his head. Evidently, this guy was either joking or he had hit him harder than anybody thought. Putting his hand on the stranger's shoulder and looking him in the eye, he asked with concern, "Are you okay? I really am so sorry."

Damian looked at Harry and gave him a crooked half-smile. Then, he saw Isabelle, and his smile widened. "Dude, seriously, don't stress. I'm fine."

Suddenly, a man who physically looked more like a bouncer, but was impeccably dressed from head-to-toe in chauffeur's attire, nervously addressed Mr. Wiggins, "Sir, the limo's just outside, double-parked. Can I get your bags for you?"

Mr. Wiggins pointed to his pricey duffel that still lay upon the filthy floor next to Harry's. "Those bags there," he said. He walked up to Harry. "Are you done here?"

"Limo? You have a limo?" Damian's eyes danced with mischief. He then sauntered up to Isabelle and whispered, "How were you planning on getting to where you're going?"

Crinkling her nose, she waved her phone and said, "Uber or Lyft or…? I'm not much of a planner. Wanna share a ride, if we can even find one?"

Damian smiled devilishly. "I think we deserve better." He then turned to face Wiggins and Harry. "You know, *we* could use a ride."

Isabelle's eyes widened. She murmured under her breath, "Brilliant!"

"A ride?" Mr. Wiggins appeared flabbergasted. "With me? In my limo? Young man, what makes you think I'm even going your way?"

Damian cradled his jaw with his hand and feigned great pain.

Isabelle chimed in, "The *young man* and I were headed toward the mall and from what I've discerned, you're headed to the mall, too, right? Oh, but wait a minute…maybe we oughta get my friend's noggin checked out at the hospital first. You know, just in case. I mean, he went down pretty hard and who knows if he has a concussion…or worse."

Damian and Harry both tried to hide their smiles.

"You did punch me," Damian said to Harry who winced at the reminder.

"That I did, Mr. Wiggins," Harry underscored the fact to the reluctant decision-maker.

Mr. Wiggins was not amused. Cocking one of his bushy eyebrows and looking down his nose at the lot of them, he opened his mouth, only to be cut off by Isabelle.

"You talk really, really loud, at least on planes," Isabelle flashed him an "I-won't-take-'no'-for-an-answer" look.

With a huff, Mr. Wiggins gestured to his chauffeur. "Well? What are you waiting for?" He led the way with a giggling Harry, Damian, and Isabelle falling in step behind.

No one could hear Harry's cell phone ringing, as it lay on the floor hidden underneath the row of chairs. The glow of its screen showed Emily's face. Her incoming call would go unnoticed and unanswered.

CHAPTER FOURTEEN

VERN & HOLLY

Familiar Faces

In the grocery store's near-empty parking lot, the beige Volvo had its hood raised and almost blended into the snowdrift it just hit. In the distance, the neon glow of the "Jewel-Osco" sign cast a reddish hue over everything it touched, including Vi and Vern who stood outside their inoperable vehicle.

Vi, her face an even deeper shade of red due to the extreme cold, began to pace. Vern adjusted the volume on his hearing aids, while shouting into his cell phone, "Can you speak up?"

He turned to look at Vi, all bundled up in her floor-length, white puffer coat. When she bought it, Vern told her the coat would make her look like the Michelin Man. He was right. It did, and he struggled not to laugh.

"Oh, give me that." Vi stepped over to him, yanking the phone out of his hand and shouting into it. "Listen here, our car won't start. We're stuck here in the parking lot of the Jewel…Hello?"

With every step, Vern lifted each foot up high over the piling snow to make sure he wouldn't be stuck, just like his car. He couldn't believe how much it had snowed in such a short period of time. He also couldn't believe he swerved right into this snowbank, almost as if he was aiming for it, or maybe the car was possessed. He looked up to the sky. It didn't look as if the storm was stopping any time soon.

"You lose the connection?" Vern asked.

Full of indignation, Vi replied, "Ugh! I think the tow truck man hung up on me. How long did he tell you he'd be before he got here?"

Vern continued to look for something in the engine—exactly what, he hadn't a clue. He always let the professionals do the real work, but he figured it looked good to any passersby to see a stranded motorist at least trying to fix the problem himself, instead of waiting to be rescued. Of course, he was well aware that passersby weren't exactly in abundance at the moment. As a matter of fact, they were pretty much all alone in that parking lot. Still, having the hood up might make them more visible to potential Good Samaritans or that tow truck driver if he does have a change of heart and decides to come out to get them.

Vern poked his head around the side of the lifted hood and said to Vi, "The tow truck driver didn't give me a time. He just said he wasn't coming—too many stranded folks. Too much snow. Blah-blah-blah." Vern shrugged and waived both his gloved hands around in the air as if swatting away at the excuses.

Out of seemingly nowhere, a female voice made them both jump. "Do you two need some help?"

Holly stepped toward them from around the back of the stranded couple's wagon. Vern took a long look at her. *Why did she look so familiar?* A moment later, and it came to him; he recognized her.

"You're the girl from that van," Vern recalled.

"What girl?" Vi asked.

"'Woman' actually," Holly corrected them. "Hear me roar!" She winked. But Vi and Vern just blankly stared back. *Dumb joke*, she thought, moving toward them, her arm outstretched to shake hands. "I'm Holly. I'm here with my colleague—*she did love the sound of that*—Ian. He's in the store."

"We were just in there," Vi softly added. "Needed to pick up some flowers…" Her voice trailed off.

"Your coworker, he's the driver of that van?" Vern cocked his head a bit, pointing to the WACK-TV van, and from the look on his face, none too pleased. "The guy who was trying to run me over back there on the highway?"

"Oh, is *that* who she is?" Vi asked. "Well, you and your friend should be ashamed of yourselves, driving like that in this weather. You could have gotten us all killed or caused some major chain-reaction accident." She then made the sign of the cross across her body. "There but for the grace of God."

"Yeah, right." Holly straightened her back, duly chastised. "Sorry about that. I tried to tell him. He has some anger management issues." Holly pointed to Ian who was now trudging his way through the snow from the store's entrance to where they all stood. In each hand, he carried a couple of large, filled plastic bags. A few Christmas-themed wrapping paper rolls poked out of the top of one bag. Holly assumed that Ian found some suitable gifts for his brother Vincent—ones that he could actually wrap. She also hoped he bought them something to eat and drink. She was so hungry.

As he approached, the look on Ian's face of *"Now what?"* needed no words.

"So, do you two need a lift somewhere?" Holly knew Ian would chew her out about it but there was something familiar about this old couple; she just couldn't leave them stranded when she knew that she and Ian could easily offer to help.

Anger swept across Ian's face. Holly could only imagine what he was thinking, finding herself impressed that he had yet to say a single word. She decided to take it as a sign that he was on board with giving these two a ride, despite knowing that probably wasn't the case.

"Go ahead and put your things in the back of the van," Holly directed the couple who began unloading their Volvo.

Ian took in the wagon's uplifted hood and watched as the elderly couple began gathering their things and transferring them into his van. Trudging through the heavy snow, Ian took the final few steps toward them, huffing and puffing as if it were more like a few hundred paces. *This is wet snow,* Ian thought. *Snowman-building snow…* But these thoughts quickly disappeared, as he was completely out of breath by the time he reached Holly.

"What's…going…on?" Ian could barely get the words out.

"We're giving them a ride," Holly stated matter-of-factly. "Their car broke down, and it's Christmas Eve."

Without skipping a beat, Ian replied, "Not happening." He then addressed the couple. "We'll call AAA for you."

"We tried that," Vi said. "Everybody says they're too busy. No one can help us, except for your lovely colleague here. Holly, is it? I'm Vi and this is Vern"

"Yes. My name is Holly. And this is Ian. Nice to meet ya. And, yes, we can. Help, that is." Holly stared Ian down.

Ian rolled his eyes and inhaled in the most exaggerated of ways. With no other real choice, he tossed his grocery bags into the van's already open back doors. He then shouted at the trio, "We're not making any extra stops. Already way late as it is."

Holly clasped her hands together, and held them up to her mouth, trying to hide her ridiculously big grin. *Why was she so happy about this? She hadn't a clue.*

Ian couldn't help but ask, "What about *any* of this has you so giddy?"

Hiking her shoulders up to her ears, Holly confessed, "No clue. Do I *have* to have a reason to feel happy at Christmas?"

Ian shook his head. "Well, don't just stand there. Come on!" With one final wave, he made his way to the driver's side of the van, opened the door and hopped into his seat.

Holly helped with the last of Vi and Vern's bags, closed the van's back doors, and helped the couple walk over to the sliding side door, hoisting them both up into the back bench seat. "Buckle up," she cheerily told them, as she shut the door, then opened hers on the passenger side to climb up into her seat.

Ian turned his whole body toward her, and after Holly clicked her seatbelt buckle, she locked eyes with him. "What…?"

"This is a giant mistake," Ian said, not caring if his unwanted passengers heard.

"Sheryl Crow. 1998," Holly responded, her chin held high.

"What the hell does that mean?" Ian barked.

Holly fluttered her eyelashes at him. "Maybe this will end up being one of your favorite mistakes, you know, like the song."

Without another word, Ian rolled his eyes, started the engine, and off they went.

CHAPTER FIFTEEN

LEO & DARCI

Mr. and Mrs. Claus

"This is one giant mistake."

Leo's crystal blue eyes were wide open and, yet, never in his wildest dreams would he have foreseen himself here in the small backstage area of the mall's theatre where events took place, dressed up as Santa, sitting on an overstuffed golden throne, passing himself off as the headlining Jolly Old St. Nick. Play acting just wasn't in him. *What was he supposed to say? Would his "Ho-Ho-Ho" sound authentic? He should have practiced his vocals and his gestures, too. Why didn't he think of that, sooner?*

Betty could tell, anybody could, from the panicked look on his face that Leo was way out of his comfort zone. "Stop overthinking this," her voice cut through the chatter of voices that lived in his head, as she stepped up onto the riser.

Leo did a double take to make sure it was *his* Betty. He looked her up and down, still not believing what he saw. There she was in all her red velvet finery, dressed as Mrs. Claus. The pointy tips of her black, patent leather boots peeked out from underneath her white petticoats and flowing dark skirt. The floor-length hem, along with the cuffs around her wrists, were trimmed in a fluffy, white fur. As his eyes traced up the curves of her hips to her neckline, Leo blushed in spite of himself. How often had he thought of Betty's curves? How many times while working at her side did he have to steel himself away from the thoughts Santa would definitely deem naughty? Maintaining his professional distance grew increasingly challenging. But at this moment, he realized, he didn't have to, and he didn't care to. They were pretending to be a married couple! What he wanted to do was soak in every inch of her, and what others thought of them was none of his business.

Leo's eyes caressed Betty's costume, noticing the off-the-shoulder top edged with furry wisps of white, swirls of gold filigree, and a sprinkle of glittery snowflakes. How she looked made him a believer. She instantly had him convinced that he could be Santa Claus, as long as she was his Mrs. He loved most, perhaps, the very top of her head—no longer styled in her usual beautiful brown coif, but now appearing as a tangle of shimmery silver locks coiled beneath a red-velvet bonnet-like cap with ruffled lace trim. Betty's costume made him think that she was the perfect complement to his own natural silver head of hair and matching beard.

"Ho-Ho-Ho!" Leo joyously roared, rising and flashing a smile that brought a sparkle to his eyes. Or maybe they sparkled because of *her*. His eyes drank her in. "Betty, I think you're going to start a new trend in women's fashion."

Betty curtsied, or at least, she tried to. Striking a bit of an awkward pose, she mused, "I feel almost as silly as I must look!"

Leo shook his head, "You look amazing!" Beaming with pride, he added, "If there were a prize for the most seasonal power couple, I think we would win it, hands down!"

Betty swung her wide skirt back and forth, throwing back her head in laughter as she did so. From its pocket, she pulled out a pair of round, wire-rimmed glasses, unfolded them, and propped them up upon the bridge of her nose. She then lowered her head and directed her playful eyes at Leo, declaring, "I will admit, this poofy skirt is a whole lot more fun than my Chanel pencil skirts."

"But equally as sexy," Leo blurted out the words, swept away in his desires, making Betty's face and his own turn bright red.

Darci's face, too, flushed as she waited in a corner of the room in silence, before intruding on the pair and their flirting. She already tried to interrupt with her announcement to no avail. This time, she cleared her throat in the most melodramatic of ways, announcing, "They are *not* coming!" That got Leo and Betty's attentions and, finally, Mr. and Mrs. Claus focused on her. Darci suddenly felt in the spotlight and nervously fidgeted.

"So sorry, Darci dear," Betty turned to address her. "Who's not coming? Your...I mean, Mr. Wiggins?"

How she wished that were actually the case! Darci hated to be reminded of the guy orchestrating the mall's demise and how everyone seemed to think that, somehow, she had any say in the matter.

"No, he's still coming. In fact, he called from the airport. Delayed because of the weather, he said, but on his way," Darci responded, sounding deflated.

"Then who's not coming?" Leo urged, standing up from his throne and making his way over to Betty's side.

"The media."

"What?" Betty crinkled her nose in disbelief. "But they always come to cover Pastor Max's Christmas Eve Kids Cheer Fest."

"I know," Darci nervously laughed. "That's what they all pretty much said," she continued to explain, consulting the notes she took on her iPad. "They said the story's been reported for years with nothing new to add to it. One news director said the numbers weren't cutting it with the ratings. Another one said it was old news. Nearly everyone I talked to added that with the surprise snowstorm, they were keeping crews available for..." She scrolled the screen, searching her notes. "Here it is: 'whatever crisis or disaster we hope the storm will create.'"

"Well doesn't that just beat all?" Leo exclaimed. "They're not looking for a Christmas feel-good story. They're praying for a Christmas catastrophe."

Unaware of the news and the now-somber mood in the air, Pastor Max practically leapt into the room where they stood in their Santa finery, singing, "Oh, by gosh, by golly…It's time for mistletoe and holly!" He spun himself around to face Betty and Leo. "Mr. and Mrs. Santy Claus…I *knew* you existed! Right under my nose all these years!" He wagged his finger in jest; then, realizing no one else was smiling, he put his hands on his hips as a puzzled look crossed his face.

"Max," Leo began. "We just heard that the media folks aren't coming."

Pastor Max looked off to his right. His Christmas spirit dimmed. A mix of anger, doubt, and fear swept his visage.

Leo knew what his friend was thinking: No media meant no publicity for his program. No publicity for the program meant no people presenting end-of-year philanthropic gifts to help pay for all the good work he and his parish did for the community.

Blowing outward and shaking his entire body, Pastor Max clapped his hands and sprang back to life. "Story of my life, Leo," he nearly sang out. "But we both know when God closes one door…"

Darci excitedly blurted out, as if she were on a game show and eligible to win a prize for answering first, "He opens a window!"

Pastor Max turned to face her, as his smile spread even wider across his face. "Look at you, Darci!" he said, matching her spirit. "You are so right. But I like to say, 'When God closes a door, STOP BANGIN' ON IT!'"

Max's accompanying act out had everybody laughing. "That door wasn't meant for you, fool!"

At that moment, two of Santa's helpers eased their way into the too-tiny room for so many people, trying to go unnoticed. But Pastor Max immediately had them in his sights.

"Ah-ha! Speaking of fools…" Pastor Max skipped over to the life-sized elves. He playfully grabbed them both by the hands and purposefully inspired them to skip over to where he could properly introduce them. "I give to you Elf Karina and Elf Randy."

Betty, Leo, and Darci applauded, cheered, and even "woo-hoo'd"!

Pastor Max could barely keep it together as he watched Karina and Randy shrink in their costumes, wanting to magically disappear. He could imagine what they were wishing: *Oh, where was Harry Potter's Invisibility Cloak now?* Karina held one hand over her face. Randy kept trying to twist free from Pastor Max's grip on him. Max, Darci, Leo, and Betty just kept giggling.

"This ain't right," Randy murmured.

"Pastor Max, this is 'cruel and unusual punishment,'" Karina said, still using her whole hand to hide behind.

"Ya," Randy added. "There's laws, and we got rights."

"Don't do the crime if you can't do the time…Oh, ya…Don't do it!" Pastor Max sang to the tune of that old Sammy Davis, Jr. theme song from one of his favorite TV shows, *Baretta*. He thought about the reruns he watched from prison. He could recite almost every line of every episode. Max always thought that one day he'd have a big, white bird named Fred, too. "You both shouldn't have been fighting on the bus. This is your payback. Speaking of which, where are the rest of the kids? I told you all to stick together."

"Man, you trippin'," Randy responded. "You think they be wantin' to hang with us lookin' like this? They all be messin' around at that game store."

Karina freed her face from its self-imposed prison and presented her case to "the court of Christmas" that stood in front of her, "The U.S. Supreme Court said that you can't impose a sentence that's disproportionate to the crime committed."

Pastor Max froze as he beamed proudly, his eyes fixated on this girl. "Guuurrrlll! *That* was seriously impressive. Somebody is doing her homework. So, somebody also—probably, maybe, most likely—already knows that the U.S. Supreme Court gave authorities *lots* of latitude in deciding what is appropriate and what punishments and crimes are complementary. I—in case you missed it—*am* the authority."

Randy faced forward, blinking several times. "My head hurts." He adjusted his elf hat, one that anyone from a distance could see was two sizes too small.

Pastor Max didn't skip a beat with his commentary. "Now don't be all Scrooge-like, Randy. I know your hat may be too small, but your heart—I know—is twice as big as them all."

Both Randy and Karina exchanged glances, muttering to themselves, "What…?"

Darci, again, couldn't help herself, laughing and interjecting, "No, no, you've got that wrong, Pastor Max. It's not Scrooge, but the Grinch. The Grinch has a heart that's two sizes too small."

All eyes of the "court of Christmas" turned their puzzled faces toward her. A moment later, and they all busted out laughing.

Darci paused and embarrassedly lowered her head. She knew they were laughing at her, but she wasn't sure exactly why. She never seemed to get the jokes, or the jokes always seemed to be about her. She tried so hard to fit in. Everyone else didn't have a problem being part of the group. Why did she? She never really felt she belonged anywhere, especially not here.

Betty approached, putting her arm around Darci's shoulders. "You, my dear Darci, are, indeed, correct."

Darci leaned into Betty just a bit. She knew she was right, and Betty's embrace made her feel better about what she had said. Still, she didn't understand why everyone thought it was so funny. Everyone knew about the Grinch and his heart, Darci thought to herself. And she of all people knew the Grinch all too well.

Just then, Darci's rose gold Apple Watch rang. She looked down at it. Mr. Wiggins was calling. Not wanting to be taken out of the group's merriment, Darci quickly placed her hand over the screen to silence the call.

CHAPTER SIXTEEN

MR. WIGGINS & DAMIAN
Making an Ass out of UME

Mr. Wiggins sat squarely in the center of the limousine's backseat, his cell phone positioned at his ear. Outwardly frustrated that his call went to voicemail, he jabbed his finger at the screen to hang up. "That girl is never around when I need her." Composing himself again, facing forward stoically, he barely moved a muscle—a technique he employed often in an attempt to keep himself calm and in control, especially in front of *others* or *the unknown*. Today, he found himself face-to-face with both: An unexpected snowstorm outside and two complete strangers inside the limo that was supposed to only transport himself and his minion, Harry. "How is it possible?" Mr. Wiggins mindlessly blurted out loud.

Harry, Isabelle, and Damian all looked at one another, waiting for more to be said. Mr. Wiggins had forced Harry to sit in between the two interlopers. Now, all three were cozily cramped, riding backwards, sharing the same backseat. With a look of disdain, Mr. Wiggins scanned all three of them. *I'm no fool*, he thought. He had watched enough movies to know just how much the lower class plotted to overtake the wealthy. All of this—from the plane ride to the punch in the face to them needing a ride—all of it could turn out to be nothing more than a ploy to rob him or take him hostage. *Serendipity, hogwash!*

"How is what possible?" Damian inquired, not worrying about what he surmised to be true: The fact that Mr. Wiggins felt multiple social classes above him.

Mr. Wiggins quizzically looked at the three of them, not quite sure what Damian meant, but extremely sure that he didn't like to be addressed by someone unauthorized to do so, especially someone so very demonic looking. He took in Damian's spiky hair and tried to resist openly sneering.

"You shouted out a second ago, 'How is it possible?'" Damian reenacted Mr. Wiggins's outburst in a slightly mocking way.

Letting out an exasperated breath, Mr. Wiggins cut him off with a reply, "You don't notice the horrendous weather outside? The traffic jam? Must I spell it out for you? With so much technology, *how is it possible* for something like this to happen? I'll answer for you. One can only conclude that human error is at fault for interpreting the forecasts inaccurately."

Damian thoughtfully studied the man's face, his tone of voice, and his posture. Damian heard him snarl and grunt out orders for a few hours on the plane, but this was the first time he had a chance to look the man in the eyes. Now, all Damian could see was a man in pain. *Why so sad? What makes you so displeased with pretty much everything that surrounds you?* A moment later, just as Mr. Wiggins was about to dismiss him, Damian winked and simply said, "Man makes plans...and God laughs."

At this, the tiniest of smiles alongside the most amused of looks swept across Mr. Wiggins's face, as he thought to himself: *Well that was a surprise...A demon quipping about God.*

"Ah...an unlikely philosopher among us," Mr. Wiggins dripped with sarcasm. "Do tell, Damian—was that your name? What is it that you do exactly?"

"Why thank you for the compliment," Damian smirked. "I do appreciate philosophy, the arts, the sciences, the study of man from all perspectives. You got my name right. But do elaborate, if you would, what do you mean, exactly, by 'do'?"

Mr. Wiggins, annoyed at the exchange and at having to explain what was to him the very measure of a man, stammered, "'Do' as in 'for a living.' From your appearance, I venture you're some sort of anarchist, or, perhaps, a starving musician?"

"Oh, right, got it." Damian wondered how long it would take Mr. Moneybags to get around to asking him about his livelihood. "While I do love music and do pride myself of being a bit of a rebel, I'm definitely not starving. I own Burn Baby Burn Bootcamps. We just made the Fortune 500 list of the 100 Fastest-Growing Companies. But I doubt someone like you would have heard of someone like me."

Harry eyed him, surprised at the response. He had heard of those workouts—not that he ever had time to go to one. "No kidding?" he said. "That's you? You're huge. Really?"

Damian puffed up just a bit. "Yes, really. No joke. And hey, man, I wasn't kidding either about that right hook of yours. You should come join one of my gyms. I could use someone like you. We also made their list of 100 Best Companies to Work For as ranked by employees. Might be a nice change of pace for you."

Mr. Wiggins rolled his eyes, dismissing Damian's offer to Harry and dig to himself and his own company. He quickly put an end to any kind of bonding between the two men. Ignoring the exchange and returning no response, he said to Isabelle, "And you, young lady? What do you do?"

Isabelle's tiny smile showed her amusement at the tense back-and-forth power struggle between the two men. "Isabelle. My name's Isabelle. I head up CSR for a global tech company." She paused for a moment. From the look on Mr. Wiggins's face, she wasn't sure he had understood. "CSR stands for Corporate Social Responsibility."

Mr. Wiggins shifted uncomfortably in his seat. "Good God, I know what CSR is. You're one of those tree huggers."

Isabelle's eyes nearly popped out of her head. She wanted to clarify, but then ended up simply nodding with a smile. She learned long ago to pick and choose her battles, and this one just wasn't worth her time. "Yup. That's me!"

Damian smirked, reading her completely. "It's all part of the *young lady's* plan, Mr. Wiggins, to be a bad influence on society. And I wholly support her. You should know, too, that one more thing I 'do' is play bass in a band, and I double as a black sheep."

Tilting her head and winking at Damian, Isabelle let out a chuckle. She looked over at Mr. Wiggins and decided to educate him. "You know, Mr. Wiggins, you're partially correct about human error being a factor in this snowstorm. The computer models showed the potential for this storm. But the data the systems needed to predict precisely when and where the storm would come to a head were probably missing. Classic junk in, junk out—that holds true for a lot of things in life, wouldn't you agree?"

Damian beamed at Isabelle. *Smart was soooo sexy!* "Mother Nature always wins." He gestured with his hands as if dropping a bomb and let out an explosive *BOOM!* sound.

Mr. Wiggins waved them both away with his hands and turned to the one person he assumed would take orders without any back talk. Wagging a knobby finger at Harry, he barked, "Make yourself useful. Find out how long this storm is going to last. And get Darci on the phone."

Harry's slouched position and brief shake of his head demonstrated how much he hated to jump at his master's command, especially in front of Damian and Isabelle who seemed like a breath of fresh air, so to speak. Reaching into his back pocket for his phone, Harry suddenly panicked as his hand came up empty. He shut his eyes, fearing the worst. "Oh, no…" He half-stood, reaching into all of his pant's pockets and, then, grabbed his coat and furiously searched every one of its pockets. He found nothing. He instantly reached in between the seatback and seat cushion behind him—*no luck*—then, felt around on the floor, begging forgiveness from his seatmates as he did so. "Excuse me, Isabelle, Damian."

The couple shifted in their seats, giving Harry full access to search. It didn't take long for him to finally conclude that somehow, somewhere, he had lost his phone.

Taking note of the obvious, Mr. Wiggins looked down his long nose, enunciating every word, "So. Very. Disappointing. And, yet, somehow, so quite expected."

"Oh, man," Damian ignored the old man, focusing on Harry. "I've been there. Losing your phone sucks. Maybe it's in the trunk?" Damian pulled out his own phone, handing it to Harry. "Dial your number. If it's here in the car, we'll hear it ring."

Harry dialed, but they didn't hear a ring. He handed the phone back to Damian and slumped down into his seat. "Well, isn't that just awesome!" In frustration, he punched his fist in the air, sarcasm dripping from every molecule of his body.

"Hey, man, seriously, you gotta join my gym," Damian quipped, trying to lighten the mood.

Harry laughed despite his circumstances. "Damian, if I had no time before, I'll have even less of it soon. My wife, Emily, is pregnant. Our first kid. She's due any minute. So not only am I *not* with her when I promised I would be, but now she can't even get a hold of me if she needs me because I lost my blasted phone!"

"A baby, that's so exciting," Isabelle exclaimed.

"Yeah, man, congrats," Damian added. "Here, just call your wife from my phone and leave her a message. None of us are going anywhere. If she calls back, I got you."

Harry accepted the phone and started dialing again. "Thanks, I really appreciate it."

Mr. Wiggins clicked his tongue in disapproval and turned his gaze out the tinted window.

"You don't have any children, do you, Mr. Wiggins?" Isabelle asked.

He turned to look at her with such disdain. "Whether I do or do not, young lady, is none of your business."

"Hey, Em, it's me," Harry spoke into the phone. "I'm hoping you're okay. I lost my phone, so please call me back at this number. I really need to hear your voice. I love you." Hitting the disconnect button, a choked-up Harry handed the phone back to Damian.

"I'm sure your wife's fine," Damian said.

"Yeah, Harry, you'll see," Isabelle added reassuringly.

"Oh, don't kid yourselves, now," Mr. Wiggins chimed in. "Hundreds of women each year die giving birth."

Harry's eyes grew big, incredulous at the comment, even for his boss. "How could you say something like that?"

"What *is* your deal, old man?" Damian snarled.

"Deal?" Mr. Wiggins coughed. "No deal. Just stating facts. Back when I…" his voice trailed off. Clearing his throat, he began again. "Well, decades ago, the numbers were almost no different than they are now. Another sign of human incompetence."

"Incompetence?" Harry's eyes narrowed as he spat out the word. "You're right, Mr. Wiggins. Humans are flawed. We make mistakes. And that includes continuing to follow people who don't merit our time, our effort, or anything we stupidly try to give them. I'll put myself in that category since I slaved away for years working for you."

Harry continued grumbling under his breath as he gazed out the window. *Waste of time…good for nothing…* Isabelle and Damian exchanged glances.

Mr. Wiggins leaned forward and opened his mouth as if about to respond. But then he looked at Harry whose eyes glassed over with tears. Isabelle and Damian avoided his stare. He shut his mouth and turned back to his window. He genuinely didn't mean for what he said to come out as it did. He actually was trying to help, but even he had to admit he had never been much good at doing that. All he was trying to say was that he knew what it felt like to love something—someone—so much that the very life inside of you wasn't much of a life without them. Chastising himself, he remembered that nothing good ever comes from showing vulnerability. Never get attached to anything or anyone. Fate will make sure you are punished. How he hated dealing with other people. Holding onto his beliefs came much more easily when all alone.

"Confounded!" Mr. Wiggins finally blurted out, looking at his watch. "How much longer are we to be trapped in this car?"

CHAPTER SEVENTEEN

DR. HAYWOOD & HOLLY

Tell Me about Nothing

Vincent sat on his bed, near to tears, clutching both his overnight bag and his gift for Ian. "Please, Dr. Haywood," he begged. "Try calling my brother again. Please!"

Dr. Haywood stood, his face a mixture of empathy and anger. He wanted to call Vincent's brother a whole bunch of things, none of them very Christian. Just as he was about to take a seat at Vincent's side, trying, once again, to comfort him and pretend that he wasn't enraged and disappointed for Vince, the nurse poked her head into Vincent's room. "Dr. Haywood, you have a visitor."

He turned to the nurse, surprised. "Thank you. I'll be right out."

"See? I told you!" Vincent exclaimed. He then shouted to the nurse, "I told Dr. Haywood that Ian would come." Vincent wiped away his tears but still kept a tight grip on his belongings. Dr. Haywood nodded to the nurse to leave. He then turned back to Vincent, taking note of him hugging his personal things. Dr. Haywood suspected that somewhere inside of Vincent, he, too, hadn't believed that his brother would really show. But what could he now say to ease Vincent's pain?

"Dr. Haywood?" the young, female voice called out to him from the doorway.

He turned to face the woman. Vincent peered at her from behind Dr. Haywood's back.

Dr. Haywood couldn't believe his eyes. His entire face exuded pure joy, "Holly...?" He took a few steps toward her, remembering that lost little girl who was left in his care at this very hospital so long ago. Look at her now. "Holly, what a lovely Christmas surprise!"

Behind him, Vincent's face fell.

"What are you doing here?" Dr. Haywood asked his visitor, moving in for an embrace.

Holly hugged him back. "I'm with my colleague, Ian."

"Ian?" Vincent's ears perked up. "Ian's here?"

Holly broke free from Dr. Haywood and looked over at Vincent. "Hey, hey are you Vincent?" she asked. "Your brother told me all about you."

Just at that moment, Ian stepped through the doorway behind Holly. "Hey, little buddy..." he said.

Holly moved out of the way, which was probably best because Vincent shot up from his bed like a firecracker. Letting his luggage and the gift box fall to his side, he literally threw himself into Ian's arms.

"Ian! You came, you came! Dr. Haywood, look. It's Ian. He came. I knew he would."

"I see that, Vincent." Dr. Haywood nodded to Ian hoping that maybe he had been wrong about Ian. Maybe this time, it would be different, and Ian *would* actually take Vincent on an overnight visit to celebrate Christmas as a family. But seconds later, he realized it wasn't very likely that he was wrong.

There was something in Ian's stiffness combined with the fact that he wasn't returning Vincent's embrace that told Dr. Haywood how, once again, this all would go.

Holly grabbed one of Ian's arms and forced it into a half-hearted embrace. She mouthed to him and spoke quietly, "What's the matter with you? Hug him!"

Ian stood as if paralyzed, letting Vincent hug him but still not fully returning the gesture.

Dr. Haywood chimed in. "How about you two visit with one another here for a little spell, while Holly and I do some catching up? We'll be right outside, I promise."

Ian slowly turned to Holly, a giant question mark invisibly hung in the air to accompany the surprised look sitting upon his face. He now mouthed the words to her: "Catching up?"

Dr. Haywood and Holly exited, leaving the two brothers alone in Vincent's orderly room.

Ian broke his brother's embrace. "Vincent, let go of me."

Vincent let go of the hug at last, his shoulders sagging with disappointment, though he was trying to be optimistic. The two stared at one another for a moment, each looking unsure of what to do or say next.

Awkwardly, Ian reached out into the hallway and pulled his two sacks of gifts into the room. "Now…no peeking until Christmas morning, tomorrow."

At the sight of the gifts, a giddy Vincent squealed with glee, grabbed his little suitcase and Ian's beribboned mystery box, and quickly hopped back to where his brother stood.

"Okay! I'm ready, Ian. Let's blow this joint."

Meanwhile in the hallway, Dr. Haywood and Holly were engrossed in conversation, unaware of the exchange occurring between the two brothers. "Holly, I can't believe it's really you." Dr. Haywood shook his head in awe. "How have you been? Tell me everything that's going on in your life."

Holly looked at her surroundings, her face illuminated as memories flooded back. She walked these very halls alone at night, pretending they were her yellow brick road leading her home. How many Christmases she spent here and how many times she gave up hope on anyone coming to visit her—except for Dr. Haywood. He always showed up to be with her and all the other throwaways, just like he was here now for Vincent. Holly's eyes glistened as she faced the man she considered her lifesaver. Swallowing back her tears, she shook her head and gave him a comical look. "Everything? Really?"

Dr. Haywood lifted an eyebrow, not at all surprised at her response. "Or…I suppose you could just tell me about *nothing*," he quipped back.

She remembered this sentence. It was how he and she started talking, way back when. It was the first thing he asked her. No, wait, it was the second. His first was, *So I understand some stuff is going on.* Holly remembered responding with a very guarded, *Oh, it's nothing.* That's when Dr. Haywood said the words that changed her life forever: *Okay, so tell me about nothing.* Wow. Now, as she took a minute to simply look at this kind man's face, she realized how much time had really passed. Had it really been nearly a decade since she had been dragged to this place? Dropped off. Abandoned. Her parents suffered enough of her "crazy" and decided they would just throw her away. She figured that she might as well just end it. Nobody wanted her. So why even bother trying to be "normal"? At the time, she felt her worthlessness was pretty clear to just about everybody else. But Dr. Haywood had proved her wrong.

She was barely 10 years old. *Who does that to a kid? Who does that to anyone?*

Their conversation was interrupted by a brutal yelp. "Liar!"

Dr. Haywood scrambled at the sound of Vincent screaming, racing into his room with Holly following.

"Vincent, calm down," a disheveled Ian was wiping away a trickle of sweat from his brow. "I brought you all these gifts. Why don't you open them up, at least?"

"What's going on?" Dr. Haywood interjected himself, knowing it was necessary. "Vincent? What's going on, buddy?"

Vincent nearly foamed at the mouth. "He's a liar! He said he was taking me home for Christmas. Now he says he's too busy."

Dr. Haywood glared disapprovingly at Ian, knowing it would have been better if he had not come at all. Why should this year be any different than all the others? At least they knew how to manage Vincent with "no shows"—they'd had so many years of practice at that. This would surely set the boy back in his progress, and Dr. Haywood's heart sunk at the thought.

"Vincent, I have to get back to work," Ian pleaded. "I already might lose my job. Even Holly could get in trouble."

"No! Don't you dare bring me into this, Ian." Holly raised her hands and stepped back.

Vincent continued his tirade. "Lies. It's all lies. If you wanted to spend time with me, you would. Dr. Haywood's a doctor and he's *never* too busy! You're a *nothing with no time and nothing.*"

Vincent marched over to the corner of his room and reached down to retrieve the ribboned shoebox that held Ian's Christmas gift. He took a few steps back toward Ian.

"Here! Here's your *stupid* Christmas gift!" He proceeded to throw the box at Ian who managed to catch it instead of deflecting the blow Vince intended.

"Vincent, don't be like this," Ian barely whispered the words. "I'm sorry…"

Vincent retreated to his bed, grabbed the covers, and cocooned himself inside. He rocked himself forwards and backwards and, like a wounded animal, he wailed.

Ian couldn't stand the sight or the sound of it. He clutched Vincent's gift to his chest, sheepishly bidding Dr. Haywood a farewell nod. He backed out of the room. "Holly, I'll be in the van," he said.

She barely heard him, and he couldn't even look her in the eye.

Ian turned toward Vincent's shaking body one last time, debating if he should even say anything. He settled on, "Merry Christmas, Vincent," before swiftly walking out the door.

CHAPTER EIGHTEEN

IAN & HOLLY

Three Snow Angels

Ian sat stone-faced in the driver's seat of the news van. He stared out the front windshield, his eyes glassy, as if hypnotized. He watched the mammoth snowflakes hit the warm glass only to be shoved aside by the wiper blades. The back-and-forth rhythm, the occasional click when they collided with the vehicle's metal parts, the hum of the engine, the blowing of the heater… Ian felt so out of sync with the orchestra of the world playing around him.

You are nothing.

Vincent's words echoed in the empty chamber of his heart. *I am nothing,* he echoed the words to himself. Ian's mind concurred with that. He was nothing.

Reminding him that she was there, Vi called out from the back seat. "Is something wrong? Shouldn't we be going? Last thing we want is to stay too long in the same spot. That's how our wagon got stuck in the first place."

Vern shot Vi an exasperated look. "That's *not* why the Volvo—Never mind." He then locked eyes with Ian in the rearview mirror. "Everything alright, son? Where's Holly got to?"

Ian held Vern's gaze for a moment. He then stared at his left hand as if it didn't belong to him and followed it with his eyes as it made its way to the door handle. His hand pulled on the lever, just enough for the door to crack open, allowing a windswept dusting of glittery snow to enter and swirl about. Maybe it was the blast of cold air that shocked his whole being, but suddenly his body wanted out of the confined van. "Hold on guys. I'll be right back. I'm gonna go get my brother."

Ian barely finished his sentence when the grinding sound of the van's passenger-side sliding door opening made him stop, swivel around in his seat, and shut his door. There stood Holly. Her eyes were full of spit and fire as she glared at Ian. Snow swirled all around her, surrounding her with a halo effect. The snow wafted into the van, but the second the flakes connected with the heat, they dissolved.

Holly braved the cold, still standing just outside the van's side door for what felt to Ian like an eternity. Vi and Vern watched the pair silently staring at one another. A moment later, the elderly couple turned their sights to one another, each shrugging their shoulders, not knowing what was going on.

Suddenly, Ian found his voice, "I was just about to go back and get Vince."

Holly looked at Vi and Vern who confirmed by nodding their heads in sync. She then asked Ian, "You were? Really?" Her entire face softened into a glow. "You don't have to."

"No, Holly, I do." Ian was surprised that she would object. "And...I really want to. So, hop on in, and shut the door before we all freeze. And if you're going to give me a hard time about it, my mind's made up. You should be happy, though, because—like you say—I'm going to do it and just 'enjoy the ride.'"

Holly's smile grew even wider. She then stepped into the van, squeezing into the space between Vi and Vern. Ian watched, a bit puzzled, and was about to remind her again to shut the door when Vincent suddenly stepped into view. His tear-stained eyes immediately locked with Ian's.

Vincent exhaled, nearly choking on his words, "Holly said you changed your mind."

Ian darted his head to look back at Holly. He was annoyed that she'd been ahead of him but felt mostly relieved all the same.

Holly exaggerated her own look of surprise. "Can't hardly believe it!! Such a surprise!" She turned to Ian. "Next thing you know, you'll be saying you're sorry and huggin' on us all!"

Ian shook his head. "A hug? Vincent, wait right there. I'm coming over to your side." Stepping out of the van, Ian slammed his door shut behind him.

All of a sudden, Ian let out a "Whoa...!" that echoed simultaneously with a THUD, as if he had fallen, which he did, and then a loud, "Crap!"

Vern cast a worried look toward Holly. "What's going on?"

She opened her mouth to respond just as Ian's voice boomed out to them from the other side of the vehicle. This time with a joyful sounding, "Heyyyy! Where are youuuu?"

Holly and Vincent exchanged glances, their eyes widening with childlike excitement, as Vincent clasped his hands and hopped up and down with glee.

Ian's voice again called out. "Come on, buddy, don't just stand where you are. Come over to my side. It's Christmas Eve. We have places to go. And angels to make in the snow."

Holly turned to Vern and Vi. "We will be right back." Then she unwedged herself from her seat, hopped out of the van, shut the side door, and together with Vincent, raced toward Ian.

In that moment, THAT'S when it hit them. Vern turned to Vi, and Vi turned to Vern. The two said it at the same time. One word: "Grace."

"Did you see her expression, Vi?" Vern's eyes showed such certainty with his realization. Vi nodded, her eyes filling with tears. "The very same as our Grace's. It can't be a coincidence, Vern."

Instantly, the couple scooted over to the driver's side windows to get a better look at whatever was going on outside. As they wiped away the cloudy film that had formed on the glass and peered through, their eyes grew brighter and their smiles grew wider at the Christmas magic unraveling before their very eyes.

They could hear the laughter and the banter from the group outside.

"What are you doing?" Holly howled at the sight of Ian flat on his back in the snow, his arms and legs flapping ridiculously.

"Did you fall?" Vincent's forehead wrinkled with worry. "Ian, are you okay?"

Ian grinned up at them both while snow dropped down upon his face. "Yup. I did fall, Vince. And, yes, I'm okay."

"Then why aren't you getting up?" Vincent asked.

Holly pulled her phone out of her pocket and tapped on the glass. Her phone lit up, displaying the time, and she waved it at Ian. "Tick-tock, mister. No time to snooze in the snow. Or did you forget about Carter?"

"I didn't forget. And, no, I'm not snoozing. I just figured since I'm already down here, and I'm trying to keep my promises..."

Vincent's face beamed. "Snow angels!" he exclaimed, his arms raised high above his head. Turning so that his back faced towards Ian, Vince didn't hesitate to execute the perfect trust fall directly into the soft snow beside his brother.

Ian giggled. "That's what I said, 'snow angels'!"

Holly tried not to laugh so that she could steady her phone and record the moment. But it was no use; Ian and Vincent were laughing and carrying on like two little kids, scissoring their legs and swinging their arms from their sides to the very tops of their heads, forming angels together in the snow. It was just as Ian had promised. How she wished her own family had come to see her for just one of the Christmases she spent alone. She shook off the sad memories and unrealized childhood dreams. She reminded herself to focus on the present—this joyful moment happening right now—and she wasn't going to waste it living in the "past lane." Nor would she stand on the sidelines any longer. Zipping her phone into her coat pocket, she spun around, fell back, and joined the fun. After all, it was the proper thing to do with this much untouched snow on the ground!

Both Ian and Vincent laughed as Holly fell to the ground and started flapping away to make snow angel number three.

As Ian lay on the ground next to his brother, he paused just a moment to watch his brother's face ooze with delight. That tiny voice inside his head, however, couldn't help but remind him that for the second time today, he had made a decision that went against his better judgement. Once again, he was at war with himself, thinking: *This is a giant mistake. No way will it be anything other than that.* Despite his voices of fear and doubt, the image of Vince laughing and enjoying life the way he did before their parents passed away made his heart soften.

In that moment, he didn't care about the consequences. Almost giddy, he returned to his angel-making. *What choice do I have?* He asked himself. *I choose this.* He answered. *I choose to enjoy the ride.*

CHAPTER NINETEEN

DARCI & MR. WIGGINS

Work-Life "Balance"

"Choices, we all make choices." Mr. Wiggins was muttering to himself as the black limo's wheels slowly rolled to a stop. Dirty, frozen clumps of slush hung onto the fenders behind them as if their very lives depended on it. As the left back door swung open, Harry emerged first.

"I'm well aware, sir, of choices," Harry said as he stepped out onto the concrete landing of Maplefield Mall's pick-up and drop-off zone. Harry added under his breath, *"If* I had a choice, I would have chosen to see my nine-months-pregnant wife before coming here with you." He turned back facing the car and noticed the hanging grey, slushy chunks of ice. Instinctively, he gave them a satisfying, swift kick. They exploded onto the curb.

Damian emerged from the limo's other side and witnessed Harry's kickboxing illustration. He shouted over to him, "Go, Harry, yeah! Show 'em who's boss."

Harry looked up at Damian. Both couldn't help but chuckle.

"Seriously, I want to see what you can do in one of my gyms." Damian winked at Harry. He then seamlessly extended his hand back into the limo and offered it to Isabelle.

From inside, Isabelle was still gathering her belongings when she noticed Damian's hand. Mr. Wiggins noticed it, too, and paused for a split second, a look of surprise on his face. Isabelle shyly lowered her eyes, assuming he was as impressed at the sight of chivalry as she was. She didn't know why, but she felt a little bit embarrassed in front of this grumpy old man. At the same time, she also wasn't sure why she felt so giddy. She wondered how her heart could be so taken by this spikey haired, self-labeled black sheep in such a short amount of time. He definitely wasn't what she always had believed was "her type." She doubted she would even give him a second glance if she swiped by his photo on some dating app. On paper, he just didn't look good. But in person, and with all that happened in the last few hours…he looked better than good. She blushed at the thought of what might be possible, catching Mr. Wiggins's eye again and noticing the look he was giving her. It made her wonder even more because it seemed as if Mr. Wiggins was waiting for her to take Damian's hand. Wait. What…? Was that the slightest bit of a nod from him? Was he encouraging her?

As if he had read her mind, Mr. Wiggins recoiled and promptly turned to exit.

Damian felt a rush of heat ignite within his whole body as he waited and wondered why Isabelle wasn't taking his hand. He admonished himself for what he thought had been a gentlemanly gesture, only to now see them as any independent woman might. *Who do you think you are? Sir Lancelot? This is the twenty-first century, not medieval times.* Damian bent at the waist and was just about to poke his head back inside the limo when Isabelle's hand reached up and grabbed onto his. She glided out of the limo; her smile radiating as her eyes fixated on him.

Isabelle felt like a princess. Well, that was until her right foot slid on the icy sidewalk, and she tumbled forward, straight into Damian's arms.

"No worries! I gotcha," he assured her as his other arm wrapped around her back, and they both fell together against the car. He had not yet let go of her hand. Both seemed frozen for a moment, their bodies pressed up against one another. They held one another's gaze until the jolt of Mr. Wiggins's harsh voice nudged them apart.

"My driver has other work to do, you two!" Mr. Wiggins called over his shoulder as he led the way into the mall.

"Oh… Right…" Isabelle lifted her hand, the one that Damian had been holding, to her hair, tucking a stray strand behind her ear. With her other, she clutched her purse to her chest.

"Clearly, you're a bad influence," Damian whispered to her as he stepped back, giving her room to stand and making sure they both now had their respective footings. Isabelle scooted away, a mischievous grin playing on her lips. She was just about to start walking toward the mall's entrance, when she paused and leaned close to whisper into Damian's ear: "And clearly, I've developed a weakness for black sheep."

Darci, with iPad in one hand, stylus in the other, and a very panicked look on her youthful face, pushed open the mall's double doors, and sprinted toward Mr. Wiggins, Harry, and the other two strangers.

Mr. Wiggins looked up and shook his head. He stopped in his tracks, nearly causing Harry to collide with his backside, and forcing Darci to run all the way to meet him where he stood. Isabelle and Damian walked over, taking their places beside Harry.

Mr. Wiggins turned to Isabelle and Damian. "I trust this is where we part? My chauffeuring services now complete?" he said sarcastically.

Realizing their journey might be at an end, Damian motioned his hand toward Harry and said, "Actually, I think I'm with you for a bit longer—at least until you can give your wife another number to reach you at?—OR until you let me know when you want to go a few rounds in the gym. I meant what I said, man. You are totally welcome anytime."

Harry chuckled.

Isabelle tipped her head in Mr. Wiggins's direction. "Thanks for the ride, Mr. Wiggins." She winked at Harry. "And YOU are going to be a great dad."

Nearly out of breath from running and finding this surprise meet-and-greet, Darci nervously began, "I am soooo sorry I wasn't here to—"

Mr. Wiggins cut her off, raising his hand like a stop sign. "I'm not interested in apologies, Darci," he said, stepping around her and toward the building.

Darci shut her eyes, wincing.

Harry recognized the girl's painful expression. He drew close to her and gently said, "Don't take it to heart. He got ten words in before being his usual jerk attitude. Don't let him get to you. Trust me, it's not you."

Darci looked up at him, a look of resolve in her eyes. Smiling, she shook his hand. "Nice to finally put a face with the voice, Harry. I knew one day we'd meet in person."

Darci nodded toward Isabelle and Damian, extending her hand to each of them as well. Harry did the honors. "This is Isabelle and Damian. They're strays we picked up along the way. Long story but suffice it to say that they *don't* work for Mr. Wiggins."

Damian wiped his brow with the back of his hand, "Phew! Have to say, I'm grateful for that!"

"You best all come inside with me," Darci directed. "The roads are all closed. I think we're pretty much stuck here together—with him—for at least a good little while."

"How long have you worked for him?" Isabelle asked.

Darci turned, gesturing for them to follow as she led the way toward the front doors of the mall. "My whole life," she responded.

Harry, Isabelle, and Damian all laughed.

"I get it." Harry nodded. "I feel that way, too!"

"We've only been with him since we got off the plane, and it feels like a lifetime," Isabelle chimed in.

Darci stopped just long enough to turn to them and whisper, "You all got off easy." Crooking her index finger, she beckoned them into a huddle. When the trio got into position, they surrounded her and leaned in to hear Darci share, "I not only work for him, but he also happens to be my father."

Just then, the subject of their discussion barked an interruption. "Darci!" Mr. Wiggins shouted from where he now stood, at the entrance's threshold, tapping his foot, waiting—something he had no patience for.

She shut her eyes, took a deep breath in, and left the group to meet up with him. The trio she left behind stayed in their hunched-over positions for a few moments, digesting the news.

Harry spoke first, "All these years, I had no idea. Her last name's not even Wiggins."

Isabelle let out a loud whistle.

Damian gestured with his hand, mimicking a mic drop, and accompanying it by his own sound effects of it hitting the floor, "Boom!"

CHAPTER TWENTY

EMILY & MR. ABDULLAH

It's All Fun and Games until...

Inside the mall, a roaring, thunder-like rumble shattered its way throughout the Games & Gadgets Galore store.

"You kids!" Mr. Abdullah lifted his long, hairy arms to the Heavens, shaking them as if they were in need of an air dry. "Enough with the Exploding Bomb Bags!"

He approached a dozen or so teenagers conspiring in the far corner of his store along with one Michael Jordan-sized elf. They all were examining, quite closely, what looked like shiny, silver Mylar pouches no bigger than the palm of one's hand.

"Come on now kids put them down." Mr. Abdullah's worn-out face turned his command into little more than a plea. He stopped short when one of those Bomb Bags sailed just over his left shoulder. He immediately put both of his index fingers in his ears as it exploded with a BANG in midair, leaving a trail of its grimy white residue to drip down his forearm.

This time, Mr. Abdullah cast his eyes upward. Taking a moment to clasp his hands together up near his mouth, his lips moved in silent prayer.

The kids immediately made a run for it. All except for Randy, who was left literally holding the bag. He walked over to Mr. Abdullah and stood facing him. The difference in their sizes was even more evident up close, with Randy measuring about 10 to 12 inches taller than Mr. Abdullah in comparison.

Mr. Abdullah opened his eyes, and for a moment, all he could see in front of him was a wall of green felt and two hands holding out the box of Exploding Bomb Bags.

"I'll take these, Mister," Randy stated. "Pastor Max will love 'em!"

Mr. Abdullah craned his neck backwards, his eyes traveling up the torso of the Amazonian elf and landing on the boy's cherublike face. He couldn't help but smile and laugh at the boy's glee.

"Come, come," Mr. Abdullah said and motioned to Randy to follow him to the front register. "I like that you are in the spirit of the season, young man!" He turned to gesture at the elf costume.

Randy followed closely behind. "Oh, this? Pastor Max made me. I sorta got into a fight. This is what he calls a 'learning moment'; I call it a 'punishment.'"

"I like this Pastor Max of yours, too," Mr. Abdullah chuckled as he worked his way behind the counter alongside other staffers and stockpiles of undelivered packages stacked from floor to ceiling. A dozen or so last-minute shoppers clutching claim tickets waited none-too-patiently for their turns to pick up their purchases.

"So, you got in a fight?" he asked, shaking his head and laughing. "I'd like to see the size of the other guy! Who would be brave—or stupid—enough to want to fight you?"

"Randy!" Karina's commanding voice startled Randy and Mr. Abdullah as she entered the Games & Gadgets Galore store. Dressed in all her elf-finery, she tapped her foot, beckoning Randy with her hands to come with her now.

Mr. Abdullah nodded at Karina. With a knowing smile, he looked at Randy. "Ah, is that your girlfriend?"

Randy's eyes grew wide and his mouth dropped open as his face skewed itself into a look of pure disgust. "Ewwww! No. No way," he said definitively. "She's the one I got into a fight with and why we now both have to wear these stupid elf costumes."

Mr. Abdullah stopped everything. He then erupted in a full-belly laugh. "Oh, my boy! Here." He gently pushed back on the box of Exploding Bomb Bags. "You go. Take these. My gift to you and to your very smart Pastor Max."

"Huh?" Randy didn't know how to respond.

"Randy!" Karina shouted, now standing with both hands on her hips. "Come on!"

Mr. Abdullah reassured him with a nod and placed the box of Exploding Bomb Bags in Randy's hands. "Go. My gift to you. You may need these."

As soon as Randy walked toward Karina, Mr. Abdullah howled with laughter.

Karina's impatience mounted as she waited for him to make his way to her. She stood in the very center of the Games & Gadgets Galore doorway, forcing others to move around her to come inside the store.

Emily tried her best to navigate her large belly and shopping bags around the tall, slender girl dressed like an elf blocking the way into the very store that held Harry's drone. It wasn't as if the passageway was narrow, in fact, quite the contrary. It was just that Emily had had enough encounters, especially of late, with misjudging spatial distances. It seemed that no matter how careful she was, every time she and baby took a turn, someone or something else ended up taking a spill.

Now, she was the one worried about stumbling; the nail technicians had outfitted her with the cutest black wedge flip-flops. It had been so long since she had her nails done, she was surprised—and grateful—that they now sold such cute accessories. She loved how the suede leather straps with their double rows of rhinestone crystal accents made her feel glamourous. Not an easy thing to do for a woman who was nine months pregnant. She couldn't very well put her freshly painted toes back into the chunky, weather-proof boots she came in, now could she? With a heel height of more than three inches, however, and the fact that she couldn't even see beyond her belly to know exactly where she was stepping, she realized a little too late that the flip-flops' cute wedge heal might cause her to tumble.

Emily couldn't confidently take another step with the teenager dressed as an elf standing in her way. She kindly tapped Karina on the shoulder, "Excuse me, Elf."

Karina turned to Emily, her eyes registering surprise at the very pregnant lady's belly.

"Can I get by, please?" Emily half-winced at her own request.

"Oh, I'm so sorry, ma'am," Karina said, as she moved out of the way, letting Emily pass. Still, Emily's hand accidentally swung and hit the girl's hip, causing the Elf on the Shelf Emily was holding to fall to the ground. She looked at the little guy splayed on the floor still sporting his wide smile.

"Here, I'll get that for you," Karina reached down and picked up the Elf on the Shelf. She looked at his felt clothes and compared them to her own costume. She couldn't help but crack a smile. "I'm Karina," she said.

Emily was grateful not to have had to bend and pick up the elf herself. "Thanks so much. I'm Emily."

Randy joined them. "Hey," he said, pointing to the Elf on the Shelf. "He's one of us."

Emily tried to hold in a chuckle. "You both look adorable. Are you part of some Christmas show or something?"

Karina rolled her eyes and reluctantly nodded. "Randy here and me, we sorta got volunteered."

Randy added, "Ya, and whatever we're a part of, it wasn't by choice."

Karina then turned to Randy, "Pastor Max said to come right away." She then turned back to Emily, handing her the Elf on the Shelf. "Here you go."

"Oh, it's not even mine," Emily said. "And, besides, it looks like he might be part of whatever show you're a part of."

Randy tried to grab the elf from Karina's hands. She yanked it out of his reach. "Who does he belong to?" she asked.

Emily was about to respond when at that very moment, Pickpocket the dog yelped out a throaty "*WOOF!*" while Rainbow the bird joined in with her equally loud "*SCREECH!*" The animal sounds made everyone in the Games & Gadgets Galore store look out the entrance's glass door and into the mall's main corridor. Mr. Abdullah strolled to the front of the store to get a vantage point. Emily, Karina, and Randy already had a front-row view as the furry and feathered pair raced by right in front of them, followed closely by another pair—a man and a woman.

The woman chasing the pets called out, "Hank, wait for me." The man immediately slowed down, allowing the woman to catch up to him. "Rainbow, naughty, naughty girl," she said.

"We've almost got 'em, come on, Andrea," the man cheered his running mate on. "We can do it!"

As this strange quartet swooshed past Emily, she extended her arm, pointing her finger at them, and excitedly exclaimed to Karina and Randy: "There! Elf on the Shelf belongs to them. Go catch them and get the elf to where he belongs."

Karina and Randy's eyes and mouths widened in awe. Without hesitation—nor thinking it through—the two human elves, one holding the toy Elf on the Shelf, raced to catch the mismatched group.

Mr. Abdullah who now stood shoulder-to-shoulder with Emily laughed whole-heartedly at the sight. He turned to her and said, "In all my years as owner of this store, I thought I had seen it all. I was wrong. A dog and a bird together here in the mall!"

Emily nodded, laughing, when all of a sudden, a sharp pain hit her, just below and to the right side of her belly. "Ooooo!" She placed her right hand on the spot and slightly bent forward trying to catch her breath. She still held her shopping bags in the other hand.

"Are you okay?" Mr. Abdullah immediately shifted himself to her other side and gently supported her with his right hand holding onto Emily's left forearm, and his left arm at the ready. "Here, come sit…"

"I need my husband," Emily panted out a breath, as she took her hand off her belly to pull her cell phone from her purse.

"Yes, yes," Mr. Abdullah assured her as he slowly walked her through his store. "We'll get him."

Emily scrolled her screen with her thumb, tapped Harry's name, and then held the phone up to her ear. Another pang to her belly caused her to look up, wincing from the pain. Just then, she saw a drone hanging from the ceiling of the shop.

"My drone," she groaned. "That's why I'm here. It was supposed to be delivered. Mr. Abdullah told me to come get it."

"Yes, ma'am, I'm Mr. Abdullah, and you have my most sincere apologies for having to come down for pick-up, especially in your condition." They continued to slowly waddle to the back of the store.

"Emily. My name is Emily. We talked earlier." She hoped to hear Harry's voice on the other end of the line, but the call went straight to an automatic voicemail message. "No answer," she said to Mr. Abdullah. She felt tears starting to bubble to the surface. Leaving a message, she said, "Harry, where are you? Please call me back. I think the baby might be coming." She paused, thinking of what else to say. "I love you. Baby does, too." Hanging up, she tried to keep her tears from spilling, but it was too late.

Mr. Abdullah noticed and hastily spoke up, trying to take her mind off things, "No worries, now. It's Christmas Eve. I have your exact drone waiting for you—no charge!"

They entered his back office where, just to the right of his desk, waited a worn-in sofa. He guided Emily to it.

"I think I need to call my doctor," Emily said as she sat down, settling back against the navy cushions. She dropped her bags and made another call.

"You rest now," Mr. Abdullah said, helping her to raise her feet in the rhinestone bedazzled wedges onto the couch's armrest. "My wife practically delivered our third child in the car on our way to hospital."

While obviously trying to soothe Emily, his words had the opposite effect. "Oh, no!" Emily's tears cascaded down her cheeks as she waited for someone to answer. "I can't have this baby now. Not all by myself." She then pleaded with her belly to cooperate, "Hang on, baby. It's not your time yet. Hold off just a little—"

Finally, her call connected, and a flicker of hope lit up Emily's face.

"Dr. Grey's office. Is this a medical emergency?"

CHAPTER TWENTY-ONE

ISABELLE & DAMIAN

A Glass of Something Red

With Mr. Wiggins in the lead, Darci, Harry, Damian, and Isabelle followed, winding their way through the mall, stepping onto the escalator, and heading upstairs to the executive offices.

Scanning his surroundings, Mr. Wiggins commented over his shoulder to Darci. "See, Darci? All your talk about how this mall draws so many people—and tourists? Look at it now. It should be packed on Christmas Eve. But what do we have? Scarcely a hundred shoppers and each with so few bags in hand. And look, not even a single child waiting in line for Santa. And not even whoever you hired to be this year's Santa in sight...?" He tsk'd as he turned his head forward, preparing to step off the escalator.

"Well, sir, we were packed earlier," Darci responded. "But with the snowstorm, people are heading home for their own safety. And the Santa story, well—"

As Mr. Wiggins stepped onto the landing, he merely waved his hand overhead behind him, dismissing Darci and her comments.

Stopping mid-sentence, shaking her head, Darci hopped off the escalator and followed him.

Harry was next in line, busy juggling a phone to his ear with one hand and Mr. Wiggins's precious mink fur duffel in his other. As he struggled to keep pace, he shouted into the phone, "No, I really can't hold any longer."

Damian and Isabelle rode the escalator just a few steps behind, exchanging glances at the conversation overheard ahead of them.

"Are you feeling all of a sudden like we've become part of his entourage?" Damian asked her. "I mean, is it just me, or are the people working here actually giving us the evil eye?"

Isabelle looked around her at some of the faces peering back at them. She then leaned over toward Damian's ear, cupping her hand to the side of her mouth. Speaking in an exaggerated spy-like, low voice, she half-whispered: "The second I get my phone back from Harry, I'm making a break for it. I advise you to join me."

The two reached the top of the escalator and stepped off, as Damian cocked one eye and nodded. "It's a deal," he said. As they continued to play follow the leader, Damian gestured to Harry, whispering to her: "Poor guy. It'll be a miracle if anybody at the airport helps him find his phone."

"You never know," Isabelle replied. "It is Christmas, after all."

"Trudat." Inwardly, Damian instantly winced. *'Trudat'? I sound so not cool. What is my problem? I'm never at a loss for words. Except when I look at her.*

Isabelle chuckled. "'Trudat,' really? You sound like my nieces, Lauren and Maddie."

Damian looked away. *Get it together, man!* Taking a deep breath and regaining his composure, he turned to face her, asking, "Your nieces? Is that why you're in Chicago? Christmas with your sister? Or are they your brother's kids?"

"It's just me and my sister now and her girls." Now it was Isabelle's turn to look away.

"How old are they?"

Isabelle paused a moment, thinking. "Good question. You know, it's been so long since I saw them last…" She did some figuring in her head. "Wow. I think Lauren's 15, and Maddie's 13-ish."

"Wow…So you're saying I sound like a teenage girl?" Damian joked, pleased he could make Isabelle laugh. "How long since you've seen them?"

Isabelle hesitated, scanning Damian's face, then thought *he's so easy to talk to, what the heck.* "Ten years. My sister and I had a falling-out at our mom's funeral. We had already lost our dad years earlier, before her girls were even born. So, when we told my nieces that their grandma died, they asked me when their grandma would come back. Lauren wanted to know if she'd be back in time for her fifth birthday." A bittersweet memory swept across Isabelle's face. A few seconds later, she continued. "I said 'No,' and then I think I said something like, 'When someone dies, nothing can bring them back to life.' To be honest, I don't really remember what I actually said. Whatever it was, my sister said I had spoken out of turn and acted *inappropriately.*" Isabelle air-quoted the last word. "She was furious. And then…we just stopped talking."

"What?" Damian's face commiserated. "What did she expect you to say?"

"Oh, probably something about Heaven and Jesus and life everlasting…" Isabelle's voice trailed off. It wasn't as if she didn't believe in all that—because she did. "Maybe I should have been more careful in my response. But I had just lost my mom, and I wasn't thinking straight. Anyway, that's why I'm here. Unannounced. Ten years is long enough to be banished and not allowed to contact my nieces. I'm going to beg my sister's forgiveness, and I hope that I can get back into my only remaining family's good graces."

"Ah, so that's where the 'bad influence' reference comes from," Damian said. He instinctively leaned over to give her a hug but stopped short when she stepped back. The look on his face was apologetic.

Isabelle hid her face with her hands. "Ugh, talk about TMI," she said, embarrassed. "I don't know why I told you all that. We just met. Ignore me."

Letting out a sigh of relief and flashing her a wicked smile, Damian replied, "It's way too late for that, lady. I can barely take my eyes off you." Now it was his turn to be embarrassed. *OMG. Either I'm at a loss for words and say stupid shit, or I blurt out a bunch of stuff and still say stupid shit.*

Isabelle blushed, quickly diverting the conversation, nearly stumbling over her own words. "So, um, how about you, Mr. Black Sheep? Why did you fly in?"

"Me?" Damian was all for getting to know her life story, but telling her personal things about himself? Different story. "That's a conversation that requires a glass or two of something red."

Isabelle's spirit lifted as she coquettishly responded, "Why, sir, are you asking me out on a date?"

A fever again ignited within Damian's soul as he nervously blurted out, "No…"

"No?" Isabelle felt her heart sink. *I am such a fool!*

What on earth am I doing? Why did I just say no? "I mean YES, absolutely!" Damian quickly corrected himself.

The two smiled at one another, still following Mr. Wiggins, Darci, and Harry down the corridor. As the group passed the Games & Gadgets Galore shop, Damian and Isabelle glanced inside.

Mr. Abdullah was nowhere to be seen, despite several customers waiting for him at the front counter.

CHAPTER TWENTY-TWO

DR. HAYWOOD & HOLLY

A State of Grace

Back at the hospital, Dr. Haywood showed off his tray-balancing techniques to the skeleton hospital crew working the nurse's station. "Watch and learn, folks. Years of food service to pay for my schooling. All lessons learned that still serve me well." He held the circular platter slightly elevated and away from him. On it, a large, plastic glass of milk, a plate of turkey with all the trimmings, and a slab of chocolate yule log shared the space. "You see it's all in using your fingertips while traveling, trusting your natural balance, and not focusing on the tray itself, but rather picking a point in front of you and focusing there."

Applause erupted.

"Thank you, thank you." He nodded appreciatively. "I just hope Vince is hungry. This is quite a feast."

"Doctor Haywood, Vincent isn't here," one of the nurses called out. "He went home for the holidays. Said you signed him out to the people you were talking to earlier." She checked the logbook on the counter. "Yes, his brother Ian, and a Holly...?"

Doctor Haywood stopped short, causing the glass of milk to topple over, crashing in a white splash onto the floor. He managed to keep everything else on the tray, muttering under his breath, "I should have known."

"Don't you worry, Dr. Haywood," the nurse continued. "I'll get someone to clean that up." As she dialed her phone, Dr. Haywood nodded a thank you, placing the tray and what was left on it on top of the counter. He glanced at the logbook. There it was: Holly's handwriting, a perfect forgery of his own signature.

How many times had she run away—or tried to—when she was a patient in the hospital? He often wondered if it was her destiny to become an escape artist, since she had succeeded at it so many times. But by the grace of God, he always brought her back unharmed. But taking Vincent out without permission or—good God—his meds, and, Dr. Haywood suspected, without Ian agreeing to look after him over the holidays… This was shaping up to be the very opposite of a 'merry' Christmas for all.

At nearly the same time Dr. Haywood discovered their great escape, Ian was conducting his own inquiry of Vincent, who now sat in the back of the van, wedged between Vi and Vern.

"There's no way Dr. Haywood or anybody at that hospital would have allowed you to do that." Ian tried to keep a stern face as he drove, watching his little brother respond from the rearview mirror.

"Yes, way!" Vincent exclaimed, giggling.

"No way," Ian responded, finding it hard not to join in his brother's giggle-fest, seeing his excited eyes and boyish grin extending from ear to ear.

"Okay, so who says I asked permission?" Vincent sassed back. "Holly doesn't ask permission. Do you, Holly?"

Ian turned to cast a disapproving look at his colleague seated to his right.

Holly opened her eyes wide, obviously startled at the question. She caught Ian's gaze and then intentionally looked away.

"Hey, how much longer in this traffic, do ya think?" She redirected everyone's attentions outside. They were at a standstill. Again. Fewer cars surrounded them but none of them could drive anywhere remotely close to the speed limit due to the snowy road conditions.

Vern used his sleeve to wipe away the condensation that repeatedly obstructed their view. He and Vi peered out the little circle of visibility he had created on the window. They both turned to look at one another. Over the years, they had gotten to know each other so well that they needed fewer and fewer words to communicate; now, they didn't even need to speak to know what the other was thinking.

"Ian," Vi hesitantly called out from the back seat. "I hate to ask, but could we make a stop just for two minutes, please?"

"Stop?" Ian glanced back at them as if they had lost their minds. "We're practically at the mall. Can you hold it until we get there?"

"Oh, no, dear," Vi explained. "I don't have to use a restroom."

"Please, Ian," Vern pointed out his side of the window. "It's St. Michael's we want. We're right here now."

"You want to go to church? Now?" Ian and Holly exchanged puzzled looks.

"No. It's St. Michael's Cemetery," Vern clarified.

Vi turned to her side where the bouquet of flowers they purchased at the grocery store sat—red roses, white miniature carnations, fragrant cedars, and tiny pinecones all bound together with a wired, golden Christmas ribbon. The bunch looked so gay and festive. She tenderly cradled them like one would a baby. "It's where our Grace is buried."

"Who's Grace?" Vincent innocently asked, unaware he was addressing the elephant in the room.

"Our little girl," Vi softly said.

"Please, Ian," Vern asked again. "It's the 25th anniversary of her leaving us."

"Our mom and dad died in a car crash," Vince volunteered. "Did Grace die in a car, too?"

"Vincent!" Ian barked, much louder than he had intended. He softened his tone, "It's not any of our business."

Holly looked into Vern's eyes. They were so full of pain and shame that she immediately, and instinctively, knew it was a suicide. "Ian, I think you should take them to the cemetery."

"Holly, we'll never get off this—" Ian began his opposing argument on why that wasn't a great idea, only to get shut down and rendered speechless by Holly's next words.

"My adoptive mom and dad washed their hands of me when I was younger," Holly said. "They never came to visit me when I was in the hospital. Even when I tried…" Holly stopped short of finishing her sentence. "They're still alive and out there, but they've never tried once to contact me. Grace deserves to know her parents are still here for her."

"I'll go with you!" Vincent triumphantly offered his assistance to Vi and Vern. He looked at Ian with puppy-dog eyes, "Come on, Ian. It's Christmas Eve. Let's make another miracle happen."

Ian furrowed his brow as he looked at Vincent in the rearview mirror and asked, "'Another' miracle? What was the first?"

Vincent scoffed, looking incredulous at Ian's question. "Well I'm here with you, aren't I? That's a miracle if you ask me."

Everyone in the van erupted in laughter, including Ian who said, "Okay, little buddy. Let's go make another miracle happen."

CHAPTER TWENTY-THREE

THE DOCTORS & THE UBER DRIVER

Ride Share

"What a crazy Christmas Eve," muttered the same Uber driver that had taken Betty to the mall much earlier in the day. He could not believe he was about to take another late shopper there again, especially not with all this snow coming down. He crawled to a stop right in front of the Alexander's Behavioral Health Center's main entrance.

Dr. Grey, bundled up in winter wear, gingerly made her way to the curb while waving at him as she approached the vehicle.

The driver rolled down his window. "Maplefield Mall?" He resisted the urge to throw a *Seriously?* in at the end.

She nodded. As she reached out with her gloved hand to open the back door, a stir behind her caught her attention. Doctor Haywood raced out the same door she had just exited, wrapping himself into his own coat, slipping and sliding his way down the icy, snow-covered walkway. While he normally prided himself on his dance moves, these lacked grace and style. Thankfully, he was able to skid to a standstill when he reached the curb. Looking up, he was shocked to see all the cars parked in the lot—including his own— buried in what looked like ten inches of snow.

"You have GOT to be kidding me!" he shouted.

"Mitch?" Dr. Grey called out to him as she stood beside the car. "That was quite an exit. Everything okay?"

It took Dr. Haywood a second to even notice his colleague standing there with, it appeared, a heated, already running car waiting for her.

"Sarah, any chance I can hitch a ride with you?"

"Where are you headed?" she asked.

"Maplefield Mall. If you're going anywhere in that direction, I'll pay." He took a few steps closer, bending his frame to reach out and open the car's back door for her.

"I'm not only going in that direction," Sarah said as she climbed into the car. "I'm going to the mall myself, and no worries, I've got it covered. Hop in!"

Dr. Haywood clapped his hands, "Good God, it's a miracle." He chivalrously shut Dr. Grey's door and then scrambled to the other side of the car to get in himself. "I can't thank you enough," he said, slamming his own door shut.

"Merry Christmas to you both!" The Uber driver tried to sound jolly. "There's water in the center console there for you," he said as he put the car in drive and eased away from the curb.

"Thank you," Dr. Haywood said, as he offered a bottle of water to Dr. Grey, who took it.

"Merry Christmas to you, too!" she said, then turning to her long-time associate, asked, "Why the race to get to the mall? Last minute shopping?"

Dr. Haywood quipped. "I'm not that crazy! No, I have a patient who's kind of gone AWOL. And to make it even worse, he's being 'aided and abetted' so to speak by my former patient. I think they're headed to the mall—at least, that's what I remember being told. Let's just say, it's complicated."

Dr. Grey blew out a breath of air. "Well, normally I might say 'Want to switch places?', but I think I'll stick with my complication. I've got a very pregnant and very panicked patient at the mall in labor to whom my last words earlier today were, 'Short of any Act of God that might befall us, I don't see any reason why you shouldn't go to the mall today'—or so she reminded me on the phone that that's what I said. I even told her to treat herself to a mani-pedi." Sarah laughed. "I was so sure she had at least another week before that baby was fully baked. Yet here we are, and she's stuck in that mall, apparently about to give birth in some toy store."

"Why not send an ambulance to get mom and bring her to you?"

"I did. But they told me it got into some wreck on the way. I'm not one to wait, and I don't think that baby is either."

"Mother Nature and Father Fate: They play by their own rules." The Uber driver chimed in. "But I gotta say, I'm glad you're not just a couple of those 'last-minute-shopping-crazies'! At least you two got purpose."

"I think this is going to be a night to remember for all of us," Dr. Haywood shared a smile laced with concern. "What's that line?" He searched his mind for the words: "'If you can meet with triumph and disaster and treat those two imposters just the same…You are a better man than most.'"

"Ah! Kipling. Beautifully put! And so very appropriate," Sarah nodded. She then addressed the driver, "Any idea how long it might take to get us there?"

He groaned, "It might take us a while—lots of traffic and this weather—but I promise we will get there in one piece. Just please don't be askin' me every two minutes 'Are we there yet?'; I got a couple of kids, and that's their favorite question."

CHAPTER TWENTY-FOUR

IAN & HOLLY

Crazy at Christmas

Ian and Holly watched from inside the van as Vi, Vern, and Vincent huddled around Grace's gravesite outside. The peaceful scene of the trio all alone, trying to use their hands to clear away the two feet of fallen snow, was shattered by the sound of Carter's ranting and raving over the news van's speakers.

"What do you mean you're not there yet?" Carter shouted. "YOU not being there yet means WE are not there yet."

Ian and Holly turned to look at one another.

"I told you we shouldn't have taken the call," Holly whispered, as Ian shut his eyes and nodded in agreement.

"I said 'no,'" Carter continued his rant. "You remember that? You said, what did you say? Oh, right, you started out with the warm and fuzzies saying 'Christmas Miracles. Peace on Earth. Goodwill to Men. That's what it's *supposed* to be about, Carter.' Didn't you say that?"

Ian tried to get a word in: "Yeah, Carter, that's what I said, but you missed the point I was trying to make."

"Oh, I didn't miss anything," Carter spat back. "Except a story on the 'snowstorm of the season' like WGN did. Or the 'Rudolph's red nose will come in handy tonight' bit that one of the idiots at WQQZ did, he even put on one of those red light-up balls on his own nose, for the love of all that's Christmas. But what do we have about the surprise Christmas Eve blizzard? *Nothing.* That's what's missing, Ian."

Holly interjected, "Carter, it's not Ian's fault."

"Oh, I know it's not *only* his fault," Carter cut her off. "I understand you and your 'do-whatever-I-want' attitude decided you'd just disappear with the camera equipment and the news van. Need I remind you that you're pretty much just a temp around here?"

Ian watched Holly's reaction. From the little he had learned about her in the last few hours, she already had her fair share of rejection in life. She didn't deserve any more negative messages about not being wanted and not belonging.

"*Enough!*" Ian exploded. "Carter, you never listen. If there's anyone who just does whatever he wants and is so closed off to new ideas, it's *you*. You have that whole newsroom paranoid to make a sudden move and too afraid to do anything that might actually put us on top in ratings. Holly's been spot-on with everything she's worked on, and she's had to do it without getting your permission, but oh, are you at the ready to take the credit when she delivers!"

Holly put her hand on Ian's forearm. Her eyes silently thanked him. She whispered, "That's enough. Cut it off," and then lifted her hand to just under her throat, comically gesturing a decapitation, complete with her eyes rolling back in her head and her tongue hanging out.

The two chuckled, waiting for Carter to say something. Anything. They could hear him breathing, seething into the phone.

"Fine. Whatever. Maplefield Mall," Carter finally broke his silence. "My old friend Betty Bryant is the lady in charge there. She called over here, asking us to cover a story none of the other stations want. Some preacher guy, a bunch of orphans or something. It's been covered every year, but the guy who owns the whole mall is shutting it down. So, this may be the last time to do this story. You said 'shopping brings out the worst'—you see, I DO listen—so here you go. Head over there and get a story—at this point *any* story!"

CLICK. Carter hung up.

Holly and Ian sat quietly, not feeling the urge to discuss the call. Instead, they again both squinted to see Vi and Vern, with Vincent in between them, all three locking arms, headed back toward the van from their cemetery visit.

"Vincent was always an odd kid," Ian spoke so softly, Holly adjusted herself in her seat to hear him better. "After our parents died, it was just me. I'd try to hang out with him. I tried to do all that holiday hoopla with him, but the more hallucinations he'd have and the voices he'd hear, to be honest, he just sort of freaked me out. I thought that what he had was something I could catch. I know that's dumb."

Holly shook her head. "Not dumb," she said quietly.

"I just wanted to keep him at bay," Ian continued. "And then it kind of grew into keeping *everyone* at arm's length and everything a secret. Being solo. That made me feel safe. Protected." Ian snorted out a laugh. Then he grew more serious. "Christmastime is hardest for me. I always have that Norman Rockwell painting in my mind. You know the one with the family gathered around in the dining room, all talking to one another, everyone with smiles on their faces and excitement in their eyes? The grandpa and grandma are standing at the head of the table, presenting this plump, cooked-to-perfection turkey that makes even my mouth water just looking at it. Have you seen it?"

Holly smirked. "You really think there's anybody who hasn't?"

"Yeah, you're probably right." Ian nodded, his eyes looking off into the distance.

Holly waited before saying anything, trying to give Ian a chance to process whatever he needed to at that moment. After a minute, she added her own thoughts: "If it's any consolation, I really hate that painting. Loathe it, actually."

Ian turned to look at her, a slow smile speaking volumes; he, too, felt the same way. "Ha! For me, it's envy," he said. "I know those people in the painting aren't real and that it's ridiculous of me to be jealous of them.

But just once…just once, I would have loved to have had experienced 'family' like that."

"Fa-la-la-la-la-la-la-la-la!" Holly belted out her best "Deck the Halls" refrain, acapella.

Ian widened his eyes at her. "Well, now who's crazy?"

"No, you dork," she laughed. "That's my festive way of saying you're preaching to the choir, get it? 'Fa-la-la'?"

"Ohhhh! Right. Got it." Ian nodded.

"I didn't grow up with anything even remotely close to what Rockwell drew," Holly confessed. "I bet there's more people like us than people like the ones he painted."

Ian nodded slowly. "Vince can be pretty stable when he's on his meds," he said, growing somber. "The minute he's off 'em, though, that's when it gets tricky."

Ian paused. Holly stayed silent, patiently listening.

"You know that line?" Ian continued. "People say they're going 'home for the holidays' or even TV commercials showing people going home for the holidays, surprising their family?"

Holly nodded and joined in. "I love that one where the little kid is in her pajamas, and the older brother in army fatigues comes through the door."

Ian nodded. "Right. That's what I'm talking about. For a lot of people, that's what 'home for the holidays' is all about. But for me, it's not. It's never been. For me, it's more about 'when madness comes home for the holidays.'"

"What do you mean?" Holly's face scrunched up.

"Never mind," Ian lowered his head, until he tapped his forehead a couple of times on the steering wheel. "It's nothing."

Holly's eyes sort of lit up. "Nothing? Okay, tell me about 'nothing.'"

Ian lifted his head and looked over at her. He hesitated, and then tried to explain himself again. "It's like this time of year, it does something to Vincent. Don't know why. Maybe he wants to be 'normal' and feel happy. He watches the classic movies and old TV shows and when he watches, he doesn't see anyone else taking meds, so, it's like…why should he…?" Ian realized he was just talking out loud, and he could see from Holly's expression that he still wasn't making much sense. Even he didn't understand what he was saying.

Holly's entire face lit up. "It's the Christmas miracle. That's what it is."

Now Ian was the one with the slightly quizzical look on his face.

She sat up. "So, for example, right now, at Christmastime…" Holly inhaled deeply, thinking, choosing her words. "People who consider themselves 'normal' talk about the virgin birth, which logically isn't supposed to be possible. They talk about Santa Claus and flying reindeer and little elves—all of these things that are arguably bizarre delusions of the season. But during this time of year, they're perfectly acceptable, heck, even encouraged. It's like it's okay for the whole world to suspend logic for a month and believe in what's really not there…like everyone's delusional together."

Ian nodded the entire time Holly talked. She got it. She understood. He bounced up out of his seat with excitement. "That's it! You're exactly right!" Ian exclaimed and looked at Holly as if for the first time. He always knew she was smart; he just didn't realize how smart until this very moment. "And while it's all allowed and even encouraged right now, the rest of the year, anything or anybody who's even a little bit outside of society's norms is dismissed, drugged up, feared, locked up. It's ok to be crazy about Christmas but not crazy any other time of year." He paused and looked outside for Vi, Vern, and Vincent.

Suddenly, Vincent's head popped up and into view, as he smooshed his nose against Holly's window and tapped on the glass with both hands. Holly jumped and turned to look at him. She exchanged funny faces. They could hear Vi and Vern fiddling with the outside latch on the news van's sliding side door.

Ian shook his head clear. "Geesh, why am I talking so much? AND I'm not even making much sense, am I?"

Holly turned back to look at him, smiling warmly. "You make a lot of sense to me."

CHAPTER TWENTY-FIVE

DARCI & BETTY

Grit and Grace

M r. Wiggins sat in Betty's office chair. The pile of gifts that were on her desk had been moved to the floor. In their place sat a laptop and ledgers of accounts that painted the financial picture leading to the shopping mall's fate.

"Well, this makes no sense at all," Mr. Wiggins spat out.

Betty, flanked by Darci and Harry, stood in front of the desk. While Darci and Harry resembled school children who had been called into the Principal's Office, Betty stood tall, with an air of defiance that surprised even her—partly because she was dressed as Mrs. Claus.

"Mr. Wiggins, what exactly is it that you fail to understand?" she asked. Her question and choice of wording drew wide eyes and not-quite-hidden grins from Darci and Harry.

Mr. Wiggins raised a scruffy eyebrow, looking at her from head to toe. "You mean other than why the head of my mall is dressed up in some ridiculous costume?"

"She's not ridiculous," Darci said, almost under her breath, clenching her hands together.

Betty looked at her, appreciation in her eyes, and gently patted Darci's hands.

Mr. Wiggins noted the exchange between the two, his face displaying displeasure. "The Saturday before Christmas is supposed to be the busiest and most productive retail day of the year," he said in an accusatory tone.

Darci tapped her iPad, turning it around to show him her spreadsheet. "Saturday's numbers were some of our best ever," she cheerily shared.

"Darci, when I want your input, I will ask for it," he said, dismissing her without looking at her screen.

Betty didn't even have to look at the young woman to know that Darci felt the sting of her father's mistreatment. Betty was one of the few to even know that fact, and with every interaction she witnessed between the two, not only did her heart ache more for the young woman, but she further understood why Darci would choose not to take 'Wiggins' as her surname. "No, actually, Darci, I'd like to hear what you have to say," she turned toward her and with her two fingers, tapped the top of Darci's iPad. "Go on."

Harry nodded his encouragement as well.

Darci took a deep breath. "The National Retail Federation projected that this year's holiday retail sales in November and December were to increase 3.6 to 4 percent," Darci began. "We surpassed those numbers. We're up 5.2 percent, this year over last year."

"That percentage of growth is a meaningless metric," Mr. Wiggins said. "It only makes sense if you have a non-zero start."

"We didn't have a zero start," Darci shot back. Her father's disapproving look met her gaze. "Sir."

"Well even if it wasn't zero, you didn't exactly start off with much of anything for any of those numbers to matter." Mr. Wiggins lifted himself up out of the chair.

"But look at the trends," Darci countered. "The rise of online holiday shopping was projected to shrink sales for traditional brick-and-mortar stores. With us, the exact opposite is true."

Mr. Wiggins stepped out from behind the desk, not really listening to his daughter, hoping to sidestep Harry and take his leave.

"Sir," Harry raised his voice, irritated partially on behalf of Darci but also because he was tired of Mr. Wiggins thinking he was the only one who could ever be right. "You've been talking about a 'retail apocalypse' for a while now. It's been your biggest argument presented as reason to shut down this mall. If Darci has information that counters that, I think you'd be wise to listen."

"Oh, you do, do you?" Mr. Wiggins visibly took offense to his underling schooling him.

Harry straightened his back and looked his Scrooge-of-a-boss in the eye. Part of him thought to himself: *What in the world am I doing? This is career suicide. Who do I think I am?* Yet another part of him, one that Harry hadn't heard from in a long, long while whispered: *Exactly. Great question. Who am I?* He suddenly felt better. "Darci, continue," he instructed.

Betty took a half-step back. Before this, she hadn't seen Darci's true colors before. She thought the girl—young woman—was her father's daughter, always concerned about the bottom line, but she was pleased to be proven wrong. And now, however things turned out, she believed she was witnessing a miracle in motion from Harry as well. She relished her front row seat.

"Mr. Wigg…" Darci cleared her throat and began again. "Yes, *father,* you're right. Some stores are shutting their doors. Retail is, indeed, in a major shakeout. And that's probably going to continue. Some brick-and-mortar stores won't survive, and neither will some shopping malls. But you sent me here to assess and evaluate this mall and build the case to shut it down. But I'm telling you that not only will this one survive, it's thriving! Truthfully, that's mostly due to Betty here."

Betty felt herself beam with pride. She almost wanted to shout out an "Amen!" No room to shrink away from the spotlight today. Her extremely professional existence, despite it currently garbed in Mrs. Kris Kringle attire, depended on self-promotion. She felt so grateful to not need to speak on her own behalf and, instead, have this incredible force of a woman do the talking for her. *How could she ever have thought less than charitable thoughts toward Darci?* She made a mental note to ask for her forgiveness later and to praise her for a job well done.

"Betty knows how to give our customers a reason to shop at this great mall instead of shopping online," Darci's speech kept gaining momentum. "She's been building these experiences for shoppers; some are hosted by individual stores and some take place throughout the shopping complex. Because of Betty, Maplefield Mall is a destination. Especially today, with Pastor Max and the Christmas Eve Kids Cheer Fest—nobody creates events like this anymore. It's what makes us unique."

Mr. Wiggins shook his head, not buying any of it. "Because nobody *wants* to see that anymore." He pushed past Harry to exit the office and stood just outside the door. He looked left and right. Few people remained inside shopping. He turned to Betty, Harry, and Darci and beckoned them out into the walkway. They followed him.

"Tell me, what do you see?" Mr. Wiggins asked. "Because I see an empty mall."

"You do realize there's a blizzard outside?" Betty couldn't hide her frustration.

"Yes. That's not really fair, sir," Harry spoke, fully understanding that the lack of shoppers had nothing to do with management and wasn't foreshadowing the future; rather, it was due to the unexpected Act of God in the form of a snowstorm keeping most people off the streets and at home this Christmas Eve.

"Life isn't fair, Harry," Mr. Wiggins said, casting a look of profound sorrow at Darci.

Darci lowered her head. Betty and Harry couldn't ignore the exchange between the two. They both could feel a sense of shame and blame that appeared to be the burden Darci carried on her shoulders. At the same time, Mr. Wiggins's grief—for whatever reason—seemed tainted by a level of resentment toward his daughter that neither one understood.

As if projecting their thoughts, there was suddenly a SWOOSH!

"What the devil?" Mr. Wiggins ducked as a sizeable white bird flew overhead, so close that the wind beneath its wings made what little hair he had stand at attention. "What is *that*?"

"That is a Moluccan Cockatoo," Betty offered up, cheerfully unfazed. "Its name is Rainbow."

The bird SCREECHED and a rowdy WOOF! answered her cry as a beefy dog raced in close behind.

"Is that one of those pit bulls?" Mr. Wiggins's eyes widened.

"No, actually, he's an American Staffordshire Terrier," added Betty, quite matter-of-factly. "His name is Pickpocket." Betty squinted her eyes at the dog. "But I don't see my Elf on the Shelf. Wonder where he's gone."

Suddenly the two human-sized elves, Karina and Randy, came bounding around the corner in pursuit of the animals. Karina held the Elf on the Shelf in one hand. The two passed quickly by, laughing and having a grand time of their game.

"Ah-ha! There he is with my other two favorite elves." Betty exclaimed. "Darci, we still have no idea how the Elf on the Shelf came to us?"

Darci shook her head no, unable to suppress her giggles at the ludicrous sight of a bird, a dog, and two human elves right in front of her in their mall. Mr. Wiggins took great offense to her show of joy. Harry noticed.

"So, *this* is what you call 'an experience for shoppers'?" Mr. Wiggins attempted to put an end to the holiday merriment. "Ridiculous!" he spat out over his shoulder as he walked away.

Harry, Betty, and Darci were left standing together. "I think he meant, 'Bah, Humbug," muttered Harry. Darci overheard him and suppressed a giggle.

"Darci," Betty turned to her. "Thank you for all you said about my work and about the success of this mall. I had no idea about all the work you've been doing. I am so very grateful. And proud of you."

Darci pressed her lips together, openly disappointed in how the conversation went with her father. "Thank you, Betty. I'm afraid, though, that nothing I ever do will be good enough. Not for *him*."

"If you don't mind me asking, what is it with him?" Harry proceeded with caution. "I mean, I'm about to be a dad. I know I'm nowhere near ready or qualified for the job, but if my little girl grows up to be someone like you? I'd consider myself lucky—and a success."

"Thanks," she said. "But I did something that my dad can never forgive me for," Darci confessed.

"I find that hard to believe," Betty's puzzled look was matched by Harry's wrinkled brow.

"What in the world could you have done that was that bad?" Harry asked.

"I was born," Darci stated simply. "And because I was born, my mom died."

CHAPTER TWENTY-SIX

DOCTORS & REPORTERS
Collisions and Candy Canes

In their Uber, while en route to the mall, Dr. Grey deliberately asked the driver's least favorite question: "Are we there yet?"

She held her cell phone to her ear. Covering the mouthpiece, she responded to the annoyed look the Uber driver flashed her in the rearview mirror, "I know, I know." She then spoke into the phone, "Emily, dear, just breathe. I'm practically at the mall entrance."

The Uber driver's eyes questioned Dr. Grey's estimated time of arrival.

"Why don't your 'Momma in the making' call an ambulance?" the driver asked.

"They did," Dr. Grey whispered, careful to make sure she couldn't be heard on the other end. "Apparently, it collided with some news van."

Dr. Haywood shut his eyes and leaned his head back, praying, "Please, don't be Ian's van."

"You focus on your breathing, Emily," Dr. Grey advised, taking a moment to look at the red bar indicating low battery on her phone's screen. Under her breath, she cussed, then calmly returned to her patient, "I'm going to conserve my phone's juice, ok? First babies take their time coming out into this world. So, no worries. I'll ring you again the second we arrive."

As Dr. Grey ended her call, the Uber driver pointed out his windshield, exclaiming, "There's the holdup. This must be that crash you were talking about."

The doctors craned their necks to get a better view. Flashing red lights and emergency vehicles flooded the scene. It appeared that a local news van and not one, but two ambulances plus three cars had all somehow collided.

"Can you make out the call letters on the van?" Dr. Haywood asked his car mates.

The Uber driver leaned forward, squinting. "Not yet," he said. "I'll let you know."

"I hope no one was hurt," Dr. Grey fretted.

Just up ahead, almost parallel with the collision, Ian inched his van forward as police officers on the scene directed traffic around the accident, funneling all vehicles into the massive highway's two left lanes.

Holly had the best vantage point looking out her passenger-side window. "WQQZ," she called out. "Man, that sucks. For them and for whoever's waiting on that ambulance. No, wait, make that *two* ambulances."

"We now know what their Christmas Eve news story lead's gonna be," Ian scoffed.

"Hey, look, cool." Vincent chimed in from the back of the van, his face pressed up against the side windows, aglow in a swirl of red light, watching a tow truck unhinge an ambulance from the rival news station's van. His eyes followed the action until they settled on the man dressed in an ugly Christmas sweater, standing—or more like shivering—in front of the whole scene with one hand pressed up against his right temple and the other holding a microphone to his mouth.

"Vincent, I don't think it's very nice to take pleasure in someone else's misfortunes," Vi gently chastised.

"It's just a fender bender." Vern craned his neck to see what he could see out the window. "I'm sure they'll be just fine."

"Oh, yeah," Vincent nonchalantly whispered, still entranced with what was unfolding outside. "I was talking about that reporter guy's sweater. Look how cool it is. It's like he's got Santa and Rudolph and Santa's sleigh all on him in 3D." He then turned to catch Ian's eyes in the rearview mirror. "You think we can find one like it at the mall for me, Ian? A sweater like that guy has, but with lightbulbs that really go on and off with a switch. Like one I saw on TV."

"You want an ugly Christmas sweater?" Ian laughed.

Vince swooned his protest, "It's not ugly. I think it's beautiful."

"So do I, Vince," Holly piped up with glee, her eyes looking over at Ian.

"Tell ya what, Vince, as soon as we get around this mess, we exit the highway and we'll be at the mall," Ian replied. "You can search for one yourself as soon as we get inside."

Vincent bounced up and down a bit in his seat, squealing with delight.

"Unless, of course, Holly thinks we should stop to grab some video on this accident? A guy in an ugly Christmas sweater. Snarled traffic. Two ambulances that can't get to the poor soul who needs help? Might be just the right footage for that reel you're working on."

Holly shrugged, dismissing the idea. "Nah! That's WQQZ and that guy's story—Mr. Ugly Christmas Sweater. Ours is waiting for us; it's the 'Brawl at the Mall'—I can feel it."

"Carter must be livid right about now," Ian tried to stifle a laugh just thinking about it.

"It's not all that funny," Holly said in her best scolding voice. She paused. "Well, okay, so it is funny." She then chuckled.

Back in the newsroom Ian and Holly abandoned earlier that day, Carter sat on the edge of an empty desk in the middle of the room, watching the television monitors. A jar of candy canes in hand, and one in his mouth, he exhaled, somewhat defeated. On the screen, the WQQZ van, the ambulances, the flashing red lights, and the nightmare traffic were in full view with the animated reporter in his holiday attire front and center. "And Ugly Sweater Guy takes the lead," he muttered to himself.

Carter looked around at the others in his newsroom. No one bothered to look up, heads down, focused on whatever stories they were working on. Carter took a moment, slowly becoming aware of their unusual silence. All that could be heard—barely—were the words from the guy in the ugly Christmas sweater on the screen, retelling his first-hand experience.

"Snow and poor visibility contributed to this collision, leaving—"

Carter muted the sound. He hopped off of the desk and addressed his team.

"You all see this?" he pointed up at the screens, as the reporters in the room looked up. "What do you think? Good reporting? Or too self-serving?"

Carter expected a response, but none came. While all eyes were on him, they looked fatigued and somewhat fearful.

"Well I think it's the latter," Carter grunted, then turned to bellow at the screen. "Good grief! It's just a fender bender. You've got a widdle bump on your big fat head. I'm sure another ambulance has already been dispatched. The story's not about you, you drama queen."

A few of the members of his team chuckled hesitantly, as Carter began circling his reporter's desks, offering each one a candy cane from his jar. "You know what we call that, ladies and gentlemen?" All heads shook no. "Making a mountain out of a molehill."

Just then, Carter's cell phone rang. He retrieved it and saw Ian's name appear at the top of the screen. He slid the green telephone icon across the screen to accept the call, and then held the phone up to his ear. Blowing out a belly full of exasperation, he asked, "Please tell me you're at the mall, and you have a lead."

CHAPTER TWENTY-SEVEN

LEO & IAN

The Calm before the Real Storm

Leo felt pretty darn silly, all dressed up in his Santa suit sitting on his king-sized throne still backstage in the mall's theatre. At least he wasn't on display in the front lobby of the mall. He was grateful there weren't any kids waiting in line to see Santa—one silver lining of the unexpected snow. He wasn't sure he could be Santa one-on-one with the little tykes. He has been gathering the courage all afternoon to bellow his best Ho-Ho-Ho during the main event…but now, it would appear, to a crowd of…no one. Peering over the tops of his phony glasses at Betty, who was still dressed as Mrs. Claus standing to his side with two steaming cups of something delicious-smelling in her hands, he asked, "So, nobody's coming?"

"Here." Betty handed him one of the frothy-topped drinks garnished with a peppermint candy cane.

"That doesn't look like black coffee." Leo narrowed his eyes, glaring at the drink in his hand.

Betty rolled her eyes. "It's not. It's the only thing the food court's coffee shop had ready-made before they, too, shut down for the night. So, for once, Leo, try something just a little bit outside of your comfort zone."

He surveyed his present situation. "This," he said while swatting at the white, fluffy pom-pom at the end of his Santa hat, "isn't enough out of my comfort zone for you?"

Betty fretted, her face showing her dismay. "It was all planned, Leo. This is supposed to be one of the highlights for our mall every year. We had more stores sign up this year than ever before! They were supposed to set up displays in their shops for Pastor Max's kids to come in and choose their gifts…but now they are closed. We had all the balloons inflated with shopping vouchers in them, ready to go."

Leo tried to interject, but Betty never seemed to pause long enough, or to even take a breath for that matter, so that he could speak.

"Each child was supposed to choose a balloon to pop and find shop cards they could use in participating stores to pick out presents for themselves and their family members," she rambled on. "We even had free gift wrapping this year."

Leo finally interrupted. "Betty, look, I know this dashing red suit may hide my real identity—Superman—but…remember me? General Counsel? Swell guy. I helped you set this all up. I *know* how much effort you've put in. I *know* how much this all means to you. But you can't expect people to not close up shop when Mother Nature's giving us not just a white Christmas, but one to rival that of the North Pole!"

"Well Father Christmas shouldn't be able to be stopped, especially when it's our last year here. This snowstorm has ruined everything," she cried out, trying to stop her tears from flowing.

Okay, now this was so not the Betty he knew, and he couldn't stand seeing her so upset. Leo stood up from his throne and exaggerated the slurping down of his sugary drink. Trying to keep his face from convulsing, he held up the empty container for Betty to see. "Mmm, Mmm! You were so right. This was delicious! I've just drank in the Christmas spirit!"

"Oh, stop." She rolled her eyes. She took a moment to appreciate the gesture and then finally allowed herself to relax a little. "Your whole face was screaming 'torture'—I know you hated it."

"Yup! But I'd drink another one for you, if it'd make you smile again." Leo tossed the cup into a nearby recycling bin. He then took Betty's hands into his. "But please, please don't make me."

Betty couldn't help but laugh, and he internally rejoiced at the sound.

"There's my girl," he said.

Just then, Karina and Randy raced into the room, interrupting, oblivious to the moment.

"And, hey look, here are Santa's helpers, just in the Saint Nick of time!" joked Leo. "Where have you two elves been?"

"Chasing some big, old dog and his pet bird," Randy offered up, haphazardly plopping himself down onto Santa's throne. "Hey, dude, this chair is totally lit!"

"Hey, Elf! That's my chair," Leo's words fell on deaf ears.

Betty blinked repeatedly. "What? That dog and bird are still running around?" She shook her head. "What were their owners' names...Hank and On-Drey-A? Huh...So, those two haven't been able to catch them yet? And why were you two chasing them?"

"And where's Pastor Max?" Leo chimed in. "Where are the rest of his kids?"

Finally getting a chance to respond, Karina shrugged. "Don't know," she said. "Some SUPER prego lady at the Games & Gadgets Galore store said the dog gave her this stuffed toy and told us to give it back to its owner." Karina offered the Elf on the Shelf, who was a little worse for the wear, to Betty.

Betty reached out to claim him. "Oh! There you are," she rejoiced. "This little guy belongs to me. Or, well, honestly, he belongs to some Secret Santa or somebody who—every year since I've been here—has had him watching over me from the day after Thanksgiving through Christmas Eve."

Karina's face made it clear she had no idea what Betty was talking about. "That sounds kind of crazy."

"And creepy," Randy added.

"No," Betty corrected. "It's actually quite lovely. He's my guardian elf!"

Betty's cell phone rang. "Hello?" she said, listening to the response. "Oh, Carter, that's wonderful. Thank you so much for sending your news crew. Yes." Betty's voice hesitated to speak her next words: "We'll give you a headline-making show. Promise."

Ending her call, Betty sprang into action, addressing her Santa and elves. "Okay, now, that was my friend, Carter, from WACK-TV. He just confirmed that his news team is already somewhere here in the mall. They've unloaded their equipment and are just waiting to be told where to set up. I'll have our security guard, Elmer, find them. Although knowing Elmer, he's probably already on it."

Leo's eyes twinkled. He loved when Betty made plans, talking out loud to herself.

"Or maybe I should send Darci, too?" Betty continued, not really expecting an answer from anyone else. Looking at Karina and Randy, she directed them, saying "You two elves, I need you to find Pastor Max and the other kids and bring them to the stage immediately."

Karina and Randy saluted, perfectly in sync, and dashed away.

As they exited, a pair of strangers entered.

"Excuse us," the woman said to Leo and Betty. "I'm Dr. Grey and this is Dr. Haywood. We were told we might be able to talk to the person in charge here?"

At that, Leo grinned, then gently nudged Betty to the forefront. "That would be Mrs. Claus," he said.

Betty took a few steps toward the doctors, but not before rolling her eyes at Leo. "What Santa means is that I'm the mall manager. And he's not really Santa. I mean, we don't dress, um, usually look like this," Betty stumbled over her words, then shaking her head, realized she didn't need to explain herself. "Oh, never mind. I'm Betty Bryant. What can I do for you both?"

"We're looking for a couple of patients of ours," Dr. Haywood said. "A young man, possibly with a news crew."

Betty nodded, a puzzled look on her face. "We understand a news crew has, indeed, arrived," she said.

"And, also, a very pregnant woman." Dr. Grey raised her eyebrows, a look of concern on her face. "SUPER pregnant. As in ready to deliver."

Both Leo and Betty looked at one another, recalling the exact words Karina had said earlier. "The Games & Gadgets Galore store," they said in unison.

Meanwhile, just inside the mall's main lobby, Vincent, Vi, Vern, Ian, and Holly were standing still in awe of the festive décor surrounding them. Ian and Holly were carrying their video equipment across the main lobby and stopped so the trio with them could admire the decorations for a few moments. Vi and Vern were glassy-eyed taking in the Winter Wonderland scene. Vincent's eyes lit up in awe of the ice castles, gingerbread cottages, and decorated forest of trees, but what made them really sparkle was when he caught sight of the brightly lit shop just off to his left with racks upon racks of ugly Christmas sweaters.

"Ian, look!" Vincent exclaimed as he pointed.

Ian followed the direction of Vincent's finger. The employee inside the shop was gathering up her belongings. No doubt they were closing early due to the storm and the lack of shoppers.

"Wow, Vince," Ian replied. "It's like they knew you were coming."

No sooner did Ian finish his thought and take a step toward the sweater shop, when BOOOOOMMMMM! an explosive roar vibrated throughout the mall. Ian froze. It didn't sound very far away.

Glancing back at Holly, he mouthed "What the hell...?"

Holly slowly shook her head and shrugged...

Vi and Vern didn't seem so concerned, however, almost as if they hadn't heard it. And Vincent was oblivious, barely able to stand still from excitement about the ugly Christmas sweater that soon would be his very own. Vincent hadn't been to a mall—let alone much of anywhere—in a decade.

Ian and Holly exchanged glances, as what sounded like a continuous moan came from the ceiling and walls. Ian whispered to her "You want to go on ahead, Holly? Check things out? I'll catch up in a second."

Holly nodded and immediately took off in the direction of the boom.

Not wasting another moment, and without showing any signs of alarm, Ian stopped, rested his load on the floor, and turned to Vincent, Vi, and Vern.

"Hey, you three," he playfully engaged them. "You know what I just realized?"

Vincent, Vi, and Vern all shook their heads in sync. Ian couldn't help but notice just how much they resembled those three wise monkeys that embodied the proverbial principle of "see no evil, hear no evil, speak no evil."

"Your names all start with the same letter *V*," Ian exaggerated his look of amazement.

"Hey," Vincent excitedly shouted out. "You're right, Ian. How cool is that!"

"What are the chances?" Ian exaggerated his surprise. "It must be some sort of sign."

"It means we're meant to be together!" Vincent gleefully put his arms around Vi and Vern in a group hug.

The elderly couple laughed and hugged him back.

"Know what else?" Ian continued.

Again, the three shook their heads.

Ian pointed to the shop. "See the sweaters over there in all colors and styles. I bet there's a perfect one just waiting to belong to somebody whose name starts with a 'V'!"

Vincent's face flitted from elation to exasperation. "They're waiting to belong to who? Vi, Vern, or me—Vincent?"

"Oh, I mean there's a perfect one perfect for each of you!" Ian said, not skipping a beat. "What do you think if you three do a little Christmas Eve sweater shopping here while I go take care of some work? When Holly and I are done, we'll come back and get you, and we'll all go somewhere together to grab a bite and celebrate? You have to hurry, though, because I think they're about to close up shop."

Ian wasn't just worried about the shop closing. Frazzled thoughts swirled inside his head: *Was it wise for them all to stay inside the mall? What were those sounds? Was it more dangerous inside or outside? He couldn't have them waiting outside in the cold. The van was running on fumes the last few miles, he hadn't wanted to waste time getting gas. How long would the gas in the tank last with the van's engine running idle and heat turned on?* He shook his head free and made his choice.

Vincent danced around, hopping from foot to foot. "Let's go," Vincent shouted, no longer willing to wait. Whirling around, he skipped his way to explore the sweaters.

Ian quickly spoke to Vi and Vern who leaned in closer to hear. Digging into his pockets and pulling out his wallet, he handed Vern all the cash he had. "Would you mind keeping an eye on him for me? I know it's a lot to ask."

"It's actually not," said Vi, a bittersweet smile settling on her lips. "Vincent makes me feel somehow like my Grace is close by."

As Vi turned to follow Vincent, Vern stepped in even closer to Ian. "I hear better than fine," he said, tapping on one of his hearing aids. "Better than most. I heard that rumbling, too, and it didn't sound good. You go now. I'll keep these turned up, and them," he pointed to Vi and Vincent, "safe until you return."

Ian nodded his thanks to the old man, and then without further delay, grabbed his belongings and ran toward the threatening sounds that grew louder and louder and more frightening with every step.

CHAPTER TWENTY-EIGHT

DAMIAN & HANK

Distractions

Pickpocket's endless barking and Rainbow's constant screeching muffled the BOOMING sound just enough for their respective owners, Hank and Andrea, to not pay it much mind. Tired from chasing their pets for a few hours with no success catching them yet, the two finally decided to take a break and sit for a bit in the food court at the far end of the mall.

As they watched the white bird sit atop the burly dog's back parading in front of the only vendor still open—The Coffee House—Hank pulled out one of the two chairs at a nearby bistro table. Struggling to catch his breath, Hank chuckled. "I feel like I'm about to have a heart attack here. I'm in worse shape than I thought. Take a seat, Andrea," he said, pronouncing her name correctly and gesturing for her to sit. "I need a minute myself."

Andrea plunked herself down into the all-metal, silver scoop of the chair's seat. "You are not alone, Hank. I've never been so happy to just sit! Thank you!"

Hank yanked on the other chair, sliding it closer to Andrea's side, and took a seat. He leaned back his head, shut his eyes, and sighed, "Cold, hard metal, and yet, it feels so good!"

The two finally caught their breath.

"I honestly just don't know what's gotten into Rainbow," Andrea said. "She knows better. She never behaves this way. And all that screeching, it's like she's trying to tell me something, but what...? I just don't know."

"Pickpocket, too," Hank replied. "He's not his usual self. I mean, if I'm honest, Pickpocket *can* be a bad influence, I'll admit it. He's the kind of free-spirited dog who's better off leash, but all of this today? I don't get it."

"'Better off leash'?" Andrea repeated, bashfully saying, "Sort of like you, maybe?"

"Look who's talking," Hank snorted. "You and all those camo colors you're wearing! I bet you don't ever color inside the lines!"

Andrea blushed. "Well, no. I guess I don't." She paused a moment. "I love colors. I imagine how beautiful everything would be, well, if I could see them."

Hank now opened both eyes to look at her. "What do you mean: 'If you could see them'?"

"Oh, I can see just fine, but my world is sort of black-and-white," Andrea explained. "I'm color blind."

Realization dawned on Hank's face. "Oh, wow. I shouted that to you when we first met. I was out of line. Sorry."

"It's okay," Andrea said.

"Uh," Hank hesitantly asked, "You do know your bird is all white, right?"

Andrea laughed. "Yes! And that's exactly why I named her Rainbow!"

Hank gave her a befuddled look, not understanding.

"White light is actually made up of all of the colors of the rainbow," she said. Nodding as if he completely understood what she was saying, Hank lowered his head, looking over the tops of his glasses. Then he grinned and shrugged a little. "I still don't get it."

"It's the light spectrum. You know, physics? That's what I teach to my junior high students," Andrea patiently explained.

"I think I must have been playing hooky during that particular lesson," Hank said. Though, if he admitted it to himself, he probably wouldn't mind being schooled in physics by this colorful creature. "So..." Hank was surprised at how fascinated he found himself at this moment. "Let me get this straight, I see your bird as all white. But you…you see the bird as rainbow colored?"

Shaking her head, Andrea found herself quite enjoying "the education of Hank." "Ok, so let me try to explain…"

"Okay," Hank slowly pushed himself out of his chair. "I'm absolutely game…but first, how about I get us something to drink before they close?" He gestured to the coffee shop where the solo staffer was starting to clean up, and some guy with spiky, gelled hair—black on bottom, blonde up top—was headed their way, carrying two festive drinks with candy canes hanging off the rims of the cups.

Hank turned just as Damian crossed in front of him.

"Excuse me," Hank stopped Damian to ask, "If you don't mind me asking, what are those?"

Damian paused, puzzled. "To tell you the truth, I'm not even sure, but they're something sweet and the only option right now. They're about to close for the night."

Hank looked at his watch. "I thought the mall was open late on Christmas Eve."

Damian turned to briefly face the couple, shrugging. "No shoppers with this snowstorm, they said. You might want to hurry if you want one of these."

Hank nodded and walked over to the counter, while Damian continued to make his way to Isabelle, who was seated at another of the little bistro tables.

Damian raised one of the sugary drinks, gallantly presenting it to Isabelle. "Here you go. One I-have-no-idea-what-this-is-but-it's-all-they-had drink for you." He sat down in the chair next to her. "And one of the same for me."

"This doesn't look like a glass of wine," Isabelle laughed.

"No, but it *is* red." Damian held the frothy concoction up to his eye for inspection. "Besides, I don't think it's 'five o'clock'…" Damian launched softly into song, surprised when Isabelle joined in.

"*It's only half past twelve but I don't care,*" they belted out, "*It's five o'clock somewhere…*"

Damian smiled, staring at her. Then he pointed his finger, tracing an imaginary circle in the air in front of and around her beautiful face. "You are definitely a bad influence."

"Tell me something I haven't heard before," Isabelle flirted back.

The two looked at one another for what seemed like a very long time.

"No, really," Isabelle broke both of their trances. "Tell me something I haven't heard before, that I don't know. About you."

"Ohhhh!" Damian tossed back his head, laughing. "I see what you want. But I think I said that that conversation required a glass of wine or two."

Isabelle raised her candy cane concoction, "Well, you just said, it *is* red…" She took a sip. "Wow!" She puckered up from its sweetness.

Damian couldn't help but imagine kissing those lips as he watched her.

"Come on, Mr. Black Sheep," she coaxed. "I told you my tale of woe, although now I'm not even sure we'll be able to get out of here so I can see my sister and my nieces…ironic, huh?"

"Mother Nature always wins," Damian quipped, lapping up some of the white foam from his drink.

"So, spill it," Isabelle demanded.

"Oh, no, couldn't do that," Damian joked. "This drink is too delicious to spill!"

Isabelle didn't laugh. She took another sip of her own drink. "Seriously. Damian. What's your story?"

"Seriously?" Damian shook his head. "You want to know my story?"

"I do," Isabelle nodded. "Although, I suppose I could make up my own story about you."

Damian was intrigued. "Well, that could be interesting."

"Fine, then. Let's see," she began. "You have your own look going on." She playfully eyed him up and down. "You're a famous hairstylist? Or maybe a designer to the stars? Oooh! Maybe you cater to rock stars. You said you were in a band."

"I did," Damian agreed, not giving anything away.

160

"But then you told Harry you own Burn Baby Burn Bootcamps…"

"I did. Have you ever been?"

Isabelle shook her head and continued: "You were born to mutant superheroes and are on this planet to save humanity?"

"Ha! Well, that would be sweet." Damian loved hearing her speak. Especially when it was about him. "But, alas, not true."

She whined just a bit, slightly frustrated. "Come on, Damian. I love a good story, and I know you've got one."

He shrugged and joked, "Okay, so I'm part of an underground resistance, dedicated to overthrowing dictatorships…and I'll risk everything for the sake of justice and truth."

Isabelle pouted. Then she pulled out her paperback novel *Of Love and Shadows* from her bag. "Oh, ha ha. Funny. Your life sounds suspiciously close to my book's hero…"

Damian laughed harder then. "I read the back cover when we were on the plane."

"Fine, then. Don't tell me anything real." Isabelle narrowed her eyes and turned away slightly, irritated at his flippancy.

"Oh, come on now, don't tell me you're mad."

"I am. I told you my story and why I'm here, but you can't be serious long enough to tell me yours. It seems a little unfair."

"You're right, Isabelle. I'm sorry." Damian took a deep breath along with a long slurp of his drink. "Here goes. I was born in England, where my dad's from. My mother is from India. They met at Oxford. I was a bit of an 'oops' for them. They ended up getting married, still are. Had a handful more kids. I've got two sisters and a brother. My family comes from money. It was tradition in both my father's and mother's families to ship the kiddies off to private boarding schools. I went to one that taught me a lot, mostly about survival." Damian's eyes darkened as old haunts casted a shadow over him.

Isabelle frowned. "Hey, listen, I'm sorry. I should never have insisted."

Damian focused in on her sympathetic eyes. "No worries, really. Honestly, it's actually kind of nice to share it with someone. Nobody asks. Nobody seems to care. Books were all I had—like it or not—and I used them to retreat into other heroes' adventures. I ended up using those stories to get me out of my own situation."

"How so?"

"I went to battle, head-to-head, with the headmaster. After I had had enough of their 'discipline,' I decided then and there when I was about thirteen years old that if they said something was white, I would say it was black. If they said to go up, I would go down, and, if they demanded obedience, I did everything I could to misbehave. Eventually I became so much of a handful that I got expelled and disgraced my family. I had finally earned the title they always believed me to be..."

"Black sheep," Isabelle supplied him with it.

Damian nodded. "Yup. That's me."

"What about your siblings?"

"They all went to different schools. They're all polished professionals, shining pillars of society that my parents like to show off whenever they can. I don't see any of them these days. I don't fit their mold, so I pretty much do my own thing."

"I'm sorry."

"Don't be. I'm not. What happened to me helped to make me who I am, and I didn't turn out half bad. Though I didn't turn out half good either," Damian joked.

Isabelle half-laughed, but her eyes betrayed her as they glassed over with tears. "'Let everything happen to you. Beauty and terror. Just keep going. No feeling is final.'"

"Ahh! I love Rilke. Damn, you are so smart, lady! *Finding Nemo* even updated that wisdom with, "Just keep swimming!" Damian chuckled, keeping his own tears at bay.

Isabelle wanted to get up and hug him. Instead, she deflected her thoughts. "So, where does the gym come in?"

"With Burn Baby Burn Bootcamps?" Damian straightened his spine. "Well, I have the headmaster to thank for that idea. He was just a bully who never grew out of punching people. I wish I had known some kickboxing moves for self-defense. But when I was sent home from school, I vowed that no one would ever hurt me again, so I started working out. Turns out I was a natural and pretty good at teaching others. One thing led to another—you know, viral videos and everything—and before I knew it, my bootcamps and I were household names."

"So, if you're not here to spend the holidays with family, why *are* you here?"

Damian sipped his drink, smiling. "I'm actually supposed to be meeting up with a preacher and the kids from his congregation right after Christmas. The guy's been killing it, paying it forward. Ex-con doing good deeds, helping other former inmates succeed on the outside with a restaurant he started. I thought that, maybe, what he does and what I do might fit together. I don't know how exactly—maybe to help motivate kids in foster care? But I wanted to see for myself first. There's supposed to be some sort of event with him here at the mall today—not that that will even happen now with the snowstorm. I wasn't even technically invited to it, but I wanted to check him out, kind of under the radar, before actually meeting him, and so, well, here I am."

Listening to him, Isabelle was lost in thought. *Who is this guy?*

"Hello…? Isabelle?" Damian waved his hands in front of her. "Did I lose you?"

Isabelle realized she had been mesmerized, staring at him for way too long. She jolted herself to the present: "Smart!" Her voice echoed; she shouted much more loudly than she had intended. She then slurped the rest of her drink, exaggerating her facial expressions on purpose with the hopes of making Damian laugh. Succeeding, she then stood up, and announced, "Okay, then, let's go find the preacher, the kids, and the p- p- p-party!"

Damian furrowed his brows, lifting his now-empty cup, "I swear these were non-alcoholic."

Isabelle grabbed both of their cups, took a few of steps over to the bin, tossed them in, and started walking away. Calling out over her shoulder, she asked, "You coming?"

He leapt up, not needing to be asked twice.

On their way out, they passed the only other couple in the food court, along with their pets that were roaming nearby.

Hank and Andrea barely noticed, both lost in their conversation.

"Yes, I can," Hank proudly boasted. "I can look at a customer the second they come into my dealership and know the color, make, and model of the car that's the perfect fit for them!"

Andrea shook her head, laughing in disbelief. "Okay, okay, so what do I drive?"

"How about I tell you what you *deserve* to be driving?"

Pickpocket, with Rainbow on his back, carefully tip-toed toward their respective people until they stood just inches apart from them. Under the table, Pickpocket used his nose to poke Hank's right knee.

Hank raised his eyebrows at Andrea, assuming, for the briefest moment that she was the one touching him.

"Woof!" Pickpocket accompanied his nose-butting with a loud bark.

"Pickpocket!" Hank jumped, happy to have his pup back at his side but also feeling slightly let down that it wasn't Andrea playing footsie with him under the table.

"Rainbow!" Andrea reached out her arm as a perch for her cockatoo. "Where have you been, you naughty girl?" Immediately, she placed Rainbow in her harness.

The beautiful bird bowed her head, spread her wings, raised her crest, and began to flap her wings, making a lot of noise.

Hank rubbed Pickpocket's head with both his hands, as he, too, clipped the leash to his collar. "Good boy! You scared me!"

Pickpocket shifted his head from side to side, ensuring a proper scratching of both his ears but, as he did so, he kept nipping at Hank's shirt and pants, tugging at them.

"What's yours trying to say?" Hank asked, as he turned his attention to the still-squawking bird while almost absent-mindedly trying to dissuade Pickpocket's love bites.

"She doesn't really speak lots of words like a parrot, so I'm not sure what's on her mind," Andrea said. "But she sure is babbling more than usual."

"Woof!" Pickpocket continued nipping at the bottom of Hank's shirt, then backed up, tossed his head, and circled him a couple of times.

"What's yours trying to tell you?" Andrea asked.

Hank shrugged, puzzled, then finally rose from his chair.

At the motion, both Pickpocket and Rainbow grew more excited. Each moved away from their owner, then came back, then away again. Each time, they'd widen the distance between themselves and their owners, moving a bit further away each time they repeated this sequence—drawing their caregivers along with them.

"It's almost as if they want us to follow them," Andrea guessed as she stood from her chair. Her actions elicited an even louder screech from Rainbow.

Hank looked at Andrea, "Shall we?" He motioned for Andrea to join him. She nodded.

"Lead the way!" they said to their creature companions.

CHAPTER TWENTY-NINE

MR. ABDULLAH & PASTOR MAX

Special Deliveries

Mr. Abdullah stood behind the front counter of Games & Gadgets Galore, rubbing his temples with his fingertips. "Kids, stop popping those exploding bomb bags!" Again, he wished that he had never stocked those cursed noisemakers.

Now, after way too may "bangs" and "booms," he couldn't wait to get home to his family. He turned to Elmer who had been keeping a watchful eye on the antics from behind his aviators, "Please…Elmer…can…"

"I got this, Mr. Abdullah." Elmer moved immediately toward the kids to help quiet the commotion and to begin shepherding them out of the store.

"Thank you so much, Elmer."

Mr. Abdullah faced the two new people who stood before him. It was a young lady tapping on her iPad and a linebacker-of-a-man who sported the collar of a holy man. He stared at the sight as his brain caught up with him. "Oh, Miss Darci and Mr.…I mean Pastor Max…my Assistant Manager said you needed my help with something? What can I do for you?" He stumbled over his words a little.

Ignoring his nervousness, Darci was all business. "Mr. Abdullah," she began. "You were one of the stores that signed up to participate in Pastor Max's Christmas Eve Kids Cheer Fest."

"Yes, yes," Mr. Abdullah nodded. "How did it go? I've been so busy in the back room."

"Well, Mr. Abdullah, it didn't actually *go*," Max explained. "And I apologize for these kids in your store; they're mine. With most of the stores closing early because of the storm, the whole event fell flat, but we're still hoping we can turn it around. We were wondering, hoping, actually, if maybe you would allow my kids to choose one item from your store—you can set the dollar limit—so at least they can have something they want for Christmas this year?"

"Mr. Abdullah, I'll make sure the mall reimburses you," Darci chimed in. "I know your deliveries didn't go out as planned. We've gotten some complaints."

Mr. Abdullah threw up his hands. "Everybody complains!" He tossed his head to the side, referencing a stack of undelivered packages leaning up against the wall. "I was going to load these last ones in my car tonight and deliver them myself. Even offer refunds…but nothing is going as planned today."

Darci continued, uncomfortable at the confession. "We thought you might have extra items on hand, like games and toys the kids would like. Maybe even open some of those packages that never got delivered? The mall can reimburse you for your inventory and, also, for compensating your customers, too."

Understanding her offer, Mr. Abdullah nodded enthusiastically and waved his arms. With the gesture, he bid Darci and Pastor Max to follow him. "Most generous of you!"

They all walked towards the back room of the store. He stopped for a moment and addressed them. "I'll make you a deal," he said.

Darci and Max stood tall, open to any and all suggestions.

In response, Mr. Abdullah shrugged. "I gladly will give to you whatever you'd like." He opened the door, beyond which Darci and Max could see pregnant Emily laying on the couch, her hair damp from perspiration.

Mr. Abdullah glanced back at them. "But some other things might still be delivered today; some very much unexpected things! How about you take whatever items you want from the store and then, you maybe take this special delivery with you, too?"

Emily looked up and strained a smile at the two new strangers. "Hello, I'm Emily," she said, propping herself up against a back rest as best she could. "Please tell me the ambulance is here or maybe, even, you found my Harry...I mean my husband, Harry?"

Darci's eyes grew wide. "Harry? Is that your husband? And he hasn't called you?"

Emily sniffled, shaking her head. "I've been calling his cell phone all day. I got a call from some spam number, but the voicemail was all garbled. My Harry came in from Dallas with his boss, Mr. Wiggins...do you know him?"

"Don't cry," Darci soothed. "I know Harry. Well, I don't know him know him, but...Mr. Wiggins I do know, or well, maybe I don't..."

Exhausted, Emily struggled to follow what Darci was saying, and then started to ramble, almost talking to herself, "Yes, I think I'd rather have Harry. Forget the ambulance." Stopping for a moment, she began to sob.

Mr. Abdullah moved to Emily's side, trying to comfort her. Emily leaned towards him, grateful for the fatherly gesture.

Darci snapped to, finally blurting out, "Oh, my gosh. I should have said this sooner, so sorry. Harry is here at the mall."

At that, Pastor Max took charge and held Darci by the shoulders. "Darci, please go get Harry. While you do that, I'll find out about the ambulance." He then turned to Mr. Abdullah and said, "I promise that we'll be right back with help for this unexpected special delivery."

Mr. Abdullah was relieved. He produced a very grateful, very broad smile in thanks.

However, to the collective dismay of all involved, as soon as Darci and Pastor Max turned to venture out into the mall, an eerie-sounding groan, quickly followed by an ear-deafening thunder, echoed through the store. The ground trembled slightly beneath their feet as they heard shrill creaking noises all around.

169

"What in God's name—" Pastor Max moved closer to Darci; the two braced themselves, with one hand wrapped around each other and the other gripped the sides of the open office doorway. Mr. Abdullah instinctively positioned himself, hovering as best he could over Emily to protect her and her baby from harm.

Then, with an ominous cracking and crunching sound, crumbling bits of powdery-grey drywall began falling from the ceiling, coating everything below with a cloud of dust. Darci and Pastor Max looked at one another, their eyes full of fear. They both looked up, just in time to see the roof up above rip open and crash down around them.

CHAPTER THIRTY

MR. WIGGINS & HARRY
Follow the Leader

Elmer corralled the last of the fifty kids, crossing the threshold from inside Mr. Abdullah's Games & Gadgets Galore store to outside its doors and onto the mall's hallway. Just as they passed through the door, the crash just behind them made them all jump and scatter for safety. Instinctively, Elmer crouched down to the floor and covered his head with his arms unlike the kids around him, who weren't that much younger than he was, but who were now screaming and crying.

"Is anybody hurt?" he shouted out, slowly rising and taking off his mirrored shades. His voice had an authoritative yet soothing tone that seemed to calm the kids and quiet their fears. Elmer turned to face the game store, its front entrance now completely blocked by the crumbled ceiling debris. A haze of dust made it difficult for him to fully assess the damage done to his surroundings.

The kids started to tip-toe their way toward Elmer as the groaning walls threatened to snap again.

"No, no," Elmer waved them back. "It's not safe here." He pocketed his sunglasses, dusted off his hands, and with one last look at the collapsed storefront, turned to take care of the frightened kids. "How about you all follow me to the other end of this place?" He pulled his ring of keys off his belt loop, raised them in full view, and jingled them. "These keys open up the food court at the other end of the mall. Who's hungry?"

Quiet murmurs confirmed the kids were ready to follow Elmer's lead. He knew there were people trapped inside the store, but he knew his priority for now was to get these kids somewhere safer than where they all currently stood. With one last look over his shoulder, Elmer gestured to the kids, escorting them away from the immediate danger as quickly as he could.

On the upper level of the mall, quite a distance from the Games & Gadgets Galore store, Mr. Wiggins and Harry were in one of the meeting rooms reviewing spreadsheets and documents when BRRRING, BRRRING, BRRRING, a throwback phone ring from well before the birth of any kind of portable phone was invented trilled its muffled way out from the depths of Mr. Wiggins's jacket breast pocket. Pulling it out, he looked at the caller ID displaying Darci's name. He moaned, holding up his left hand, gesturing for silence to Harry who sat hunched over his laptop at the other end of the conference room's long table. He put the phone to his ear and took the call.

"Darci, now is not a good…" Mr. Wiggins immediately cut himself off as the panicked voice of his daughter pierced his ears, reminding him of another similar-sounding, distressed voice from long ago that still haunted him to this day. His eyes widened and he put the call on speakerphone so that Harry could hear, too.

"Slow down, Darci," he said as Harry rose from his seat to come closer to the phone to hear better.

Darci coughed into the phone, her speech breathy and labored, "The roof caved in," she managed to stammer out.

"What?" Mr. Wiggins seemed stuck in place, unable to do anything but listen to Darci and cast a most worrisome look at Harry. He finally stammered out, "Darci, where are you?"

Harry gestured for Mr. Wiggins to give him the phone. Surprisingly, the old man did. Harry shouted into the speaker, "Darci, this is Harry."

"Harry!" Darci's voice broke. It was clear to both Mr. Wiggins and Harry that she was trying to choke back tears. "Emily…"

Harry froze at Darci's mention of his wife's name.

"Emily…she's here with me. It's just us and Pastor Max and Mr. Abdullah," Darci's voice was strained.

"Here? She's here?" Harry wanted to leap into the phone. "Where's 'here'? Darci, where are you? Why are you with my wife? Harry's eyes darted back and forth bouncing among the questions racing through his mind.

Mr. Wiggins shook his head, confusion clouding his face. He said to Harry, "They *can't* be in the mall. Roof collapse? We would have heard something."

"Darci?" Harry shouted as he paced, "Talk to me."

"We're in Games & Gadgets Galore," Darci's voice seemed so far away. "The far end of the mall, new addition. We're trapped."

"That's way on the other end of the mall from us here," Harry whispered to Mr. Wiggins, as he grabbed his keys from the credenza in the conference room. He circled and slammed his laptop shut, then unplugged it and jammed it under his arm.

"I heard something, a faint something, earlier, but…" Mr. Wiggins's voice trailed off.

Harry ignored him. "Darci, are you okay?" he asked. "Are Emily and the baby okay?"

Mr. Wiggins's eyes locked onto Harry's as he tried to steel himself away from his surfacing memories…his own wife…Darci's mother…her final moments…the feelings of helplessness. His inability to do anything but watch her die.

"Darci…?" The sudden silence on the other end of the phone visibly unnerved both men who stared at one another, not as boss and subordinate but man-to-man, father-to-father. Now equals, both of their eyes filled with concern and a sense of dread.

Harry commanded, "Darci, you sit tight right where you are. We're on our way. Just hang on—" Suddenly the phone call dropped. Three dial tone beeps. And then it went dead.

Mr. Wiggins's eyes pleaded with Harry. He wanted to say something. He wanted to tell him what to do. But he didn't know. Just like the day Darci was brought into this world, and his wife, Lynn, was taken out of it.

Though distraught, Harry saw something in his boss's eyes that he had never seen before: A fearful ask for help. Harry felt compelled to put his hand on Mr. Wiggins's shoulder. Then with a nod, he sprang into action, taking charge and leading the way, and a grateful Mr. Wiggins followed.

"I'm calling 911," Harry announced as he hurried out the door.

Near the main lobby of the mall, Isabelle and Damian cocked their heads to listen to the creaking and popping sounds that seemed to be getting louder. "You do hear that, right?" Isabelle asked the question as Damian immediately nodded, a look of alarm on his face.

The couple had walked from the food court to where they stood now, trying to find their way back to the executive offices that they knew were somewhere on the upper level near the main entrance doors. That's where they assumed that they would find someone—anyone—to connect them with Pastor Max and the Christmas Eve event, if it was even still taking place.

"Hello?" Damian shouted out at the top of his lungs, his voice bouncing off the walls and echoing as if they were deep within a hidden cave.

"Shhh," Isabelle put her hand over his mouth. "What on earth are you doing?"

He covered her hand with his own, kissing her palm, eliciting a dreamy look from Isabelle that he returned with his own, then removed her hand from his mouth. "It's way too quiet, like eerily so," Damian said, looking around at the emptiness.

But suddenly, a loud, reverberating… "Hello!" answered back. It was a delayed response to Damian's call followed by a childlike laugh.

Vincent loved the sound of his own voice repeating and bouncing back to him. The mall was so great for that.

From across the way, Damian and Isabelle saw a laughing young man sporting a very ugly Christmas sweater. Somehow, the 3D ornaments and bulbs sewn into it actually lit up, pulsing on and off in bright waves of red, blue, green, and yellow lights. His chest puffed up as he stood so proudly alongside an elderly couple also wearing their own ugly Christmas sweaters, holding shopping bags with their puffy, winter coats stuffed inside. They all were just hanging out near the doorway of what appeared to be the only store still open, but seconds later, the lights of this shop, too, grew dark.

Amused and intrigued at the sight of the trio, momentarily alleviating them of their concerns over the ominous sound they heard earlier, Damian and Isabelle walked hand-in-hand to meet them.

Damian broke the ice by calling out, "LOVE your sweater, man!"

"Thanks!" Vincent beamed back at him. "I love your spiky hair." He took a few steps forward with his hand raised, evidently intent on a tactile experience, but Vi gently pulled him back.

Damian saw his enthusiasm. "Go ahead," he said to Vincent, lowering his head as he approached. He then shot a sideways glance at Isabelle. "Everybody wants to touch it!"

Vincent reached up and let Damian's hair poke his palm. "So cool!" he shouted with glee. "I'm Vincent. This is Vi and Vern; they're my friends."

Damian grinned at him, holding out his hand so Vincent could shake it. "I'm Damian and this is my friend, Isabelle." Vincent enthusiastically returned the handshake and Damian continued, "We heard there was supposed to be a Christmas Eve event here. But I don't think—"

"That's why my brother, Ian, and his friend, Holly, are here," Vincent offered. "They have the cameras with them. They're working."

Vern stepped forward then, looking a bit grave and shaking his head. "We all came in the WACK-TV news van. They were supposed to be covering that Christmas thing with a pastor and some kids, but I think something else has maybe taken priority."

"Ian said to stay here until they came back to get us," Vincent added.

"Came back to get you?" Damian asked. "From where?" He looked at Vern, then at Isabelle. Something wasn't right.

And then, another thunderous boom, this one unmistakably the result of some kind of explosion, sounded out from somewhere inside the mall.

They all twisted toward the sound, bracing themselves against one another, unsure whether to run or stay put, let alone where they should go.

Damian took a deep breath as he attempted to step up and lead the group. "How about you three stay here or, better yet, maybe outside where it might be safer?"

Vi put her right hand on the side of her face. "It's freezing out there!"

"Right." Damian wasn't sure what to do. As he tried to get a grip on his thoughts, Isabelle rescued him.

"Then you stay here, and we'll go check it out," she said, trying to sound reassuring.

"No!" Vincent shouted, becoming a ball of untamed energy; he was obviously ready to take action. "I'm not waiting. Ian needs me. I'm not scared. We need to go. Now!"

Vi again gently took hold of Vincent's forearm. "Yes, dear, I think you may be right." She turned her eyes to look at Vern's. "Honestly, what choice do we have?'

Vern let out an exaggerated breath, lifting his arms as if in surrender. "Okay, we'll all go." He turned to Isabelle and Damian, shrugging his shoulders.

"All for one and one for all!" Vincent shouted out his battle cry. "Like the Three Musketeers." He pointed to himself, then over to Vi, and then Vern. He paused. "Only now we're like the Five Musketeers with Isabelle and Damian." He laughed and did his best version of the Running Man, dancing his way forward, leading the group. "Follow me!"

CHAPTER THIRTY-ONE

IAN & CARTER

This Side of Normal

Racing with his gear in tow, Ian skidded to a stop in front of the Games & Gadgets Galore store; its broken sign with neon lights haphazardly blinking was hanging precariously from wires that swung and extended down to the mall floor. Ian blinked a few times at the scene, trying to take it all in, recalling what Holly had said to him earlier that night in the van about how people's bizarre delusions of the season were accepted as "normal." The sight in front of him of a Santa Claus, Mrs. Claus, two human-sized elves, a distinguished-looking couple, and Holly with her camera hoisted onto her shoulder, all standing there against a backdrop of destruction was bizarre, indeed, although definitely not "normal."

Ian struggled to find his words, watching the cloud of dust swirl about fallen steel beams that crisscrossed in tandem with fibrous broken-up pieces of cement sheets. The gaping hole in the roof above seemed to shine a light on what had been the entryway to the Games & Gadgets Galore store, its access now blocked by a mountain of debris. Snow fell through the open roof, and the sight was oddly beautiful in its strangeness.

"Ian," Holly snapped him to. "This is Ms. Bryant, mall manager."

Betty stepped up, a worried look on her face, and extended her hand. She swallowed back tears, saying, "Call me Betty. This is Leo, our general counselor." Leo also shook hands with Ian, as Betty continued, "We thank you for coming. We know it wasn't for this. There are people trapped inside…" her voice trailed off.

Holly interrupted, "Ian, come on. I got Carter on already."

Squeezing his eyes shut for a moment, Ian shook his head in an attempt to clear his foggy thoughts. Opening his eyes wide, he nodded at Mrs. Claus and the rest of the group resembling the misfit toys from the North Pole. Then he dropped his equipment bag to the floor, unzipped the top and pulled out his microphone and other cables to exchange with Holly while positioning himself in front of the scene and the camera's lens.

With a nod from Holly and the red recording light atop of the camera's viewfinder aglow, Ian cleared his throat, speaking into his microphone. "Carter, are you seeing this?"

Ian and Holly exchanged incredulous looks. "Put Carter on the two-way speaker," Ian called out to Holly, getting an immediate nod from her in response.

Across town, in the WACK-TV newsroom, Carter again sat impatiently on the edge of one of the desks. A handful of reporters were seated surrounding him. Balancing a jar of candy canes in between his knees, he pulled one of the few remaining candies out and began sucking on the minty treat.

Ian's anxious-sounding voice echoed on loudspeaker for the entire newsroom to hear. "Carter, we're transmitting video right now. Tell us when you've got 'em up."

With a look of disinterest, and a roll of his eyes, Carter watched the monitors and waited. As visuals began to take form on the screen, with angular shapes appearing, silhouetted against a backdrop of white haze, Carter's interest grew, as did the others in the room. Snapping his fingers at a crew member sitting at the controls, Carter pointed from him to another monitor in the room with some unspoken yet understood direction that caused switches to be flipped and images to appear on multiple screens.

"Ian, what the devil am I looking at?" Carter squinted at the video transmitting before his eyes, his brow furrowing. The people around him began to stand at attention, each one fixated on the ghostly figures emerging on screen.

Ian answered, "You're looking at part of the roof that just collapsed here at the mall. Holly's getting it all on camera. Are you seeing the full picture over there?"

Carter's jar of candy canes slipped from between his knees as he stood. "Holy crapsicle! It looks like a bomb went off. Where is everyone? Anybody get hurt?"

Ian stepped into the frame, bizarrely accompanied with what appeared to be Santa Claus and Mrs. Claus.

Ian deferred to Mrs. Claus who responded to Carter's question. "Almost all of the mall's shops already closed down due to the storm before this happened. It's a miracle so few people were still around," said Betty, her face filling the camera.

Carter took a closer look at the person on his screen, recognizing her. "Betty?" He tried to stay somber, given the scene, but seeing his old friend in such a costume made him choke back a chuckle. "Betty, what the devil you doin' dressed up like that?"

"Carter, if you're thinking of making any smart remarks, I'd caution you to think twice about doing so." Betty wagged her finger into the camera—just like any good Mrs. Claus would do—not realizing how much funnier it made her appear to those watching.

Then Santa Claus himself piped in because Leo couldn't help but find the humor in it all and wanted to add his two cents to the situation, "You're already on the naughty list, Carter," he warned. "Don't ruin any chance you may have of getting something other than a lump of coal in your stocking."

Carter squinted at his screen. "Leo?" Realizing that his old friend was doubling as Old St. Nick compelled Carter to turn away from the screen to try and rein in his laughter.

"Don't ask," Leo said, rolling his eyes.

From outside of the frame, Dr. Grey then crossed in front of Leo and stepped into view. She addressed the camera authoritatively, "I fail to see the humor here," she said.

Dr. Haywood stood by her side, his look of disappointment squarely focused on Ian and Holly.

Carter cleared his throat, composing himself. "And who might you be?"

"I happen to be the OB/GYN to the *extremely* pregnant woman we think is in labor—and still inside that store!"

Then, two adult-sized elves—Karina and Randy—stepped into view. The pair moved behind Dr. Grey and waved at the camera. "I saw her!" Karina called out over Dr. Grey's shoulder. "That lady is ready to pop."

In the newsroom, watching the bizarre transmission, another intern lifted his iPhone so Carter could see the photo on its screen. Once again, he squinted at the tiny image, bringing it closer to his eyes, and moved his lips to read the image's caption. He then looked back up at the large monitor, as if he was seeing double. The same female elf appeared on both screens. "So, this is you here?" He turned the cell phone toward the camera, shaking it. "You posted…" He turned to the intern, "What is this called, this type of photo?"

The intern kept a straight face and responded, "A selfie, sir."

"Right, a selfie." He turned back to address Ian and Betty and the others. "So, one of your elves there posted a *selfie* on Instagram of her in front of the store after everything came down?" Carter shook his head thinking: *What in the world goes through the mind of anybody in the midst of a crisis these days?*

As Betty flashed Karina a disapproving look, Carter continued, unable to mask his chastising tone. "So, after you took the time to post a picture of yourself on social media, did anybody think to call 911? Should any of you even be there? It doesn't look safe at all."

Holly's excited voice chimed in, "Carter, it's Holly. You gotta realize that *this* is the story nobody else will get."

Ian put himself back in front of the camera so he came into center view. "She's right, Carter. There's maybe a handful of people still in there.

I know it's not exactly the safest place to be, but I don't think we can wait for help to find us. Not with this weather. On our way in, we passed two ambulances and WQQZ's news van—"

Carter cut him off. "I know. They broadcasted it. We saw it." He blew out a breath of air in frustration, and carefully considered the situation, taking his time to respond. "Look, I'm all for getting the story and 'if it bleeds, it leads' and all that, but what I can see from your video spells structural damage and danger. You have no idea what other support columns or gas lines or electrical wires are going to come down, explode, or catch fire around you. Story or not, it's not safe for you all to be standing where you are right now, or even for us to be talking about all this. I think you need to get somewhere safe. Get out of there. Now."

Still on the camera, just behind Ian, Dr. Grey poked her head into view, and argued back at him. "We can't just leave those people in there and wait around for help that, to this point, is nowhere to be found."

Off screen now, Betty's voice came in, as if shouting. Carter straightened his back, attentively listening. Sounding determined, she said, "And Pastor Max and Darci may be in there, too. Who knows who else, Carter? We can't leave. We have to try and help them."

CHAPTER THIRTY-TWO

ELMER & IAN

Calling All Heroes

Deep in the underground belly of the mall, Elmer and the kids swiftly walked through the secret maze. "Let's go everyone." Elmer jingled his keys, a makeshift pied piper distracting the kids who followed him away from destruction and towards the promise of good eats. It wasn't that long ago that Elmer was a growing teen himself, and so he was well aware of the allure that a mall's food court might bring. As a bonus, he knew of so many ways to get there. This path through the tunnels beneath the mall was one he knew well, and one he was sure they'd enjoy given its novelty and safety away from the collapsing roof.

"Where are we going?" A few of the kids whispered to one another.

"Where are we?" a few others asked as they marveled at the smooth walls and overhead hanging fluorescent lights lining the tunnel.

Elmer already told them they were headed to the food court, but he realized that the route he was taking wasn't exactly direct, nor was it publicly known. The labyrinth of hidden passages ran the length of the mall underground. They were put in place when the structure was first built in order to expedite travel from one end to the other, as well as allow for the delivery of precious cargo like the rare diamonds and fine artwork that came for the mall's high-end stores and seasonal exhibits. The tunnels also once helped media-shy celebrities shop without being noticed back when the mall was even more alive with year-round shoppers. Today, no one used the tunnels. Elmer thought it was something that Betty might consider putting to use again, but he had hesitated to make the suggestion. He feared that reminding Betty about the secret tunnels, his own personal escape of sorts, would put an end to the very place he called home for the last several years.

"We're almost there," Elmer called over his shoulder at the whispering teens behind him. Over the years, the passageways had fallen into disrepair, but he knew that they still proved to be solid and more structurally sound than any of the new construction additions to the mall, especially those of late like the recently replaced roof above Games & Gadgets Galore. The nearly new roof caving in was pretty solid evidence of cutting corners.

Arriving at a doorway, Elmer flashed a mischievous grin. He placed both hands on the door and was about to give it a push when he turned and noticed the looks of wide-eyed wonder on each of the kids' faces. He gave them a wink. "I'm not sure I can do this on my own. I might need a little help opening up this secret door here. Any takers?"

Elmer didn't have to ask twice. The kids gleefully rushed toward him.

Just outside of the destroyed Games & Gadgets Galore store, Ian was reporting live to the world on the events of that evening.

"As people rushed to finish their last-minute Christmas Eve shopping, Mother Nature rushed to deliver a surprise winter storm that's been breaking dozens of records." Ian's somber face filled the television screen as he delivered the news, microphone in hand.

He was having a hard time fighting distractions though. The sound of his brother laughing made him look off camera. Vincent was approaching the scene, followed by what seemed like his own entourage. It included Vi and Vern, but now his brother had collected a few others that Ian didn't recognize. One guy had spiky hair, that much he could see. Close behind, there was also, bizarrely, a dog and a bird along with four other people: Three men, two of them in business suits, and a woman in some multicolored ensemble.

It seemed as if Vincent was in charge, leading the way. Ian couldn't help breaking into a wide smile as Vincent waved to him and pointed at his chest—as if Ian could miss him with that ugly Christmas sweater he was wearing. Ian could tell, even from this far away, how proud his little brother was of his prized sweater. Vincent's boosted self-esteem showed in how tall and confidently he was walking at the moment. Ian couldn't help but beam, almost as brightly as the lights on that sweater, at Vince's courage, determination, and love for others—every stranger was a friend to him.

Ian noticed that the men in suits were carrying briefcases. The younger of the two had a long tube under his arm. Both seemed utterly panicked.

Ian nodded toward the group as they grew closer and gestured for them to stay to the sidelines. The younger man in the suit ran his hand through his hair, clearly upset, and then mouthed four-letter cuss words in Ian's direction.

Focusing on his reporting, Ian continued. "Sorry. folks. It's hard to stay focused with so much going on. Let me try that again," he said, repositioning himself so as not to be in such full view of all the background activity. He repeated himself: "As people rushed to finish their last-minute Christmas Eve shopping, Mother Nature rushed to deliver a surprise winter storm that's been breaking all sorts of records."

He stepped as far as he could away from the others. "So far, nearly two feet of snow has fallen outside in a matter of hours, causing shoppers to rush home or be stranded, roadways to become accident sites or parking lots, and mall stores to shut their doors early, despite typically remaining open on Christmas Eve until late at night."

As the camera zoomed out, Ian turned a little aside, gesturing to reveal the destroyed Games & Gadgets Galore storefront. "But that's not all this powerful force of nature has served up tonight." In the lower left corner of the screen, the WACK-TV call letters glowed. "Here, live now at Maplefield Mall, as you can see behind me, a portion of the mall's roof has collapsed." The camera followed as Ian took a few steps over to where the Games & Gadgets Galore sign swayed in mid-air hanging from frayed wires that dangled down from the torn-up ceiling. "Access to this popular gaming store is completely blocked. Emergency vehicles have been called but seem unable to make their way here through the deep snow and yet unplowed roads. While we don't yet know how many people in total are trapped inside this store—Games & Gadgets Galore—we do know that one is a woman who is nine-months pregnant, and from what we understand, she's about to give birth."

Ian couldn't help but notice the young man in the suit, listening intently to his words, tears forming in his eyes, his entire being looking like a used washrag. *Who was he?* Ian then shifted his eyes to Vincent who was now playing happily with the dog and the bird. Then he turned his sights onto Dr. Grey. He had hoped to call her into the camera's view for an interview, but one look at the doctor's sullen face told him that he hadn't a prayer of that ever happening. So, Betty was next on his list to address. He waved her over.

"I'm told we do need to evacuate, but where to is anybody's guess," Ian said. "And before we do, we are taking this opportunity to bring you as much as we know so far about this exclusive story. Spirits are hopeful here and perhaps one of the most optimistic people in charge at the mall is here to talk with us for a few minutes. I have with me the Maplefield Mall manager, Betty Bryant. Betty, would you mind answering a few questions for our viewers?"

Betty, dressed in all her Mrs. Claus glory, entered the frame.

"Hello Ms. Bryant, or should I say Mrs. Claus?" Ian's attempt at introducing a tiny bit of levity to the grave situation was met with a curt-yet-still-polite scowl. He cleared his throat. "What can you tell us about this Christmas catastrophe?"

Ian was surprised at his own words as soon as he heard them. They sounded so stupid. *He* sounded so stupid. He was even more surprised at the sick feeling he got in the pit of his stomach.

Betty spoke then, addressing Ian and the audience on the other side of the camera: "This has been quite a Christmas Eve, as you well know, Ian. In all my forty years as mall manager, never has anything like this ever happened." Betty repositioned the wire-rimmed glasses onto the bridge of her nose. "A traditional Christmas Eve for us normally includes our annual Christmas Eve Kids Cheer Fest. Our holiday costumes are due to this event organized by Pastor Max who runs the Open Kitchen non-profit restaurant downtown. He is one of the people trapped inside Games & Gadgets Galore along with the shop's owner, Mr. Abdullah, and we all are just worried sick about it."

"Our thoughts are with Pastor Max and the others, of course," Ian empathized with Betty and cast another glance at the young man frantically pacing, who looked as if he was trying to not just assess the damage, but find some passageway inside. *What was going on with that guy? What was going on with himself? Why were his words sounding so stilted? He cared. He did. So why was he struggling?*

Betty cleared her throat, bringing Ian out of his head and back to the present. Stammering a bit, Ian asked, "Have you had contact with any of the people inside? Do you have any insight into what may have caused the roof's collapse and how you will be getting them out?" Again, Ian chastised himself at asking such stupid questions when there were clearly far more important ones at hand, and when time might be better spent with less talking and more taking action.

"We aren't speculating as to the cause right now, although the weather may be a contributing factor," Betty said, trying her best to brave a smile. "Our priority is to rescue the people still trapped inside the store. Until we do, we need to be able to offer them our support in any way we possibly can. We understand that there were about fifty or so children from Pastor Max's group who were standing around the Games & Gadgets Galore store just moments before the roof collapsed. I received a call from our mall's security guard, Elmer, who, fortunately, took them all to safety. We're so very grateful for that. Things would have been a lot worse if more people were still shopping inside the store when the roof collapsed."

"A nearly deserted mall on Christmas Eve, in this case, is definitely a silver lining," Ian added, nodding his head.

"I do wish my colleague Darci, who we believe to also be trapped inside, would call—" Betty's comment was interrupted, as the young man growing increasingly distraught entered into the conversation, shouting from off-camera.

"Darci did call, Betty," Harry huffed, nearly hyperventilating.

Ian extended his arm to wave Harry into the camera's view. As Harry approached, Ian placed his hand on his shoulder to comfort him and to draw him closer.

"Sir, I've been watching you on the sidelines," Ian gently spoke. "You seem frenzied."

Harry scoffed, the expression on his face teetering between crying and laughing. "You would be, too, if it was your wife who was nine-months pregnant and about to give birth while trapped in there." Harry pointed to the debris.

Ian's eyes grew wide, as he searched for what to say. "I am so sorry," he blurted out.

Harry nodded, lowering his head a bit while wiping away tears that threatened to spill.

"You said you did receive a phone call from those trapped inside?" Ian pressed.

"Yes. We found out that four people and my baby are trapped inside: My pregnant wife, Darci who works at the mall, the shop owner, and Pastor Max. But the call dropped before I could learn anything more..." Harry said, his voice trailing off.

Ian froze, as did the entire room. For an uncomfortable few seconds, no one seemed to know what to say, and, yet, they were on live TV. Holly peered over her camera at Ian and the others, then carefully took it off her shoulder and mounted it atop the tripod stand. She panned the camera from side to side to show each person's raw and very real emotions. Then, she zoomed in on Harry who, at that moment, looked directly into the camera and said, "I'm sorry, everybody, but this sideshow isn't what we need now. I have to get in there to my wife."

Holly zoomed out so that the camera frame would take in Harry's awkward exit off to the side. She then turned her sights back onto Ian, catching his eye and mouthing to him to say something.

In the newsroom, Carter and the other staffers waited, mesmerized watching the feed on the monitors. Carter gestured at Ian's dumbstruck expression. Nodding and waving his arms, Carter coached Ian through the screen, "Go on, man. I'm listening. We're all waiting to hear what you have to say next."

Finally, Betty stepped into view, addressing the audience. "I know the situation seems dire," she said, her eyes glistening. "This undoubtedly is not at all what we had planned for today—Christmas Eve—our last one here at this mall. But I believe in miracles. And I'm asking all who are watching to say a prayer and to ask for a miracle to happen tonight here on Mall Drive, so that everyone is safe and for families and loved ones to be reunited."

As Betty took a step back, Ian caught sight of the little elf Betty had removed from her skirt pocket and was now holding in her hand.

"We all share your wishes for everyone's safety, Betty," Ian said, gently touching her arm, keeping her on camera. "If I could just ask something further?" he continued with Betty's nod. "You said this was the last year for the mall? Is that your assumption because of this roof collapsing or…?" Ian let his question dangle.

"Oh, Heavens no," Betty responded. She then looked square into the camera and matter-of-factly stated, "The mall is being shut down by the real estate development company that owns it."

"Why is that?" Ian was surprised and slightly pleased to have more than just a scoop about the roof collapse.

"Good question, Ian." Betty paused, needing to swallow back the lump in her throat. "I guess when it comes down to it, the real estate company thinks that profits are more important than actual people."

Ian opened his mouth for a follow-up, but seeing how visibly upset Betty was, he couldn't do it.

As Carter watched them on the monitors, he realized it, too, whispering, "As a follow-up, Ian. Bring it back to the miracle of Christmas Eve."

Almost as if Ian heard Carter's words of encouragement, Ian looked directly into the camera. "Well, Betty, you said it: This is Christmas Eve and a night for miracles. I couldn't help but notice, is it also a night to call in reinforcements?" Ian said, gesturing to the elf she held. "Is it usual for Mrs. Claus to carry around a mascot?"

"Mascot…?" Betty shook her head, not understanding, and then followed his gaze. "Oh…!" She giggled and brought the Elf on the Shelf into the camera's view. "This is a mystery, Ian. Every year, just after Thanksgiving, this little fellow keeps appearing in my office, in the staff lounge, throughout the mall… He seems to know my holiday routines better than I do. I guess he's keeping a watchful eye on me and all the boys and girls out there to help Santa know who's been naughty and who's been nice."

"Huh, a Christmas mystery…?" Ian winked at the camera, intrigued.

Betty continued. "No one will tell me just how my Elf on the Shelf moves throughout the mall. He is quite magical."

As Carter watched, he sniffled and called out to the monitors, "Now bring it home—"

But no sooner did Carter utter the words than a large white bird flew into the camera's view, flapping her wings while letting out a loud SCREECH.

"What in the world…?" Carter bellowed, as the others in the newsroom laughed. The view zoomed up to reveal, not just the bird flying around Ian and Betty's heads, but also a large, barking dog, his leash trailing behind him, who leapt up to snatch the little elf away from Betty's hand, once again carrying it off in his mouth.

Both Ian and Betty were shocked into surprise and then laughter. Ian made a feeble attempt to grab the furry beast's collar but was distracted by Rainbow's wings flapping in his face, thwarting his efforts.

Ian and Betty both jumped at the chorus of voices erupting nearby just out of view from the camera. The man shouted, "No, Pickpocket!" And the woman, holding the bird's harness in her hands, shrieked, "Rainbow, you

Houdini! Get back here!" And, then, just like that, in full view of Carter, the newsroom, and the audience watching the broadcast, the dog, the bird, and the felt elf hopped across the threshold, past the broken Games & Gadgets Galore sign, through the collapsed rubble, and disappeared deep into what remained of Mr. Abdullah's store.

Carter and the newsroom shouted out a collective, "Ohhhhh!" Clasping his hands together, Carter howled, "Now that's a show."

"Okay, then," Ian wiped his brow in jest, addressing the camera. "It appears it's all hands, paws, and wings on deck! We are taking any and all assistance to help get our trapped friends to safety. Anything else you'd like to add, Betty?"

Betty adjusted her Mrs. Claus cap. "Actually, yes, Ian. I just want to say that I do so appreciate the media and all of you people out there who have made Maplefield Mall your community meeting place for decades. I know you will be sending prayers for a Christmas Eve miracle and happy ending to our story. I must bid your viewers a good night and help in our search and rescue efforts." Betty nodded a farewell into the camera and stepped out of view.

Ian stood still as if frozen in time. Once again, his face filled the entire screen's view as the camera moved in for a close-up. Holly peered over the viewfinder. Slowly, she framed Ian's face even tighter, his emotions were bubbling up. Tears formed in his eyes.

Suddenly, Ian snapped back to his current reality and looked straight ahead into the camera, his eyes piercing through the screen and making direct contact with whoever was still watching. "You know for the past three years…Wow!" Ian again paused, looking down at the ground. "Seems so much longer than that." He shook his head, half-laughing, then lifted it, and started again to address the camera and its audience.

"I've been coming into your homes for years now, reporting the news, if you could call it that," he said. "To be honest, I never really did. It didn't seem like news to me. I was assigned to cover Little League, the

Police Blotter, Neighborhood Council meetings, school lunch programs, promotions and ribbon cuttings. I didn't get to report about anything or anyone I cared about. I…what was it you said about me, Holly?"

Ian walked right up to the camera, his face becoming blurry to the viewers at home. He took hold of Holly's arm, pulling her out from behind the camera and positioned her directly in front of it alongside him.

Taken aback, Holly's eyes grew wide as she mouthed a "hello" and gave a little wave to the viewers.

Ian continued his reporting. "Everyone, this is Holly. She's WACK-TV's best-of-the-best when it comes to visual storytelling, and she's not even done with school yet. Holly here made me realize that I was 'sticking to the script' and 'sitting on the sidelines.' I was…what was that you said to me? 'Proclaiming the good news like some sort of trumpeting Gabriel'—and now I realize that I was doing exactly that. But, at the time, I didn't believe any of it. I didn't think it mattered. I considered all of this 'non-news' all a waste of my time."

By then, Holly had exceeded her level of comfort of being in front of the camera, backing away, saying, "On that note, I'm gonna go back to where I belong now—behind the camera." With a nod and a half-salute toward the camera, she disappeared from view, leaving Ian standing solo.

Smiling, Ian continued: "We—that is, every news station tonight—had to decide what stories warranted being on the air this Christmas Eve. Every one of us wants to win at the ratings. And, like Holly reminded me, we all want to have stories that go viral and, as of late, that seems to be the stories that show us humans at our worst—and that get people riled up enough to take sides. For Holly and me, we started out this Christmas Eve hoping to find the next 'Christmas Mall Brawl' kind of story. We were actually on our way here to the mall in search of it. You know the story, the one where the whole 'goodwill towards men' attitude goes out the window when there's only one toy left with two different parents throwing punches at one another in a battle to make sure that their kid is the one who gets the prized toy. Other TV stations decided to send their reporters out to get weather-related Christmas car pile-up stories—the more banged up, the better."

Ian looked off-camera for a moment. There was no turning back now. He kept going.

"This Christmas Eve, fifty kids—who, through no fault of their own, have been thrust into the foster care system—came to this mall to be a part of something that, for at least a little while, helps them feel the spirit of Christmas kindness. Betty, who you just heard from, opens up the mall's kitchens and puts out a feast, so to speak. Pastor Max and many of the shop owners here at Maplefield Mall like Mr. Abdullah—both of whom are trapped right now inside the store behind me—made it possible for these kids to pick out gifts for free, not just for themselves but also to give to members of their families, if they have any contact with them. Some of these kids are completely alone. Some who do have parents or siblings have been separated from their family members for a very long time. For others, Christmas Day might be the one day of the entire year they get to see someone they love and call family. This year, with this program, this lucky group of kids had the chance to play Santa Claus, so to speak. All courtesy of Pastor Max and his mission. In the past, Pastor Max was able to bring double the amount of kids to the mall for this special Christmas Eve shopping spree, but this year, his parish is hurting financially and only had room in the budget to care for a smaller group of children. Look, I know we can all say, 'maybe next year,' but tomorrow is never guaranteed for any of us. And, as you heard Betty say earlier, this mall will be closed soon. So, sadly, this year may be the last year of joyous holiday celebrations here at this landmark. Ok, sure, other news reporters like me could have come here to the mall to cover the annual Pastor-Max-Christmas-Do-Gooder story. Our broadcasts could have reached thousands of viewers who may have opened their wallets to give donations to the parish, but, heck, *that* story's been done before, and who wants too much good news when there's so much bad to go around and around and around…?"

Ian trailed off. Then, once more, he went quiet and grew pensive.

Carter and the rest of the team watched in silence from the newsroom. Carter's face reflected both concern and fury at the same time. He loved that Ian was getting a scoop, and that WACK-TV had the exclusive on such a big story but, at the same time, Ian was getting a little *too* emotional and *too* opinionated. Carter didn't like that, not at all.

CHAPTER THIRTY-THREE

IAN & ELMER

Man Makes Plans, God Laughs

In a neighborhood not too far from Maplefield Mall, picturesque storybook homes quietly sat swaddled in snow. Outdoor Christmas lights peeked through snow-ladened branches of evergreens and manicured bushes, as holiday lawn ornaments of reindeer pulling Santa's sleigh, oversized gift boxes wrapped with glittery bows, and life-sized nativity scenes braved the cold. From each brick dwelling's front windows, the Christmas Eve celebrations of the families inside were in full swing, and as far as they were concerned, Mother Nature could continue to let it snow.

Through the bay window of one Tudor-style home, the glow of a television set cast a blueish halo around the icicle lights hanging from its shingles. Inside, with cell phones in hand, and their eyes glued to the 70-inch, flat-screen TV hanging over the fireplace, two brown-haired, brown-eyed sisters's faces were illuminated, partially from the flickering flames of the roaring fire they faced but, also, for another reason altogether.

"What in the world are you two girls doing?" A singsongy voice called out to the two teenagers who sat on the Persian rug in the center of the living room floor. "What could be so interesting that you're actually watching the news on Christmas Eve?"

"Mom," the 15-year old turned to call out over her shoulder. "I think you should come in here and see this." The teen turned back to the girl at her side, whispering "Is that her?"

"Ya, she looks just like mom except for no blonde hair," the 13-year old nodded in return. "Mom is gonna freak."

As their mom entered the room, she noticed that one of the four red, velvet Christmas stockings, the one embroidered with the word "MOM," was tilted and overlapped the stocking next to it with the leather applique of the word "DAD." She walked over to it and separated the two, saying, "Why can't things stay put? And why can't my stocking say 'IVY'?; it's the same number of letters." She looked over her shoulder at her girls, realizing they weren't listening. With her OCD activated, she then straightened the other two more modern-looking socks, one bedazzled with the name "Maddie," and the other written in cursive with the name "Lauren."

"Mom. Seriously." There was a typical impatience and derision in the teen's tone. "Do you even see what we're seeing?"

As their mother continued to adjust the Christmas decorations hanging from the mantel and pull on the stray wisps of the snow blanket drooping underneath the ornate Dickens Victorian Village display that sat on top, she asked, without focusing on anything in particular, "What? What is it that I'm supposed to be seeing?"

The girls both raised their sculpted eyebrows, exchanged glances, and scrunched up their faces in what appeared to be discomfort. Almost in unison, they pointed to the TV and said, "Isn't that Aunt Isabelle?"

Snapping to attention and no longer preoccupied with her perfectly picturesque porcelain figurines, she immediately turned her focus onto the flat-screen TV. A puzzled look crossed her face as she joined her two daughters, both of whom presented as younger versions of herself, to watch the unfolding scene at the mall.

"I haven't heard that voice or seen that face in so long," their mother whispered wistfully. "Izzy...?"

On the screen, they watched as Ian interviewed Isabelle in front of a destroyed storefront.

"The roof at Maplefield Mall collapsed," Lauren offered to her mother who seemed in a trance.

"Aunt Isabelle's talking about her work and how she helps companies help the world," Maddie added.

The once-familiar voice spoke out from the television, "…Christmas, community, and corporate social responsibility," Isabelle's face turned to the lens, as if looking straight at her sister and two nieces. "The three are part of the same family and a way to give back." Isabelle concluded her comments for the camera with a nod and a smile before taking a step back.

"Wait," objected Ivy, shouting at the TV. "That's it?"

Ian nodded, "Thank you, Isabelle," as she exited off screen.

Suddenly, Ivy sprang to her feet. "Girls, get your coats."

The teens excitedly rose to their feet, and almost in unison asked, "Where are we going?"

Their mother, still staring at the television screen, responded, "To be with family."

Emily was dealing with her own family issues. Trapped inside Games & Gadgets Galore, she was trying to be grateful that the back room she was in still had its roof intact, providing some shelter from the snow and cold, unlike what she understood to be the destruction suffered by the rest of the store. Losing power, with the only light coming from whatever Mr. Abdullah was able to jury-rig, Emily tried to focus on the fact that she wasn't alone, despite feeling very much so. She spoke fast in order to get her words out before another contraction hit. "Now, I'm NOT complaining, mind you."

It was too late. "Ooooooh! Ooooooooooooh! Oooooooooooooooooh!" She leaned farther back onto the armrest of the sofa she had laid on for what seemed like hours. She tried not to scream out, but holding it in was causing her face to turn an even brighter shade of Christmas red.

Darci knelt beside her and pressed a damp handkerchief to Emily's forehead. "It's going to be okay, Emily. You're not going to die."

Emily's eyes widened. "Die? Why would you say that? I have no intention of dying. Is something wrong? Ooooooh! Oooooooooooooh! OOOOOOHHH!"

Pastor Max handed Darci a small bottle of water. "Look I found a few more."

Darci uncapped the water bottle and rewetted the handkerchief.

"Pastor Max, am I dying?" Emily's eyes welled up with tears.

"Oh! No, no, no," he knelt alongside Darci. "You're gonna be just fine and so is your baby. Now what is it that you didn't want to complain about?"

"Ooooooooooohhhhhhhhhhh!"

Mr. Abdullah rushed in. In his hands, he held portable cell phone power banks and external battery packs. "Ah-ha! Here we are. While I may not have everything we wish we had to deliver a baby in this store, I do have these!" He raised his arms and did a little dance, shaking the wires and cables that dangled from his fingers.

Emily tried to smile, obviously holding in the excruciating pains she felt.

Mr. Abdullah dropped everything he was holding and, instead, took hold of her hand. "My dear, dear Emily. I have six children of my own. With every birth, my beautiful wife swore like a sailor; I think that is the American expression, yes? And she screamed and cried and called me some names she still apologizes to me for. With every colorful comment, I loved her more and more. You need to just let go! It helps with the pain."

"Oh, I couldn't," Emily breathed heavily.

"Yes, yes! You can." Mr. Abdullah nodded. "Come on. We all will join you." He patted Emily's hand and gently placed it on her swollen belly. Standing tall, he began to vocalize his sympathy pains. "AAUGH! Owwwwww! Get this baby out of here!" He then turned to Darci and Pastor Max, giving them a look that told them they better chime in.

Pastor Max chuckled. Then he belted out, "Sweet baby, Jesus!" almost as if he were at a church revival. "Deliver us, Lord!"

Darci giggled and added, "Screw you, Mother Nature! We're having a baby and there's nothing you can do to stop it!"

Emily erupted in laughter at the sheer silliness of them all attempting to make her feel better. But a moment later, she dissolved into tears. "I can't do this without my Harry and Dr. Grey."

"And you shall have them!" Mr. Abdullah grabbed Emily's phone and one of the cables. "Just give me a few minutes to connect everything and charge the battery a few minutes, and we'll get them both on the line. It will be as if they are right here in the room with you!"

From somewhere not too far into the caved-in storefront, Harry turned on his borrowed cell phone's flashlight, trying to follow the path of the giant dog and big white bird that had just raced by him. At least he swore that's what he saw—unless his worries were getting the best of him, causing delusions. The beam provided little in the way of illumination, and whatever it was that whooshed by, it was now gone from sight. All he could really see, at most, was a yellowish haze and pulsing glow of the chalk-like dust that filled the air. The smoky substance made it difficult to breathe.

"Harry, I am ordering you to come back here at once!" Mr. Wiggins's command echoed throughout what had been the entryway to Games & Gadgets Galore and now, where Harry stood. Although he knew he barely made it a few hundred yards inside, his employer's voice sounded so far away—or was that just his wishful thinking on his part?

He had to get to Emily and their baby. As he looked around at the destruction caused by the collapsed roof, Harry couldn't help but feel shame at the sight. After college, he aimed to use his civil engineering degree to build things, to work with his hands to make things better. Instead, he had turned his love of construction into the very opposite career path. As he listened to the creaking walls, he imagined them wailing. It was as if this old mall knew what was in store for it, and rather than be bulldozed by someone else's hand, it willed itself to fall apart on its own terms, perhaps as some sort of final act of defiance.

"Harry!" Mr. Wiggins's voice roared once more.

For ten years, he had listened to the unforgiving and insufferable man who seemed hell-bent on wrecking other people's hard work and accomplishments. How Harry wished he could disobey his orders this time, to find his way to Emily and save her and his baby and the others, and finally say good riddance to his boss and this business that was stealing his very soul.

Harry aimed his pathetic little light up above him and then down below him and then all around him one last time. Ceiling tiles, steel beams, chunks of drywall and exposed wires obstructed his path, making it impossible for him to take even another step. His eye was drawn to one particular support beam. It looked a bit odd, but he didn't have time to examine it before he heard his name loud and clear.

"Harry!" The concern in Leo's voice made Harry more cautious. From outside the fallen entryway, Leo pleaded, "If you can hear me son, please answer me."

With a sigh of regret, realizing the only safe option was to turn back, Harry decided to do just that. "I'm okay," he shouted. "I'm coming out."

As he continued reporting live from the front of Mr. Abdullah's store, Ian glanced over at Leo and the others. But his eye caught sight of Vincent waving at him, which gave him an idea.

"Hey, Vince, come over here," Ian called out to his little brother.

Vincent, smiling from ear to ear, stepped into view, twice circling where Ian stood and, all the while, looked up at his brother with adoration.

"Look into the camera, little buddy," coaxed Ian.

Vincent did as he was asked, still smiling.

Ian continued his report. "Everybody, I'd like you to meet my younger and only brother Vincent." Ian hesitated. Taking a deep breath, he continued, "This is actually the first Christmas Vince and I have spent together since we were kids. Right, Vince?"

Vincent nodded, clearly just happy to be with his brother.

"Is it okay with you, Vince, if I share with everybody our story…?"

Vincent beamed, "'Our' story. Yes. It's true and you should always tell the truth."

Ian smiled, nodding slowly. "That's right, Vince. No more pretending." Then looking into the camera, Ian said, "Vincent has schizophrenia." Almost as if he was socked in the stomach, Ian sucked in a giant breath, both relieved and terrified that he finally spilled a secret he was keeping and was ashamed of for so long.

From the newsroom, Carter and his team watched Ian and Vincent on the TV monitors. As his voice carried across the loudspeakers, Ian's voice cracked as he tried to get out his words.

"I haven't told many people about Vince, not if I could help it," Ian said. "I've kept myself as far away from any association with him and his mental illness as I possibly could." He turned to make eye contact with Vincent. "Even refusing to come see you and keep my promises to you. Right Vince?"

Vince looked down, nodding.

Shaking his head at what he was watching unfold on his news station, Carter began coughing, choking on the piece of candy cane he just angrily bit off. Clearing his throat, he snarled, "Good God, what is he doing? This isn't the Oprah show."

The image on the screen now of Vincent's face, his shy smile locked in place on Ian's proved too much for Carter who barked to no one in particular, "Get Holly on the phone."

Almost at that same moment, a phone sitting on one of the news desks rang. Carter noted it. One of the news team members picked it up and started a conversation. Seconds later, another phone rang. Moments later, another. Soon, it sounded as if every phone was ringing in a coordinated symphony.

Carter shut his eyes, grunting. "Here it comes," he said at the top of his lungs. "People complaining about Ian's on-air meltdown."

As phones continued to ring, and staffers continued to answer, one of the members of the news team called out to Carter: "Sir, people aren't complaining. They're phoning in to say they love it. Ian's honesty. They want to congratulate whoever's in charge. They want to know how they can help."

"Help?" Carter's face softened, his anger turning to a look of confusion, then giving way to an ear-to-ear grin.

Elmer couldn't help but smile at the fifty kids he had separated into five teams of ten members each. Setting up camp, so to speak, in the food court, far away from the roof that had collapsed, Elmer planned to keep the kids safe and preoccupied with a little cooking contest. After all, he surmised, these kids were under the care and keeping of Pastor Max, so they *had* to have had some training in the good reverend's Open Kitchen cooking school, right? Now it was time to see what they had learned. "I'm open to whatever it is you want to cook," Elmer said with his best circus ringleader impression.

Each group stood in front of one of the food court eatery counters. Each teen had the same look on their face: "This is gonna be lame"! They shifted from foot-to-foot and murmured, not exactly on board with the plan.

Elmer knew he had to get back to help the people trapped inside the Games & Gadgets Galore store, but he also knew he couldn't leave these kids unattended or without something at least a little bit entertaining to keep them occupied.

He had to think fast. "Kids, we don't know how long we're going to be here. We're safe where we are, or at least we're safer here than anywhere else we can get to right now. So…I don't know about you, but I can always eat…?"

The kids shrugged and half-heartedly nodded in agreement.

Elmer raised his ring of keys. "I've unlocked the doors to the food court kitchens here. Each team sticks to one eatery—the one you're standing in front of right now."

The kids looked up at the signs behind them, slowly understanding and advancing behind their assigned kitchen counter.

"Now it may be more of a challenge to cook because the gas has been turned off, but I know you're Pastor Max's finest, so you will find a way," Max continued. "Your job is to use whatever ingredients you can find and turn them into a dish worthy of being called 'Christmas Eve dinner' OR 'Christmas morning brunch.'" Elmer had a pretty good feeling that they all would be here well into the night, if not through to tomorrow morning. He hoped that if the kids didn't realize it already, that this exercise might help them accept the inevitable.

One of the kids shouted out what they all were thinking. "Mr. Elmer, how the heck are we supposed to cook without the gas oven?"

Elmer grinned. "Great question. All these kitchens have electric burners, too. Use what you find in their pantries and refrigerators. Get creative. Look for what you can do, not what you can't. Use your imaginations."

Again, one of the kids asked what they all were probably wondering: "Dude, why don't we just wait for somebody to come get us out of here? Why we be doin' so much work?"

Elmer masked his look of disappointment, recalling just for a moment his own memories of a childhood full of abuse, waiting for someone to save him, and finally running away, living on the streets, and fending for himself since he was 13. He saw his younger self in these teenagers standing before him—and he wanted desperately to make an impact on their lives, so maybe they could have a better time growing up than he did. He shook his mind free from his thoughts. "Alright, now, I hear you," he shouted out. "But I've learned first-hand that to wait for someone else to swoop in to rescue you is never a good idea. You know it, too, don't you?"

The kids shuffled their feet, some nodding, others embarrassedly looking down at the floor.

"If it's to be, it's up to me." Elmer watched as each kid's face looked up at him, reflecting an understanding of what he was saying. Then he continued, holding his keys high and jingling them. "Kids, you're competing for the keys to the kingdom! Remember why you all came here? Pastor Max's Christmas Eve Kids Cheer Fest? I've seen some of the gifts set aside for you. So, what if we have ourselves a taste-testing contest, and the team that cooks the best eats gets first pick of the gifts?"

The kids grumbled. One spoke up, "Dude, no offense. But that's not much of a prize."

Another kid added, "Especially since we already were promised our pick of free stuff and a feast to eat!"

Scratching his head, Elmer had to agree. "You're right," he said. He thought it over for a moment before speaking again. "People make plans. God laughs. You ever heard that expression?"

The kids looked at him, blank stares abounded.

Elmer continued, "Sometimes, the best plans don't work out, at least not in the way we want them to, and that's what happened here tonight. So how about just this once…what if you just did what I'm asking without any prize or anything like that?"

"So, like, we be doin' all the work and getting' nothing for it?" One kid's voice called out, prompting the others to grumble in agreement.

Elmer was animated. He had to do something to motivate these kids. "Hey, why does there have to be something in it for you in order for you to do something? What if you just did it 'cause it's the right thing to do, and if you don't do it, maybe nobody else will?"

Silence filled the room. The kids barely breathed as they stood staring off into space.

Elmer couldn't tell if they were in or out, or whether they were considering his words or totally tuned out in their own little worlds. He prayed there weren't any more questions and that the kids would just go along with his plan. After all, he hadn't really thought through any of it. How would this all work out? If they even agreed to do it, who would actually do the taste test and judge the winner? How? And as for those gifts the kids were even supposed to get before this whole mess started, how many would there be? Elmer knew there were some gifts in Mr. Abdullah's Games & Gadgets Galore store, but any more details than that, Elmer didn't have a clue. Were the gifts even still intact? Did they get smashed when the roof collapsed? Elmer slowed down his breathing, reminding himself of one of his favorite quotes from Dr. Martin Luther King, Jr.: "You don't have to see the whole staircase, just take the first step."

Finally, one of the kids burst forth in excitement. "We need names!" Team names! Like we could be Team 'What the Fork'!"

Everyone laughed and Elmer was relieved at the sound.

"We can be Team 'IncrEDIBLES'!" another voice shouted out.

"That's it! Now you're cookin'!" Elmer high-fived the air as all the kids began talking within their teams, excitedly making plans to prepare their winning feasts. "Okay! So, we need the older kids," Elmer looked out at them. "I need the three oldest to raise their hands." A handful of kids, the tallest of the bunch, as it turned out, stepped forward. "Thank you. Now you three need to be in charge while I try to go back and help those people who are trapped, you understand?"

They nodded.

Elmer nervously nodded. "Okay, then, you all stay right here. Do your thing. Make sure no one here gets hurt, or burned, or worse. So, let's say you've got two hours." He had no idea if that time frame was feasible. Nor did he have any sense for how long it would take the kids to actually cook. He certainly hadn't a clue about the amount of time it would take, let alone if it were even possible, for him to rescue the people trapped and get them back to safety.

The kids raced over to their respective kitchens.

"Ready? Set? BAKE!" Elmer had always wanted to shout that out, ever since he started watching a few episodes of that *Great British Baking Show*. He was so grateful to have everything he needed here at the mall—and that for all the years he had been living in its underbelly, his make-shift home had never been discovered. He cried when he learned that the mall was going to be shut down. He knew that he'd need to gather up his belongings, what little he had, and find somewhere else to call home. *But where will I go?* He couldn't think about all that right now. He had to get back and help the people trapped in the game store.

Elmer took one last look at the kids as they eagerly began exploring their surroundings and scrambled to see the food available to use for this challenge. He thanked God for small favors. Looking up to the heavens, Elmer quickly said a little prayer, asking for help. Then, just as quickly, he took off back through the secret passageway door from where they all just came.

CHAPTER THIRTY-FOUR

MR. WIGGINS & THE ELF

Out of the Mouth of Babes...and Old Fools

Mr. Wiggins and Leo stood peering into the tiny opening where Harry had entered the store to try and reach those trapped inside.

"We really shouldn't stay here," Leo stated matter-of-factly, turning to address everyone within earshot. "None of us. It isn't safe."

"Oh, hogwash!" Mr. Wiggins growled.

"Betty," Leo raised his voice to drown out the man who was speaking. "We need to go."

Betty shook her head. "Leo, I'm not ready to give up yet. Not on getting everyone out, and not on this mall. Not on Christmas Eve."

"I don't think you're going to get your miracle, Betty," Leo said, his eyes full of empathy. "Let's issue an official statement. We get out and give it over to God."

Just then Harry emerged from the rubble; his clothes, face, and hands were stained with ash and soot. He overheard just the tail end of what Leo was saying and immediately responded. "Get out? No way. I'm not going anywhere. I should be with Emily in a hospital birthing room, and if this is as close as I can get to her for now, then this is where I'm staying."

Harry didn't bother looking at anyone when he said it and kept his focus on the task at hand. He marched himself right to the table to grab the rolled-up mall blueprints. He threw them onto the floor, plopped himself down beside them, and unrolled them, immediately setting forth to find another way in.

Mr. Wiggins shook his head and hissed. "Just because that news guy over there is having an embarrassing meltdown, it doesn't mean we all should turn into marshmallows. I, personally, oversaw this addition, and we are not going to make it easy for those vultures to sue us by running off, tail between our legs, saying it's 'unsafe' and giving them something to use in court to extort us out of millions."

Far enough back, but still within earshot, Damian balled up his fist and took a step forward. Isabelle took note and with both hands, grabbed his, unclenching the fist. He looked down at her hands that were now softly laying over his and then peered into her eyes.

"Somebody needs to deck that guy," he whispered, leaning into her. Instead of pulling back, he instinctively kissed her.

Isabelle kept hold of his hand and kissed him back. When they separated, she leaned in and whispered, "I bet you'd get farther if you kissed that old man. It works with me."

Suddenly, Harry scrambled to his feet, looking to the Heavens, shouting out, "You!" His outburst attracted everyone's attention. After quietly studying the blueprints for just a few minutes, he straightened his frame and marched himself to stand nose-to-nose with Mr. Wiggins. "You," he said in a quiet yet threatening voice. "*You* did this. *You* are the cause of this!"

Mr. Wiggins attempted to mask his fear with a sinister-sounding response, "Careful, Harry. You wouldn't want to be dismissed with a baby on the way."

Damian stepped forward then, still holding onto Isabelle's hand. He faced Harry, saying, "Hey, man. I need an upstanding guy, one who can throw a mean punch, to work with me at my bootcamps," He flashed a wicked smile. "I'll match whatever he's paying you AND make sure your personal life takes priority. Oh, and I'll never make you carry my bags."

Harry's rage slowly dissipated. His entire demeanor relaxed in the few minutes it took to realize what he was being offered. "I accept," he nodded to Damian. Then he turned to Mr. Wiggins, triumphantly stating: "I quit."

Mr. Wiggins snickered. "You foolish, foolish boy."

Without skipping a beat, Harry responded. "You're an ignorant, greedy old man. You 'personally oversaw' this part of the mall's addition. We all heard you say it. What I want to hear you actually say is that you cut corners to keep costs low and put more profits into your own pocket. You know, I thought that beam I saw inside the shop looked odd. Your little face-lift of this mall included lightweight framed parapets. Didn't it?"

Leo stepped forward to Mr. Wiggins, "As your general counsel, sir, I should be advising you to mitigate risk for the company, but I can't abide by your actions. Take this as my notice that I'm stepping down."

Mr. Wiggins snapped, "Oh, confound it, man. There's nothing illegal about those building materials I used." His entire demeanor seemed off-balance and confused.

Harry spat back, "Illegal? How about unconscionable? You never bothered to analyze and augment the existing roof framing to see if it could support any weight-bearing across the newly created bridge between old and new, did you?"

Mr. Wiggins stumbled over his words. "I…well…it wasn't mandatory. Costs would have been prohibitive. Betty, you wanted that addition—"

Leo angrily chimed in, "Don't you dare bring Betty into *your* mess."

Harry continued his rant, advancing step-by-step with every word until he had forced Mr. Wiggins back up against a wall, "You selfish fool. Your negligence and cutting corners didn't account for extreme weather circumstances and especially not the weight of snow. And now, because of *you* the roof framing collapsed. *You* are responsible for my wife and others being trapped with no way to help them."

A hesitant voice interrupted the tension. "Excuse me?" Randy asked, dressed in his elf outfit. He and Karina had witnessed this whole scene from the sidelines. "Can I say something?" The whole room turned toward him. Karina's whole mouth gaped open in utter disbelief that this boy would enter into the fray and actually ask to speak.

Betty took a moment to inhale deeply. "I think we all need to calm down. Whatever Randy has to say, might provide the breather we all need. "Go ahead, Randy."

"*RimWorld*." Randy beamed as if he had just accomplished world peace.

A few seconds of silence followed, until Leo, furrowing his brows, asked the question on everyone's minds: "I'm sorry son, but what do you mean, *RimWorld*?"

Randy laughed at himself. "Oh, I forgot how old you all are." He then began his ramble: "*RimWorld* is an online game I play. The other day when I was expanding my territory, I forgot to put a no-roof-zone over a door in my base's outer wall. So, obviously, the roof collapsed, and one of my guys got his leg crushed. I was too far from any support, even though there was a pillar, like, two squares away. I figured out that in order to get to my guy, I needed to build a roof from above on a diagonal angle so that everything wouldn't collapse and cave in. Same thing could be done here, you know, to get inside."

While Randy beamed with what he had just shared, everyone else had a look of utter confusion on their faces.

Harry took a deep breath, equally as perplexed with Randy's plan, but eager to try anything to get to his Emily. "Okay, Randy. I have no idea about this *RimWorld* thing but tell me more about what you're saying. I'm open to anything. Give it to me again."

CHAPTER THIRTY-FIVE

PAST MR. WIGGINS & PRESENT MR. WIGGINS

Inner Workings

Inside Games & Gadgets Galore, Emily was struggling. Her hair was plastered to her head, and her face was glistening with perspiration. Despite Darci's best efforts to cool Emily down with wet handkerchiefs, it just wasn't enough.

Perspiring almost as much as Emily, Pastor Max had assumed the role of midwife. It wouldn't be the first time he had helped deliver a baby but never in conditions like these. And while Max tried to mask his gut feeling that something didn't quite seem right with this delivery, Mr. Abdullah could see it on his face.

"Dr. Grey," Mr. Abdullah called out, after he attached new battery packs and tangled wires to the portable speaker now connected to Darci's cell phone. "Can you hear me?"

The OB/GYN's voice came in loud and clear, followed by a collective sigh from everyone in the room, except for Emily who, panting to try and ease her pain, spat out, "You said this baby had another week to bake!"

"Emily, you aren't an Easy Bake Oven," Dr. Grey's voice filled the void with laughter, even making Emily chuckle. Dr. Grey continued: "There's no exact timer we can set on when a baby will be born. Part of the miracle of birth is that each baby decides when he or she is ready to enter this world. Science isn't as exact as we may think it is. That's why we call it 'practicing' med—"

Cutting her off, Emily's contraction hit with full force, "Owwwwww! Ooooooo! Haaaarrrrrrryyyyyy!"

Harry's voice crackled as he came in over the loudspeaker and tried to soothe his wife's pain. "I'm here, Em—I wish I were there, holding your hand. I love you."

Emily whimpered, "I love you, too."

A second later, Harry's voice, now full of confidence, continued, "We're going to find a way to where you are right now. And an ambulance is on its way, Em. We're working on a plan, but we're sorta flying blind. It'd be faster if we had eyes on the path to get to you."

Then, seemingly out of nowhere, the snowy white Cockatoo swooped in.

Emily let out another scream paired by Rainbow's SCREECH. Chasing his companion, Pickpocket had a more difficult time squeezing his muscular body through the tiny openings of fallen debris, but he managed, bounding in and adding his own low-pitched howl to the chorus. Still in his mouth, Elf on the Shelf hung by one arm, flopping around as if dancing to the beat of his own drum.

"Well, look who has come back to visit us," Mr. Abdullah sang out.

Pastor Max fixed his eyes on the fanfare of feathers in the air. "This is a Christmas miracle." He stood tall, his eyes wide, his arm extended outward in an attempt to get the bird to land on it. "It's Fred."

Darci tee-heed. "Who's Fred?"

Pastor Max answered: "He's the bird from that old TV show *Baretta*. I've always wanted my own Fred."

Darci stood, hand on hip, correcting him, "That's not Fred. It's not even a 'he.' Her name is Rainbow. At least, I *think* that's her name. And that giant dog is called Pickpocket." Darci coaxed the big ball of fur to her side and rescued the elf from its jaws. "And this little fellow is Betty's mystery Elf on the Shelf. How in the world did they get in here?"

Emily's eyes widened in disbelief at the conversation, "Helllllooooo…?" She winced. "Remember me? Woman in labor about to be split wiiiiiiiiddddddddeeeeeee OWWWWWWW!!"

Dr. Grey tried to soothe her patient through the phone, "Emily, I want you to breathe,"

"Em, I'm here." Harry's voice sounded more panicked. "If that big dog could get to you, I will, too."

On the other end of the phone, there was nondescript chatter and the sounds of furniture being moved.

"What's going on over there, Harry?" Emily cried out.

Dr. Grey responded: "Emily, hon, don't you worry about anything other than yourself and that baby."

"Mr. Abdullah?" Harry's excitement came through loud and clear. "You must carry drones in your store, right?"

"Yes! Of course." Mr. Abdullah exchanged knowing glances with Emily as her eyes widened.

"Harry, that's what I got you for Christmas, a drone. I knew it was what you wanted." Emily's sudden burst of jubilation gave way to yet another contraction. "Oooooohhhhhhhh!"

"Em, I love you so much," Harry's voice cracked. "Mr. Abdullah, can you fly that drone of mine out of there and turn the video on? If you direct the drone to us, we can watch the video it takes and see exactly what we'd need to navigate along the path back to you."

Immediately, Mr. Abdullah sprang into action. "Yes, yes, right away." He hopscotched his way to the boxes where he kept Emily's drone and got to work.

Through the speaker, Dr. Grey fiddled with her own phone and shared another idea. "Pastor Max, I know you're doing a fine job helping Emily, but now it dawns on me that in the past I've used Facebook Live to work one-on-one with patients who are unable to come into my office. We can make the settings private from…oh, shoot," she stopped mid-sentence. "I just got locked out of my Facebook account—too many failed password attempts! Good Heavens! But…maybe we could set it up from Harry's phone…? I know there's a private audience setting where you can invite ONLY 'specific friends' to join the livestream—and not the whole world. Right, isn't that how it works?"

Harry chimed in, "Yep, I think so. I don't have my phone, but we could use Damian's to log into my account. Pastor Max, could you or Mr. Abdullah log-on to the Games & Gadgets Galore Facebook page using one of your phones? Then, we can 'friend' you from my account, and you can invite me to join the private livestream?"

"It's definitely worth a shot," Dr. Grey said. "I should be able to use the feed to see what's going on and direct you all on what needs to be done to deliver that baby. Just make sure to double check the settings before you start the live video!"

Pastor Max's shoulders dropped, relieved. "I think I've done this before! I'm on it, Doc."

Darci chimed in, "I'll get you one of those flexible tripod stands for the phone." She rose to her feet. "We can wrap the bendable, octopus-like legs around something here to hold the phone up to give Dr. Grey the best view and keep you, Max, hands-free."

As if in stereo, both Pastor Max and Dr. Grey cheered, "Awesome."

"I think we should all hang up now to conserve our battery power," Darci commanded. "We don't know how long we'll be here."

The others nodded, but just as their fingers were about to hit their respective power-off buttons, another voice shouted through the phone, stopping them.

"Darci?" Mr. Wiggins called out; his tone uncharacteristically shaky.

Darci skipped a step and paused, but only for a moment. She looked at the speaker, then dismissed him and forged ahead on her mission, calling over her shoulder, "Not now, father. I'm busy."

The CLICK of Darci's disconnect seemed to echo throughout the mall where Mr. Wiggins, Harry, and Dr. Grey had set up home base just outside Games & Gadgets Galore. Mr. Wiggins still stood hunched over the phone, looking alone and distraught in the hollow hum of silence that followed. As Harry and Dr. Grey busied themselves with their plans, he absent-mindedly, caressed the mink fur of his Fendi suitcase sitting to the right of him. He'd given this $10,000 bag its own seat at the head of the table, as if this stupid bag held such prominence as to merit it.

A few moments more and, finally it was Betty's voice that pierced the stillness. She walked up behind him, offering her advice, "Your girl, Darci, is more competent than you think. You can be proud of the daughter you raised, Mr. Wiggins."

It took a minute for Mr. Wiggins to recognize who that voice belonged to. Not because he wasn't familiar with Betty's voice but because he fully expected every one of the others to voice responses in hateful and accusatory tones. He'd expected it most from Betty. After all, he was the one purposely railroading her into early retirement. He was also discrediting her life's work by closing the mall's doors—shutting down everything she had worked toward for the past forty years. He knew that if the shoe had been on the other foot, he wouldn't hesitate to respond with rage. Actually, who was he kidding? He had already behaved in such horrible ways without any reason. No… he knew without a doubt that he deserved their hostility, and, yet, Betty gifted him with the very opposite. Taking another moment to digest the actual meaning of the words Betty spoke, he found himself rendered speechless. Despite all the malevolent business trickery he had been directing her way, Betty chose to comfort him rather than condemn him, and it made him feel something he hadn't for decades: Shame.

Mr. Wiggins looked up from his wasteful, opulent purchase and met Betty's kind eyes as they looked back at him through her wired spectacles. He would never had told her but, when he first saw her dressed up like Mrs. Claus, for the tiniest of moments, he allowed himself to unearth from his memories a similar encounter from when Darci was just a toddler. He remembered he took Darci to visit Santa Claus at one of the malls he owned. A woman, dressed very much like Betty was now, approached them with a kind smile and a candy cane. At the time, Darci was just starting to form words. He could still see his little girl's eyes lighting up at the sight of Kris Kringle's better half, and he could still hear her squeal in delight trying to pronounce the words: "Merry Christmas, Momma!"

Momma.

The words made him ashamed. And angry.

It was the first—and last—time that he ever took his daughter to visit Santa. He could barely remember himself as *that* Mr. Wiggins, Darci's father. What he did recall is how that moment may have been the instant he started to withhold his love for Darci altogether. What a fool he had been. How much time had he already wasted?

He looked at Betty's arm from which hung a vintage black and red leather bag with straps so frayed, he thought for sure it would break free and fall to the floor at any moment.

"Thank you, Ms. Bryant, for your kind words." He looked up at her, the corners of his mouth rising meekly. "I have done a great many things in my life, but one thing for which I deserve absolutely no credit is the raising of my daughter. I am most grateful that she has had you as her mentor for the last little while."

Standing nearby, Harry cleared his throat. "Let's get back to reality. Randy, this *RimWorld* game, how can it help us get to Emily and the others? How do you win at playing that game?"

Randy lumbered his giant elf-self over to Harry. Karina followed closely.

"*RimWorld* ain't about winning," Randy replied.

He took a seat at the table next to Mr. Wiggins's fur bag. Before he actually sat down, however, Mr. Wiggins grabbed his bag and tossed it unceremoniously to the floor. He gestured to Harry to sit where the bag once rested. Harry shook his head and remained standing while Karina seated herself at the head of the table.

"I don't get it," Harry said to Randy. "I thought you said…well, I'm not exactly sure what you said, but I know the endgame was getting into the room where they are trapped."

"*RimWorld* is a story kind of game," Randy explained. "You pick a storyteller—mine is the totally unpredictable Randy Random…"

"You be trippin'," Karina interrupted. She giggled.

"No, Karina, it's legit." Randy became more and more animated as he continued to educate them on the game he loved. "It's like sci-fi meets your generation's Wild West."

"My generation?" Harry chuckled.

"Yes, sir, that's what Pastor Max told me," Randy explained. "He's the one who got me and some of the other kids playing this game. He said that this teaches us strategy and…" Randy paused, his eyes reaching to the Heavens to recall the words. A moment later, he continued with a Cheshire-cat-sized smile spreading across his face. "Oh, right! Strategy and 'diversity of human conditions'!"

Harry rubbed his eyes with his forefingers in frustration. "Randy…"

Randy shrugged and raised his hand in a "stop" gesture. "Wait. People. Listen. You, like, land on this planet, and you gotta learn how to build stuff you need and grow food and get along with the other colonists—some of these be so dumb!" Randy scoffed, until he saw the frustration on Harry's face. "Look, man, what I'm tryin' to tell you is when one path gets closed off to you, you gotta build tunnels underneath or bridges overhead and make you a whole new way to get to where you want to go. The first thing you gotta build, though, is your storage room. That's where you stockpile stuff and then sell it to trade ships."

"He's not actually wrong," Mr. Wiggins gingerly entered into the conversation.

"I got this," Harry waved his hand, immediately dismissing his former boss's input.

"It's in the blueprints," Mr. Wiggins straightened his frame and turned to address everyone. "I remember seeing them when we first bought the building. Underground tunnels of sorts. They're like a maze, if I recall. I thought they may have been used for smuggling or transporting…"

Randy shot straight up, his arms in a victory pose high overhead, and exaggerated his words. "Pirates' Boooo Teee!"

Harry craned his neck back, blowing out air through clenched teeth. "Damn it!" he shouted, lowering his head and locking eyes with Mr. Wiggins. "This is the last time we will work together." He then stepped aside, giving the old man access to the blueprints. "Show me these tunnels so we can *RimWorld* our way in."

CHAPTER THIRTY-SIX

HOLLY & A BABY

Disclosing Disclaimers

H olly heard Randy's earlier outburst and piped up, "Pirate's Booty. You know, I'd kill for some. That's my favorite snack!" Walking out from behind the tripod with her camera in hand, Holly plopped herself on the floor beside Ian, both taking a break from reporting.

Ian reached into his pocket, pulled out a mini candy cane, and handed it to her. "Courtesy of Carter," he said. "Not Pirate's Booty, but still a snack!"

Holly patted her tummy. "Thanks, but no thanks. I'm in the mood for something savory not sweet."

The two laughed together, whatever invisible walls had stood between them earlier that day were gone. Holly shrugged. "Besides, I can still hear Carter crunching them in my ears."

"He does love his candy canes," Ian snorted.

Suddenly, the sound of Vincent laughing made them both turn to the side. He was in a corner with Vi and Vern, apparently trying to teach the pair how to rock their ugly Christmas sweaters with some of Michael Jackson's dance moves.

Ian indicated towards his brother, "He is something."

Holly nodded. "Yup. He sure is." She twisted off the lens cap from the camera she held. "You are, too. So, what happened to you earlier?"

"What?" Ian looked off into the distance.

"You know, Carter called me during your little on-air meltdown."

"He did? Crap. But it wasn't a meltdown."

"I figured but...what was it, then?"

Vincent's laughter filled the space, again drawing Ian's attention.

Holly noticed, but pressed on, "Church confession?"

"Yes....maybe." Ian thought about it for a moment. He then shook his head. "No, actually it wasn't. I *wasn't* confessing—I felt more like I was unloading. I'm just so sick of pretending everything in my life is okay. I'm tired of keeping Vincent and his schizophrenia and my family's link to mental illness secret. Everybody has their breaking point. It's not all Norman Rockwell; sometimes, it's—"

Holly chimed in, chuckling, "A 'Brawl at the Mall'...?"

Ian nodded, smiling. "Christmas and crazy just seem to go hand-in-hand for me. Everything that's supposed to be 'normal' like family parties or even just wanting to be with your family..." He trailed off in mid-sentence.

Holly reached into her pocket and pulled out a prescription bottle filled with pills. "Normal's overrated. And pretty boring, if you ask me." She shook them and held the orange, plastic vial out in front of Ian so that he could clearly read the label.

"Duloxetine. What's that for?" Ian asked, puzzled.

"It's a poor girl's Cymbalta. Antidepressant...but I take it for anxiety."

"Anxiety? You?" Ian couldn't mask his surprise. "I thought you were fearless."

"Nope."

Ian chuckled. "Well, news flash. In case you didn't know, most people in the newsroom fear you."

"Muwahahaha!" Holly exaggerated a wicked laugh. "I thought I was doing pretty well at keeping my demons in check. You should have seen me when they first put me on this drug." She gave the bottle of pills one last shake and pocketed them once again. "It made things worse. I felt like that Crazy Eyes chick from *Orange Is the New Black*. You ever watch that show?"

Ian shook his head.

"My eyes were like buggin' out. I wanted to punch people in the face for no reason."

"Can't help but think that you still do," Ian interjected.

"Ok, true," she admitted. "But now I'm like that kid, Kevin, in *Home Alone*." Holly acted out the film character's line: "Hey, I'm not afraid anymore! I said I'm not afraid anymore! Do you hear me? I'm not afraid anymore!"

Ian chuckled. "Maybe I need my own prescription."

As if on cue, Dr. Haywood tapped Holly on the shoulder. "I suppose I should give you credit for being clever enough to sign Vincent out *and* remember to get his meds."

Holly winced. "Yeah, about that...you really should re-educate your nurses so they can spot a scam."

"Holly...Really...?" A disappointed sounding Dr. Haywood responded. "Not only was it irresponsible, but what you did was illegal."

"Doc," she said, looking up at him with puppy dog eyes. "I blame it on the meds. You know this drug I'm on might increase certain behaviors. I've memorized them. I'm supposed to talk to my doctor if I have 'thoughts of suicide, symptoms of aggression, irritability, panic attacks, extreme worry, restlessness, abnormal excitement,' or the side-effect I'm going to go with in this case, 'acting without thinking.'"

Dr. Haywood leaned forward, as if wanting to respond.

Holly didn't give him the opportunity, smacking herself on the forehead. "Hey, I forgot one. 'A 2011 study, published in the International Journal of Clinical Practice, found that weight loss was reported among some users explained by a loss of appetite, another common side effect of the drug,' but just for the record, that has NOT been my experience AT ALL."

"Not funny, Holly," Dr. Haywood chastised, as much as his tiny smile betrayed him.

"I know. Have you seen me eat? Why couldn't I get that side effect and not the others?"

"Holly, you know what can happen when someone like Vincent is taken out of his environment. Even with his meds, he's going off routine, over-stimulated, and might build up unrealistic expectations," he cast a look directly at Ian. "These things can set Vince back, who knows how far."

Holly lowered her head. "I know. I didn't mean any harm. I was trying to help."

Vincent snuck up behind Dr. Haywood. "Ho-Ho-Ho! Have you been naughty or nice?"

Dr. Haywood looked over his shoulder, and, in his best Groucho Marx impression, repeated one of his favorite responses to the question, "Always nice…sometimes naughty! As it should be!"

Vincent circled around, placing himself in the center of the trio. "Best Christmas EVER with my two favorite people: My brother, Ian, and you, Dr. Haywood."

"Hey, what about me?" Holly joked.

"You didn't let me finish," said Vincent, very seriously.

"Okay, finish."

"And my newest favorite person, you, Holly!"

"Don't forget Vi and Vern," Holly pointed over to them.

"Right! And Vi and Vern." At that, Vincent's face clouded over, and he was visibly confused for a moment.

"You okay, buddy?" Ian nudged, carefully.

Vince nodded, connecting his thoughts together. He took a moment but then addressed Holly. "Yeah. Ian. I'm good. But, actually, Vi and Vern were talking about Holly."

"Me?" Holly sounded surprised.

"It's ok," Vincent was quick to reassure her. "It's not anything bad. Though everything was sad. They were talking about Grace. She's who we visited in the cemetery. Remember?"

Holly nodded, treading carefully. "I remember. But what about me… and Grace?"

Vincent sported a somewhat goofy grin. "They said that when they look at you, they see her. They said Grace had a little baby. They said that maybe they're your real family. Grandma Vi and Grandpa Vern and grandbaby Holly."

From the looks on Holly, Ian, and Dr. Haywood's faces, it was obvious that Vincent had dropped a bomb without even knowing it. Noticing their collective expressions of shock, Vincent panicked and began flapping his arms, doing a bit of what looked like the chicken dance. "Uh-oh," he said. "I think I gotta fly!"

Just then, a drone buzzed its way into where the others had made camp. Mr. Abdullah succeeded in flying the drone through his collapsed area—hopefully recording a pathway to rescue the group trapped in Games & Gadgets Galore. Alongside it flew the white bird, Rainbow, and Pickpocket the dog trailed not far behind. To Vincent's delight, the drone and bird circled near where he stood, and then approached the table where Harry and Mr. Wiggins worked. The two were hunched over the table studying blueprints of the mall. The drone hovered overhead, just above them. A moment later, it gently landed on the center of the table.

Rainbow and Pickpocket finally rested and sat next to Vincent.

Harry couldn't contain his excitement. He looked like a little boy opening presents on Christmas morning. "Sweet! I have SO been wanting one of these!"

At almost the same time, Isabelle and Damian looked up from Damian's phone and shouted out: "Harry, we're logged in to your Facebook." The two looked at one another, and said, "Jinx!"

Damian continued: "And we are already in the live video stream that the Games & Gadgets Galore store invited us to join."

Isabelle looked down at her own phone. "Hey, I just got a Facebook notification on my phone," she said, reading it out loud: "Games & Gadgets Galore is now live. Hmm…I must have accidently logged into Harry's account from my phone, too. Oh well, no biggie."

Now, even more excited, Harry moved to Damian and took his phone. "Thanks, man!" He called out, "Dr. Grey? Emily's on."

Immediately, Dr. Grey sprang into action, crossing over to where she could see. Quickly, she sang out, "Fantastic, where are we at with momma and your baby. Emily, can you hear me? Emily?"

Betty and Leo came to the table, both reaching out for the other's hand. They looked at one another, nodding and smiling.

"This is the kind of Christmas miracle the world needs to see," Betty exclaimed.

As Ian and Holly neared, Leo looked at them, adding, "Here's your news story."

Everyone gathered around Harry, their faces so bright and hopeful as they all watched the tiny screen. Damian patted Harry on the back. Hank and Andrea poked their heads over others' shoulders and in between arms to get a peek at the birth. On the screen, they could all see Pastor Max who was standing at the foot of the couch where Emily lay. Darci was kneeling near Emily's head, wiping her own brow and brushing back her hair with her one hand while holding onto Emily's hand with her other one. Emily didn't seem to be moving. Mr. Abdullah slowly paced back and forth with the remote to the drone in one hand, while keeping an eye on his cell phone's streaming video from the freestanding tripod. The scene looked anything but cheery and definitely not what they all had expected. One by one, every face watching the scene shifted from joy to concern.

"Harry, is there any chance you can switch this to a bigger screen?" Dr. Grey asked, a slight note of concern in her tone. "And I don't think they set it up right. Why can't they hear me?"

"Oohhh, I see. We can hear them from the Facebook Live event, but they can't hear us! They didn't remember to click to invite Harry to join them on camera! I'm sure they were moving so fast to set up the event, they just forgot. All we need to do is call them back from another phone," Isabelle said as she quickly redialed Darci's number. "No need to add another thing to their plate and ask them to set up the livestream a second time when we could just talk to them through speakerphone."

Harry nodded in a silent response to Isabelle, never taking his eyes off of the tiny screen. "I gotta get in there!"

Damian stepped in, reaching over to grab the drone. He studied it for a moment and said, "Wiggins, do you have a USB cable in that fur bag of yours?"

Mr. Wiggins moved to retrieve his bag. "I'm sure I do," he said, simultaneously lifting his laptop and handing it over to Damian.

Harry shifted the view of Emily's birthing to his laptop. He robotically fell into a chair. With a few keystrokes, Emily and the delivery of his baby appeared now on the laptop's screen. With a shaking finger, he clicked the button to unmute the sound. That was when they heard Pastor Max shout, "Stay with me, Emily! Don't you DARE give up now!"

CHAPTER THIRTY-SEVEN

EMILY & HER FANS
A Virtual (and Viral) Birth

G rim faces surrounded Dr. Grey at the table from which she commanded orders through the speaker on Isabelle's cell phone: "Emily? Emily, it's Dr. Grey. Can you hear me, hon? It's time to meet your baby." All eyes were glued to the laptop screen; the cell phone rested on the table just next to the computer.

"She's not responding!" Harry's voice trembled. "Em, honey, it's me," he shouted. "Open your eyes, love."

As Damian and Mr. Wiggins worked on the other laptop, plugging in USB cables to try to download the drone's footage, Damian noticed Mr. Wiggins concealing the tears forming in his eyes. Although surprised, Damian involuntarily reached out his hand to place it on Mr. Wiggins's shoulder.

But before he could do so, the old man lowered his head and took a step back.

Damian empathetically nodded, slightly relieved; he then typed on the keyboard and clicked on various dialogue boxes that popped up on the laptop's screen until finally the drone's footage appeared for them all to see.

"Pastor Max, can you hear me?" Dr. Grey spoke in a forceful yet calming tone.

An exhausted voice responded, "Yes."

"I want you and the others to do exactly as I tell you. Understand?" Dr. Grey continued as she watched Darci, Mr. Abdullah, and Pastor Max all tend to Emily and the unborn baby. Emily's face had turned from beet-red to ash-white. Her clothes stuck to her body and she lay stiff and still. Her three caregivers also stood still as statues; the look on each of their faces displayed their worried thoughts.

"Do you understand? I need you all to give me a nod," Dr. Grey prompted. "Now is not the time to give in to fear and let it paralyze you." Her voice grew in volume as she directed them: "Now, everybody… MOVE."

Mr. Abdullah was the first to snap to, hearing her words. "Yes. Right." He turned to address his team. "Darci, Max, the doctor is speaking, and we need to listen."

"Okay, good. Now, listen to my voice," Dr. Grey saw them turn to look toward the phone's camera, still broadcasting the Facebook Live event, as if to ask her "What do we do now?".

Back in the newsroom, one of Carter's young reporters looked down at the Facebook notification that popped up on his iPhone. It read: "Games & Gadgets Galore is now live." He stared quizzically at the livestream, watching as three people who seemed to be in a panic were racing around, propping up someone who looked asleep or even passed out. Squinting to see more clearly, his eyes grew big at what now he knew to be a live video feed of three people helping a very pregnant woman in trouble. Looking up for a moment, he caught Carter's eye.

Carter looked at the young man, noticing his tense posture and dropped jaw. "What is it?" Carter yelled out. Moving closer to stand just behind his direct report, Carter peered over his shoulder and focused on the tiny screen. "Holy moly! Put that up on the monitor. And somebody get Holly and Ian on the phone. NOW!"

"How long does it take to go less than a mile?" Lauren cried out from the backseat of their massive, silver pickup truck as they maneuvered their way along the unplowed side streets.

Maddie, sitting shotgun, excitedly shouted over her shoulder to her sister, "I see the Maplefield Mall sign. We're so close."

Their mother, Ivy, revved the engine. "I fought your father for months on getting this truck. I hated it, but he was convinced it would help us in the winter months. Remind me to thank him when he comes to pick up you girls tomorrow."

Lauren leaned forward, putting her head in between her mother and sister, and with a broad grin, coyly asked, "Maybe daddy can stay, and we can all have Christmas together?"

Maddie giddily added, "Maybe even Aunt Isabelle can come?"

Ivy looked over at her daughter's hopeful faces. "Maybe," she said, causing the girls to squeal with glee.

Maddie's cell phone dinged. She pulled it into view so that both she and Lauren could see the alert on her screen. "Games & Gadgets Galore is now live." Maddie was about to dismiss it when Lauren stopped her and tapped the alert to join the video feed.

The pair watched as three people hovered over an obviously pregnant woman who clearly was in trouble. At the same time, both girls shouted out, "MOM!"

Back at the mall, Dr. Grey continued to direct the scene as best she could. At her side, Harry leaned in, chewing on his fingernails. On the screen, they were watching, along with the others in the room, as Pastor Max, Darci, and Mr. Abdullah feverishly worked together to get Emily into more of an upright position. As they moved her, Emily began to respond with the slightest of movements.

"There!" Harry saw it, pointing. "She moved." Harry held back tears as he looked up, whispering, "Thank you. God, thank you."

Mr. Wiggins pounded his fist on the table and blurted out, "Thank God." He surprised himself with his show of emotion, and clearly surprised everyone else whose eyes were now on him. Almost immediately, Mr. Wiggins's embarrassment showed on his face. He lowered his eyes and rounded his back, inching farther away from the others.

Shifting their attention back to the screen, they all watched as Emily began to awaken. Slowly, she started making noises, becoming aware again, and looking around at her team of helpers. With another contraction, Emily cried out, panting again.

"Welcome back, Emily!" Dr. Grey cheered into the speaker, relaxing just a tiny bit. A second later, she saw Pastor Max, Darci, and Mr. Abdullah applauding. She turned to Harry, and whispered, "Camera's too far away for me to really see much, since the phone is perched at a bit of an angle. I'm not going to tell them that. But I want you to know, Harry. It's family and friends and prayer now."

Harry was about to respond when suddenly Emily came fully alive, doubling over and grunting through another push. She grabbed onto Darci with one hand and Mr. Abdullah with the other for support, while Pastor Max positioned himself to receive the newborn.

Harry and Dr. Grey exchanged a hopeful nod, and then with her full attention on the screen, Dr. Grey shouted out, trying to sound nothing but positive. "That's it. Your body knows what to do, Emily. The female body is made for giving birth. I want you to relax. Everything's going to be just fine. Your baby's head is going to hit a nerve bundle near the base of your spine, momma. Your body's contractions and a little gravity are what's going to help push this baby out."

Behind her, Vincent had turned away from the screen and sat down on the floor in the corner. Dr. Haywood watched him for a moment and then decided to join him.

"Hey, Vince," Dr. Haywood said as he lowered himself to a seated position by his side. "You doing okay?"

Vincent looked into Dr. Haywood's eyes. "Is she going to be okay?"

"She's really tired, Vince. But she's awake and people are helping her."

"We need to help more."

Dr. Haywood bowed his head. "How about we say a prayer to get some more help?"

"Praying doesn't work," Vincent's face grew a sour expression. He turned his head away, trying to hide it from view.

"Why do you say that?" Dr. Haywood asked as he nudged Vincent to look at him.

Vincent shrugged. A moment later, he turned and, with tears in his own eyes, he looked into Dr. Haywood's. "I pray to be normal. That doesn't work."

Dr. Haywood nodded sadly. The two sat in silence for a moment. He then asked Vincent, "Why do you think you're not already normal?"

Vincent opened up his hand to reveal three pills, each one a different color, shape, and size.

"Oh...right." Dr. Haywood's face showed an expression of understanding. "You think it's because you take pills? You hate taking those pills, don't you..."

Vincent nodded. "Normal people don't have to take pills."

As Vincent and Dr. Haywood sat on the floor, Holly walked over to them.

"Hey, can I join your party?" Holly asked, catching a glimpse of Vincent's drugs just before he curled his hand into a fist to hide them from her. She gave both Vincent and Dr. Haywood her best sympathetic smile as she sat down facing Vincent. "Hey, Vince, thank you. You just reminded me, it's time for me to take my meds."

As Holly's words sank in, Vincent's puzzled look was soon followed by a smile. He looked back at Holly and said, "You, too?"

Holly nodded.

Vincent looked at her in awe.

"So, Vince," Dr. Haywood chuckled. "Holly is anything but 'normal,' but I think that's part of what makes her a great person. What do you think?"

Vincent locked eyes with Holly. He lunged forward to hug her, exclaiming happily, "Want to take them together?"

Holly raised the water bottle she had in her hand and reached down into her pant pocket with her other hand to pull out her own prescription bottle. "We can share my water."

Dr. Haywood swallowed back tears, happily chuckling at them both.

From the far side of the space, Ian waved his arms to get Dr. Haywood's attention.

Dr. Haywood saw him and could see the serious, panicked look in Ian's eyes. Turning to Vincent, Dr. Haywood said, "You start your prayers without me, Vince. I'll be right back."

As Dr. Haywood rose to leave, Holly took over, saying, "I'll get started praying with you, too. Is that okay, Vince?"

Vince nodded, calmly smiling ear-to-ear. He cheerily said to Holly, "I'm anything but 'normal' too, and that makes me great, just like you."

"You got that right, Vince," Holly winked.

Just a few feet away, Ian walked to meet Dr. Haywood and leaned in close to whisper into Dr. Haywood's ear.

"We got a call from Carter in the newsroom," Ian said. "The *private* Facebook Live, um, somehow…it's broadcasting everywhere."

"What's everywhere…?" Dr. Haywood took a moment. "Good Lord," he said jerking his head back. "You mean Emily…?" He glanced over at Dr. Grey and Harry and the others, all huddled around the laptop screen. "How? They went back and forth to make sure that they only invited Harry to join."

Ian shrugged. "Somehow, despite whatever they did—or think they did—it wasn't set to a private audience—only inviting specific friends—and so it's now a live feed for everyone to see," he explained. "And to make matters worse, it appears they used Mr. Abdullah's Games & Gadgets Galore Facebook page to go live."

Dr. Haywood shut his eyes and exhaled. "How many people?"

"The store has a TON of followers, so anyone who's friends with the store, or who follows the store, got a notification." Ian continued. "SO many people are watching... It's going viral. Since the store is the host of the livestream, they are the only one who can control the settings, and they would be able to see the number of viewers on their screen... but that's not really the first thing on their minds right now... So... The question is, do we say something?"

Without a moment's hesitation, Dr. Haywood's eyes narrowed as he shook his head. "No. I think that to distract anyone from the task at hand is a definite...no. Making sure Emily and the baby come through without any more challenges is the only thing that matters right now."

As if they could hear him, the action inside Games & Gadgets Galore picked up pace and played out on the screen.

Pastor Max's voice shouted out, "Here comes the head!"

"You're doing it, Emily!" Darci encouraged.

"Come on, Momma," Mr. Abdullah cheered.

Dr. Grey added, shouting into the speaker, "Push, Emily, push!"

With one loud cry, Emily pushed with all her might.

The following cry was even louder, as the baby that Pastor Max now held in his arms wailed.

"Ha-ha! It's a girl!" Pastor Max rejoiced.

Both rooms—the one Emily was in and the one watching—erupted in celebration. Harry, who had been holding back tears throughout the entire ordeal, finally let himself release his emotions. "Emily," he shouted at the screen. "I love you, Em!"

Carter and his entire crew whooped and hollered at the live birth they witnessed, now streaming on their monitors in the newsroom and on live TV throughout the entire Chicagoland area.

One of the interns hollered out ecstatically, "Carter, we just hit 5 million views!"

Carter nodded, wiping away happy tears and letting out a "Woo-hoo!" He then pointed at the screens next to his WACK-TV feed. Three other local news stations were now also broadcasting Emily's live birth. Bursting with pride, Carter said, "Love that WACK-TV logo. Don't those call letters just POP?!" He then grabbed a newly replenished container of candy canes and waved them in the air. "Wish I still had my cigars, but this will do. Candy canes for everyone!" As he said the words, the phones in the newsroom, once again, began ringing. "Uh-oh," Carter joked, "Every time a bell rings, an angel gets its wings."

As the celebration continued around where Holly sat with Vince, Holly suddenly took note of all the strangers-turned-friends; there were so many different faces but each one sharing in this experience showed such love and joy. She scrambled to her feet and quickly loaded her video camera onto her shoulder. Holly pointed her lens at the community before her and began documenting the people and their interactions. Vi and Vern embraced. Damian and Isabelle kissed. Andrea and Hank, along with Rainbow and Pickpocket, jumped and fluttered about. Dr. Haywood and Vincent patted one another on their backs. Harry grabbed onto Dr. Grey, mouthing over-and-over again the words "thank you" as he tightly held onto her. And, Mr. Wiggins, Holly noticed, with his finger still on the laptop's trackpad, sported the broadest of smiles as he looked around and seemed to revel in everyone else's jubilation. He was watching and re-watching the drone's footage of the seemingly impassable passageway into the Games & Gadgets Galore store when so many voices burst out in cheers. When his eyes connected with Holly's through the lens of her camera, she peered over the top of the viewfinder to smile at the old man. He nodded in response.

Holly then shouted out to everyone, "Hey, let's give our audiences a real feel-good Christmas Eve story."

They all sounded off in agreement.

Ian positioned himself in front of the group so that viewers could observe their collective merriment. He motioned to Dr. Grey and Harry to come over, grabbed his microphone, and turned to Holly, silently communicating his intent to interview the two doctors with a point of a finger.

Holly read his mind, and already had her camera pointed at the proud papa and the good doctor, making sure to position the laptop screen in the background. Then, suddenly, a painful cry from Emily coming through the speaker pierced through the revelry.

"Oooooohhhhh!" Emily's scream commanded instant attention from all who were watching and hearing.

Dr. Grey immediately spun around and took in what she saw on screen. Her face shifted from glee to gloom as she slowly repositioned herself in front of the laptop's screen. She saw her patient doubled over again and she knew something was very wrong.

"Emily? Emily talk to me. What are you feeling?" Dr. Grey called out, making sure that Isabelle's cell phone was still on speakerphone and connected to the group inside the store.

A look of panic, once again, swept across Harry's face as he pulled out the chair beside the doctor and nearly collapsed into it. His eyes were glued to his wife.

"Something's coming," Emily cried out. "I think it's another baby."

"What?" Dr. Grey expressed utter and complete shock. "It can't be." She turned to Harry, shaking her head. "I saw Emily less than 24 hours ago. One heartbeat. One baby."

As they watched, Pastor Max and Mr. Abdullah resumed their original birthing positions, almost instinctively. Darci held the first baby girl in her arms, rocking back and forth. Emily panted and breathed and yelled.

"Sweet baby Jesus!" Pastor Max exclaimed. "I do see another head."

Darci shrieked, "Emily, you're having twins."

"One more time, Momma." Mr. Abdullah sang out. "You can do it."

Harry and Dr. Grey, now with everyone else surrounding them, watched yet another miracle unfolding before their very eyes.

Holly moved in closer with her camera. On screen and all around, pure excitement and exhilaration filled the air. Holly lifted her head to scan her surroundings. She thought she heard a strange sound like a drumbeat, and it seemed to be getting louder and louder. Soon, the beat turned into the sound of stomping feet that were walking closer and closer to them. She realized that she wasn't the only one who heard it. Everyone stopped talking and laughing as they turned away from the laptop and focused their attention in the direction of the sound.

Firefighters wearing heavy gear from head-to-toe marched in. Holly counted five of them in total. The guy in the lead shouted, "What are you all doing here?" He didn't bother waiting for any answers. Shifting the axe that he was holding from one hand to the other, he gestured to his engine company. "Round 'em up. Everybody out of here now!"

Holly resumed filming, following two of the first responders as they moved toward the former entryway of the Games & Gadgets Galore store.

In response, Vincent shot straight up, excitedly hurrying toward one of the firefighters. Vi and Vern followed while Hank and Andrea made their way toward the exit.

"Don't touch me. I'm not going anywhere!" Harry shouted when one of the firefighters tapped his arm to escort him out. "My wife and babies are in there."

Leo intervened then, calmly explaining to the firefighters. "His wife just gave birth. Looks like another baby is coming. Three other adults are helping her. All are trapped."

Dr. Grey stepped forward. "I'm his wife's doctor," she explained to the firefighter barking the orders as she pointed to the laptop screen for him to see.

Giving a nod of acknowledgement to Dr. Grey, the firefighter responded, looking at both her and Harry. "With all due respect, Doc, we'll take it from here."

And with that, the firefighter in charge ended the call and slammed the laptop shut.

CHAPTER THIRTY-EIGHT

ELMER & THE CAREGIVERS

When God Closes a Door...

From her "birthing room" in the Games & Gadgets Galore back office, Emily screamed, "Harry!"

"Emily, listen to me," Pastor Max's smile failed to mask his own concerns. "I think I heard that the firefighters are here. They'll be charging through to us any minute."

Both Darci and Mr. Abdullah exchanged worried glances.

"But... Harry..." Emily cried out and then screamed with another painful contraction.

As Mr. Abdullah ended the Facebook Live video, he chimed in, "Harry is going to be fine. We all are." He exchanged glances again with Darci as they both looked around the room, neither one quite sure that what he had said was true.

Pastor Max set his attention to the second delivery. In a soothing voice, he encouraged Emily onward. "We're almost there, Emily. Let's get this baby out, and then, let's get us all out of here."

Darci nodded, seconding him, bravely voicing what she felt in her heart: "When God closes a door..."

She paused, giving Pastor Max a knowing look which he returned with a wink. They all then shouted out the response: "STOP BANGIN' ON IT!"

Despite their circumstances, Emily, Pastor Max, Mr. Abdullah, and Darci laughed out loud. "This isn't funny!" Emily exchaimed, but she couldn't help laughing through her tears. With one last growl of frustration and pain, she let out a final push.

Emily's attendants shouted out in encouragement. They knew they only had this moment—with no idea what to expect next. Then Emily's second baby emerged, immediately exercising its lungs with a healthy-sounding cry. Pastor Max held the child in his arms and tearfully choked up on his next words, "It's a boy."

There was a loud CLAP and a booming celebratory shout of "Yes!" that echoed throughout the room. Emily lifted her head, turning her gaze from her newborn son to the daughter who was only minutes old and was safely swaddled in Darci's arms. Emily's eyes scanned her surroundings and then she saw him: The security guard, the one with the kind eyes and the ring of keys, poked his head out from a crawl-space-sized opening on the floor.

Elmer climbed out of the secret tunnel and then gestured to the door in the floor. "Excuse me, ma'am. As soon as you're all done here, I think it best that we all go."

Back at the Games & Gadgets Galore destroyed storefront, two of the firefighters flanked the opening, testing the ceiling with a pike pole, standing poised to enter and scurry through the debris to the trapped group. Suddenly, a shattering vibration just inside the opening shook out with a BOOM!

The two firefighters jumped back, joining the others in the center of the area. While one firefighter crooked his neck to speak into his shoulder-mounted radio, the other turned over the chairs and shifted the table into a make-shift protective barrier.

"Folks," the firefighter in charge barked, "Those sounds coming from deep within that passageway are telling me that more of the structure is falling. All of you need to leave immediately."

Holly, who was still videotaping, continued to capture it all.

"Turn that thing off, please," the head firefighter yelled at Holly. "We need to secure a collapse zone, and you all—including you media—need to get out of here."

Ian had just raised his microphone to his mouth, but then knew better than to disrespect the firefighters. He nodded to Holly, who had lowered her video camera from her shoulder and pulled the plug to the feed.

Harry stepped around her, leaning in almost nose-to-nose with the firefighter. He opened his mouth to speak, but the firefighter didn't give him the chance. Placing both his hands upon Harry's chest, the firefighter said, "Buddy, I'd feel the same way you do if the shoe was on the other foot, but you're not helping here. Having to deal with you guys out here means that we can't do our job and get to them in there. So please. For your wife, your kids, those other people in there, go with my guys. Let us do what we know how to do."

Harry searched the other man's eyes for a moment, as his thoughts warred within: *How can I leave when Emily and my two babies are still trapped? My God, I'm a father. And I'm failing. Already. I'm supposed to protect them.* And then, the firefighter's words rang in his ears: *The longer they had to deal with him, the longer it was taking for them to rescue his family.* Harry's shoulders sank. He didn't like it, but he understood. He took a deep breath.

The firefighter took his hands off of Harry's chest. "We got this," he said confidently, meeting Harry's tearful gaze.

Betty chimed in. "The footage from the drone," she offered up to the firefighter.

"Right," Damian shouted out, as he handed the laptop over. "We flew a drone and took video of the collapsed path, moving all the way from where they're trapped inside to us out here. It shows all the pitfalls and possibilities. Well, at least, before whatever just happened now. Mr. Wiggins and I were just watchin' it. He mentioned that he might have traced a way through."

Damian looked around for Mr. Wiggins. He asked the others, "Where's Wiggins?"

As they all looked around for the missing old man, Damian detected a motion out of the corner of his eye; something—or someone—just darted into the opening of Games & Gadgets Galore. "Oh, crap," Damian exhaled, pointing toward the entryway. "I think the old fool decided to crawl through on his own and be a hero."

For the past hour, the monitors in the newsroom had been showing the twin births and the celebrations, broadcasting live from both the social media page and Holly's video feed. However, the newsroom staff were now silently staring at blank, crackling screens for longer than they should have.

"Good grief!" Carter murmured under his breath. Surveying the others, he asked aloud what everyone in the room was thinking: "What the heck just happened?"

"It's not just us," a member of the news team said while punching buttons on a console. "The other stations lost eyes on it all, too."

Suddenly, up on one of the monitors, a snowy image started to appear. Carter peered at it. "What is that?" he asked.

The picture came into focus. Outside of the mall, two fire trucks were parked alongside the front doors. Firemen worked outside their rigs, trudging through the two feet of snow that fell that day. They were pulling line and carrying equipment, trying to enter the mall. The camera panned across the parking lot to capture the ambulance literally inching its way around the corner of Mall Drive.

"Finally," Carter exclaimed.

Ian stepped into the frame holding his microphone up to his mouth, trying to quiet his chattering teeth. "This is Ian McConnell for WACK-TV coming to you live from the parking lot of Maplefield Mall. If you've been following us this Christmas Eve, then you know that a section of the roof on the far end of the mall collapsed earlier today. Inside, several people were trapped in the Games & Gadgets Galore store. One of those was a pregnant woman in labor who now, thankfully, is a mom to twins. The delivery of her babies was shared live just a little bit ago. Although we lost our video connection with them, we have since learned that mom and the babies—along with the three other folks who were also trapped—are no longer broadcasting on Facebook Live. We are trying to get an update on how they're all doing."

He continued. "Now, we are reporting from the chilly outdoors, since we were escorted out of the mall by first responders just moments ago. As you can see behind me, emergency vehicles were finally able to make their way through the roadways that have been virtually impassable today due to this surprise winter storm. So far, Mother Nature has dumped a couple of feet of snow on us, turning highways into abandoned car parking lots with dozens of accidents along the way. We know that firefighters are already inside the mall working on rescuing the group trapped inside. More firefighters are now trooping through the mall's main entrance behind me. We also know that at least 50 local teenagers who were participating in the annual Christmas Eve Kids Cheer Fest are safe inside another area of the mall that—to our knowledge—does not have any structural damage."

Ian's chattering teeth were now matched by Holly's trembling which was causing the video to shake.

"We'll come back to you when we have more information to share," Ian continued. "We're planning to go back inside, if they'll let us. Reporting to you live, this is Ian McConnell for WACK-TV."

"Good grief!" Darci huffed, looking down at her ringing cell phone. The caller ID displayed: MR. WIGGINS (aka DAD). The glow from the screen illuminated her face, highlighting the wisps of damp hair that framed it. "For decades, my dad barely spoke to me. Now he can't seem to go a couple hours without calling me."

She curled her fingers around the phone and repositioned herself onto the backend of Elmer's little golf cart. With her other arm, she wrapped herself around Emily, who was bucketed as securely as could be into the cart's tiny cargo bed, cradling both of her swaddled and sleeping newborns in her lap.

An exhausted Emily looked up at Darci, "I don't think Elmer's club car here was designed as a seven-passenger vehicle." The two softly giggled. Emily then paused, a sad look sweeping over her face. "You're not going to answer his call?" she asked.

Darci shook her head. "I'll call him back later."

Pastor Max was wedged into the front seat in between Mr. Abdullah to his right and Elmer, who was driving, to his left. He chimed in now, "With everything going on, it could be important."

Darci used her index finger to silence her phone. "Yeah. Maybe," she responded. "I'm still going to have it go to voicemail." She then looked at Pastor Max. "Great expectations are great expectations. But with my dad, they never end up being what I hope for, so I just stopped expecting much of anything." She paused, turning away. Then said, "I'll listen to his message as soon as we get to wherever it is that we're going; I promise."

Elmer sped up just a little bit. "Food court, that's where we're headed, Miss Darci. "Almost there. This one curve coming up is a tight squeeze." Elmer cocked his head a bit and took on the exaggerated tone of a movie studio tour guide, saying, "All hands and feet inside the vehicle at all times, please."

The group chuckled.

Mr. Abdullah stroked the leather trim that adorned the golf cart's interior. As if in a trance, he murmured, "I want one of these. Yes. Yes. This is going on my Christmas list for next year. My next new toy." He then leaned forward to address Elmer. "How did you ever get your hands on something like this, Elmer?"

Elmer beamed with pride. "She is a beauty, I know. Officially, she belongs to the mall. Unofficially, she's my baby. She makes getting around this place and hauling things from end to end, especially from down here, so much easier."

Elmer slowed down, expertly navigating the curve with the narrowest of widths that left no room for error.

242

Pastor Max took in a giant gulp of air. "Everybody, breathe in and lean in."

"No worries, Pastor Max. My baby's got this." As soon as Elmer cleared the corner, he increased speed and flashed an "I told you so" kind of smile to Max. He was enjoying playing chauffeur so much, fantasizing about driving his own brilliant white Mercedes Benz convertible, that he momentarily forgot about where he lived in reality. As he drove through the narrow passageway, he realized that his home was just up ahead in one of the alcoves—and he had no way of rerouting or hiding his secret from his fellow passengers.

Sure enough, it was too late to do anything about it, and the group set their sights on what looked like a homeless encampment. Clearly, someone was living here.

That someone was Elmer.

"Elmer, don't tell me you live down here," Pastor Max nearly tripped over his words as he took in the tell-tale signs of the supplies homeless people tended to collect: A folded blanket in need of a good wash, a foam pad to sleep on that looked a bit like Swiss cheese with all its divots and holes, a lumpy old pillow, and a couple of trash bags filled with clothes. He had seen folks sleeping on the streets more often than he cared to recall.

Darci twisted her body and raised her head to peer over Mr. Abdullah's shoulder. Her eyes scanned the sight. She then looked at Elmer, who stared stoneface straight ahead. Her voice was barely audible as she whispered, "Elmer, I don't know…"

He cut her off. "Miss Darci," Elmer explained, a slight stutter starting to creep into his speech as he did. "I keep my place picked up and never take anything I don't pay for. I'm not doing any harm."

She realized he feared some sort of accusation or punishment at her hand. "No, Elmer, it's okay." She caught herself. "I mean, it's not okay. But not in the way you think." She became a bit tongue-tied, swallowed to regroup, and then tried to sound as nonchalant as she could manage. "I just wish I had known. That's all. You have taken such good care of us when we should have been the ones taking better care of you."

CHAPTER THIRTY-NINE

IAN & HOLLY

What Makes You, You

Outside the mall, a reluctant and very vocal Ian was the last member of the group to climb aboard the fire truck. "I don't need anybody taking care of me," he shouted over his shoulder as the rig's door slammed shut behind him. He saw all the faces he had gotten to know over the last several hours staring back at him. Damian and Isabelle huddled intimately in the back corner. Andrea and Hank were curled up alongside Pickpocket and Rainbow, as Karina and Randy pet the animals. Leo and Betty took their places together on the fold-down chairs mounted against one of the side walls, just beneath the yellow pouches that held the firefighters' masks hanging from the hooks above. Ian could see they were holding hands. Vincent sat up front in the driver's seat. He was the only one not looking at Ian. He was enthralled with the controls that lit up the driver's dashboard. Ian knew what held his brother's full attention: Two red switches on the console. God, he hoped Vincent wouldn't touch anything he shouldn't. It was then that he realized Dr. Haywood was on the passenger's side sitting in the captain's seat. Ian exhaled, grateful for the doctor's watchful presence. Dr. Grey had been allowed to stay with the firefighters to help with Emily and the babies. It was the only way that Harry, who sat all alone in the shadows of the rig's rear, would agree to leave and come wait here. Each one of these people seemed to care more than they should about others. Why couldn't he?

Holly slid into one of the open seats next to Vi and Vern in the jump seat area of the truck. She let out a deep sigh of satisfaction, shutting her eyes and leaning back her head. "Heat," she said. A moment later, she opened up one eye as she sensed that Vi and Vern were staring at her intently, almost as if they were studying her face.

"You look so much like her," Vi said, reaching her hand out to touch her, but stopping short of actually doing it.

"Okay," Holly sprung forward in her seat, full-on alert. "Let's lay the cards on the table. Your daughter, Grace. You think she's my mom, don't you? Lay it on me. Looks like we're gonna be here a while, and I'm not a fan of mysteries."

Vern chuckled, "Just as spirited as she was, too." But then he grew somber. "Holly, we made mistakes with our Grace."

Vi tried to comfort her husband, "Vern, don't."

"No, Vi," he shook his head. "We did. Lots of them. We were so busy following what we thought was right, what we thought were the teachings of the Good Book. We were so afraid to be seen as less-than-perfect people." He stopped to stare into this stranger's eyes that were anything but unfamiliar. "We forgot the greatest lessons we were really meant to follow: Fear not; judge not; love all."

Holly scoffed, "My parents must have belonged to your same church."

Dr. Haywood had turned around and was eavesdropping on their conversation. He pointed to Ian who was still standing, lost in his own world. "Hey there, Ian. Hello?"

Ian snapped to and looked at him.

Unfolding his frame from the passenger's seat, Dr. Haywood rose from his chair and gestured with his hands to swap places with Ian. "Why don't you spend some time with your brother?" He stepped over the center console and through the row of jump seats, moving toward the back, just as Ian stepped toward the front.

Holly's glistening eyes connected with those of her old doctor, realizing with gratitude that he was, once again, coming to her rescue. She pointed at him and said to Vi and Vern, "Doc here was more of a parent to me than the ones who I actually got stuck with. Seems like that was maybe something else your Grace and I shared in common?"

Vi and Vern hung their heads in shame at her direct accusation.

Dr. Haywood looked over at them, then at Holly. He knelt down to face her and spoke softly, "Holly, why not hear what they have to say?"

"Why bother?" Holly fired back. "What does it matter now? Even if it's true, and I am their grandkid, my whole childhood was messed up because of their daughter—my *mom*, I guess. She was just another parent who didn't care enough to keep me. And now…what…? She gave me away to two people who cared even less than she apparently did. When I needed help, they decided the best thing to do was lock me away!"

"She cared," Vi's voice trembled. "Grace wanted to keep the baby. I was the one…"

Vern interrupted, gripping hold of Vi's hand. "No… *We. We* were the ones."

Holly tried to hold back angry tears, but she failed. Vi reached over and, very gently, wiped away the tiny trail that started to run down her cheek. "I'm so sorry, Holly," she said. "I worried more about what the congregation would say about an unwed pregnancy, and so I made Grace give the baby away. It was the biggest mistake of my life." She paused and stared off into the distance. "It ended up destroying her to the point where she couldn't take it anymore."

Holly caught her breath. She pulled up her sleeve to reveal the scarred-over cuts on her wrists. "Grace did herself in?"

Vi and Vern clutched each other's hands again.

"What a messed-up family!" Holly turned her face away.

Dr. Haywood repositioned himself so that he could connect with her eye-to-eye. "That's right, Holly. It might be *your* family. Families aren't perfect. It's possible that a family can mess up sometimes and will probably mess up again…just like you will. Just like every one of us does almost every day." He paused, tired of her avoiding his gaze. With his index finger, he gently tilted up her chin, connecting and communicating face-to-face without uttering a single word. Gently, he said, "Holly, when are you going to stop wishing for a better past? 'Cause you're never going to get it. But right now, you *might* have this… a chance at reconnecting and who knows what else in the future? Isn't that worth something?"

While the intense conversation progressed between Dr. Haywood, Holly, Vi, and Vern, Ian sat up front with Vincent in a very awkward silence. He turned to spark a conversation, but nothing coming to mind seemed worth saying.

"I'm sorry, Ian," Vincent barely whispered the words; his gaze still fixated on the dash. Ian leaned in closer to hear his brother. "You're sorry? Buddy, what do you have to be sorry about? You don't owe me any apologies. If anything, I owe you one."

"I called you a liar."

Ian hung his head and chuckled. "Yes, you did. And I am, or, I should say, I was."

"I called you a *nothing*."

Swinging his head from side to side, he turned to face Vincent. "Yes, you did. But it's okay, Vince. I know you didn't mean it."

Vince turned to face Ian, nodding his head and in the sincerest of tones said, "Yes, I did. I did mean it when I said it."

Ian winced at his brother's honesty. "Ouch!" He then thought a moment and said, "You know what? That's what I thought about myself, too, earlier today. I'm a nothing. A big giant nothing."

"But you're not," Vincent jumped in. "I was wrong, Ian." He once again looked up at his brother with his adoring coal-colored eyes. "You're not nothing because you're my brother. You're always going to be my brother and that's something. A big something to me."

Ian never thought of himself as having a true purpose, especially not one that mattered so much to someone else. Vincent thought he was important—his life meant something—just by being there. Ian snickered at his brother, thinking how ironic it was that Vincent was now the teacher and he the student. At the thought of it, Ian spontaneously leapt up out of his chair and wrapped Vincent into his arms. He let himself hug his brother and be hugged in return, squeezing his eyes shut. It felt so good. Finally, he was so proud to have Vince as his brother.

Several moments later, Vincent piped up. "Okay, Ian, you can let go now. You're sort of smothering me."

Throwing his head back in laughter, Ian released Vincent, knowing that this was the first time in his life that he wasn't the first one to break loose from a hug.

"Hey, you know what I didn't yet open?" Ian reached into his camera equipment bag and retrieved Vincent's gift to him. "The gift you threw at me."

Vincent objected. "No, I gave it to you."

"Well, okay, you did. But, technically, you threw it at me."

Vincent nodded. "I did. I threw it at you because you deserved it."

"Well, good thing I can catch. Okay if I open it?"

Vincent nodded. "I made it just for you."

Ian unwrapped the ribbon from the slightly bent, brown box and pulled off its lid.

Already, Vincent was bouncing in his seat, applauding.

Ian looked inside the box, then reached into it with two fingers and pulled out six, large puzzle pieces. Each piece was made of wood and stamped with a part of a photograph.

"I made it in arts and crafts for you," Vincent said, directing his brother with both hands to take action. "Put it together."

Ian set the pieces out on the wide dashboard in front of him and got to work. In seconds, he locked each piece, one hooking into the other, to reveal the image.

"It's you and me," Vincent exclaimed. "Remember? Before mom and dad died."

Ian looked down at the younger versions of themselves. Two brothers. Laughing and making snow angels side-by-side in the front lawn.

"Vincent..." Ian barely whispered.

"You like it?" Vince squealed. "It was hard to make all the pieces fit together."

"It's perfect, Vince. It's the best gift I've ever gotten."

While the two brothers were talking, Holly couldn't help herself. She had quietly crept up on them and was doing her best to videotape them from behind without their knowledge. The camera angles were horrible, and maybe she wouldn't get anything useable for her reel, but she *had* to tell this part of their story.

Then, the back doors of the rig slowly eased open. The grinding metal door hinges sounded like the aching moans of something prehistoric. With the rush of cold and snow flurries that swept inside the truck, so, too, did the voice of Emily. "Harry?"

Harry lifted his head at the sweet sound of his wife calling his name. A second later, he vaulted his way over to her.

Holly immediately swung around and positioned herself perfectly to capture Harry and Emily's reunion on film, and dad's first meeting with his two newborns.

With firefighters at her side for support, there Emily stood in the doorway, carrying two bundles, one in each of her arms. Harry choked on his words, unable to say anything but the very start of her name. "Em—"

The firefighters lifted Emily and the babies up and into the truck.

"Oh, Harry!" She exclaimed, he embraced her and his two tiny children.

"Waaaahhhhh!" One of the babies started wailing, which only prompted the other one to join in.

Harry took a tiny step back to look at his newborns. "They're so small." With tears in his eyes, he looked up at Emily.

She laughed, "And so loud!"

"Here, Em," Harry ushered her and the babies to the back, helping her take a seat. "You rest. Let me help."

Dr. Grey stepped into the firetruck and climbed her way over to the crying twins. "Good, strong, healthy lungs! Healthy momma, too." She paused a moment to check on the new little family. She stroked the second baby's peach fuzz on its head. "Where were you hiding little man?" She marveled, shaking her head. "Two! What a little miracle you are." The babies stopped their wailing. "Both of you."

The firefighter outside the rig gently prompted, "Folks, if you all could step as far in as possible so we can get everybody inside where it's warm." He then helped Darci, Elmer, and Pastor Max aboard.

"Betty!" Darci lit up at the sight of her own personal Mrs. Claus.

"Darci, dear," Betty reached out to pull her into an embrace. "I'm so thankful you're okay." She then looked over Darci's shoulder at the others. "That you're all okay."

Darci pulled the Elf on the Shelf out of her pocket and presented him to Betty. "This little guy would have it no other way!" She handed him over to her. "And Elmer. He's the one who got us out of there. Betty, we need to talk about him."

Betty nodded as Pastor Max announced, "Here come the kids." He stood just inside the still-open doors of the fire truck, pointing to the 50 foster kids marching out of the mall and toward the fire engines.

"Ooooo!" Elmer hooted, as he joined Pastor Max at the doorway awaiting the kids' arrival. "Those are some unhappy campers."

"Well they're about to get unhappier," Holly quipped, her video camera capturing the troops trekking toward them. She then looked around at the already cramped quarters in the rear of the truck. "Hate to be cliché, but there ain't no more room at the inn here. Where are they planning on puttin' them?"

Elmer shrugged. "Good question." He then turned to Pastor Max and started laughing. "Did you see their faces when those firemen told them to stop cooking and start moving out?"

Pastor Max nodded. "Cooking!" He chuckled. "I had no idea these kids even knew how to turn on the stove."

"Who said they did?" Elmer joined in, laughing at the irony of it all.

"I always tell the guys at the Kitchen, 'Where there's a whisk, there's a way'!" Pastor Max sung out.

"As long as you have the secret ingredient," Elmer added. "Love."

"Amen!" Pastor Max put his hand on Elmer's shoulder, looked up to the Heavens, and shouted out, "Preach, brother." He then paused a moment and in a more serious tone said, "When we get out of here and things settle down, I think you and I should talk, Elmer. Maybe there's something I can put together for you to work at the Open Kitchen?"

Elmer nodded, then turned his attention again to the parking lot outside, watching with growing excitement the kids and his potential future marching toward him. He nearly missed what else was traveling toward them in the parking lot until Ian called out from the front of the rig.

"What in the world is all that?" Ian shouted, pointing out the front windshield of the fire truck. Damian and Isabelle rose from their seats, making their way to the front for a better look. Everyone peered outside, marveling at the cavalry: Leading the way with their emergency lights flashing, lighting up the night sky, was a trio of ambulances and massive bookmobile vehicles.

Damian laughed, "I guess those are going to be our make-shift housing units until they can get us all out of here."

"Look at that line of cars, and—" Isabelle stopped short of finishing her sentence as she squinted at one huge silver truck in particular at the head of the pack. Three passengers inside seemed to be waving frantically *at her*.

Watching her reaction, Damian chuckled. "What...? What are you looking at?"

Tears trickled down her cheeks, as Isabelle started waving back just as enthusiastically at the approaching vehicle's trio. "Oh, my God, Damian. Those are my nieces, Maddie and Lauren. And I can't believe it, but that's my sister Ivy driving that truck."

Before Damian could even respond, Isabelle bounded out of the rig. He watched as the silver truck fell out of line and stopped abruptly. Three women flung open their doors, stepped out into the cold, and hopped as best they could through the snow-covered parking lot towards Isabelle, all of them meeting somewhere in the middle for a major group hug. Damian swallowed back the lump in his throat. Maybe this was the year he would try reconnecting with his own family.

The line of vehicles plowed through the two-lane path that had been created by the fire engine. Behind them, Ian could see a news van, but it wasn't one of theirs. Its side door was open with what looked like a video camera peeking out. Someone inside must be holding it and taking footage.

Behind that, however, was what had caught Ian's eye the most. For as far as he could see, there were dozens of headlights shining through the darkness belonging to all sorts of vehicles. He had a hard time believing it, but it looked as if strangers had decided to get into their cars and SUVs and pickup trucks to come to the mall and be part of this whole wacky Christmas Eve experience.

"Look, Ian!" Vincent gleefully shouted. "It's the news guy with the beautiful Christmas sweater we saw earlier today!"

Ian squinted. He couldn't help but grin. "You're right, Vince. It is him. I'd recognize that ugly sweater anywhere!"

Holly wiggled her way to the front. Peering over Ian's shoulder she half-snorted. "Carter's gonna freak. You want to join me outside for all this?"

With a laugh that put her at ease, Ian turned. "Let's let ugly sweater guy get one win tonight. Or at least a head start. I'll meet you out there in fifteen. We already have our own story—a pretty great one—to share," he said. He looked toward the back of the rig once again at the people that he now considered to be family and friends. Only a few minutes ago he couldn't grasp the bonds the others had created today, but with Vince's gift, and Holly's new friendship, he now completely understood.

Holly nodded and turned to head outside with her camera when the fire captain, the man who had been barking orders earlier, addressed the group.

"Everyone," the firefighter began. "We've got a couple more units coming just around the corner. They'll be here in a few minutes so we can safely take all of you back to your homes. It's been a long day for all of us." He looked at his watch. "Actually, a long couple of days, since it's now officially Christmas Day."

"Excuse me," Darci stepped forward. "I don't see my father, Mr. Malcom Wiggins?"

Damian joined Darci, adding, "He's the older gentleman we thought may have tried to…"

"…Right." The firefighter raised his hand, stopping Damian from continuing. "I remember. And you were right. He tried to be a hero."

Damian instinctively put his arm around Darci's shoulders.

The firefighter looked at Darci's expectant expression. "That last collapse in the building...Your father didn't make it, Miss. I'm sorry. We found him inside."

As Betty, Leo, Pastor Max, and the others moved to surround Darci, all she could do was stand in a dazed silence. So many emotions swept across her face as her thoughts raced to process what the firefighter just said.

Your father didn't make it.

Stunned momentarily, Darci struggled with a swirl of emotions she hadn't expected. Slowly pulling her cell phone out from her pocket, she looked at the screen. A notification still appeared, reminding her of the voicemail message she had yet to hear.

CHAPTER FORTY

FRIENDS & FAMILY

One Year Later

Tapping her iPad with her stylus pen, Darci felt the car slowing to a stop. That didn't deter her, however, from continuing to work.

Her driver looked into his rearview mirror, knowing full well he'd have to say something with his "outside voice" to get his regular passenger's attention.

"What a difference a year makes, eh, Ms. Timbers?" his expressive eyes waited for hers to acknowledge his words. It always took a minute or two for her to be fully present; he was used to it.

A moment later, finally looking up, Darci responded. "Yes, Joe." Looking out the window, she smiled at how much Maplefield Mall had changed—and how much she, too, had grown. She turned back to Joe, saying, "And you'd think after just about a year as my driver, you'd call me by my first name." Her confident gaze met his, a tiny smile and a wink made him as nervous as a schoolboy. He looked out his side window. Darci followed his lead.

Darci loved this time of the morning, the moments where darkness gave way to light. This very break of day, when the morning sun emerged, always started her off with the feeling that anything was possible if she just believed it.

As she raised her left arm, she glanced at her rose gold Apple Watch and noted the time. She had just a few more minutes to wait until the Heavens started painting on their canvas in a design that she thought looked like pink and blue angel's wings. Today, on this Christmas Eve, the emerging picture in the sky did not disappoint; it was more miraculous than ever.

"Whoa! Look at that, Darci. You seeing what I'm seeing?" Joe pointed to the wisps of clouds taking shape. He lowered his window. "You let me know if this gets too cold for you."

Darci shook her head in response, curiously peering out at the sky, while trying to roll down her own window which wasn't cooperating. "Window's locked, Joe."

Joe looked back as he lowered Darci's window for her. "My kids," he explained. "Gotta childproof things when chauffeuring them around."

Darci poked her head outside and watched the undeniable heart-shaped cloud that hovered above. "Merry Christmas, Mom…and Dad," she whispered.

As she looked up at the beautiful sky, the scores of shoppers gathered outside of Maplefield Mall's main entrance patiently stood in the line that wrapped its way around the mall farther than either of them could see. Few were wearing coats given the unseasonably warm weather predicted for the day.

"It's supposed to be a high of 60!" Joe exclaimed. "They're saying we might even break a record."

Darci leaned back into her seat, raising the window as she did so. "I don't know about that, Joe. You can't really predict the weather. It's one of those things that even when you think the numbers add up, you can never really be sure they do. Nature does what nature does." Gathering her jacket and other belongings, she opened her door and handed Joe a $100 bill. "Merry Christmas to you and the family, Joe!" She stepped out of the car.

He looked at her generous gift and then at her with a grateful smile. "Same to you, Darci."

Darci exited the car and stood for a moment, watching him drive away. When his vanity license plate, I DRV DRC, became barely visible, she gave a tiny salute with her free hand. With the other, she tried to get a better grip on her father's old Italian fur duffel bag and headed toward the mall's entrance.

"Merry Christmas, Darci!" Excited shoppers called out to her. "No need for a snow shovel this year, right Darci?" Another shouted out. "Or an ambulance!" Someone else added.

Darci laughed and nodded in response. "Maybe we should hold Pastor Max's Christmas Eve Kids Cheer Fest outside this year?"

The crowd chimed in. "Sure, why not?" One voice shouted. And another added, "Anything's possible!"

Elmer, sporting his signature mirrored shades, had already swung the front door open, holding it for Darci to pass through. As he waited for her to reach him, he removed his glasses. Turning his emerald green eyes to the crowd, he, too, greeted the waiting shoppers. "How ya'll doin' on this fine spring day?"

They chuckled with their responses. "Sure does feel like spring!" They showered him with their season's greetings.

As she crossed the threshold, Darci grinned with satisfaction. "Thank you, Elmer. Boy, was Betty ever right. You are the guy to see here at the mall. With all those keys on your ring, it's clear you're the one to know to gain entry to those Pearly Gates!"

Elmer jingled his keys, "Just taking care of my family," he quipped, a wide grin on his face. "Ms. Bryant's already inside."

He shut and locked the door behind Darci. She paused just a moment longer and pulled a large black and white envelope from her bag. It almost looked like a tuxedo jacket with its color-blocked design. "I don't want to forget to give you this," she said as she handed it to him. "A superhero needs to be outfitted appropriately. This is just a little something to help you buy something tailor-made for your college graduation."

"Aww, Ms. Darci, you didn't have to do anything." He couldn't help but notice that the envelope, with its squared-off, hard-edged design, was the complete opposite of the festive paint-splatter print she wore.

"No, I didn't." She nodded, leaned in and patted his forearm. "Neither did you."

Elmer used the envelope as a prop to "tip his hat" to the woman who now managed the mall. He watched Darci turn on her heel and glide across the main lobby which, this year, was decorated with more lights than ever before. This year's holiday theme was This Little Light—and it topped last year's decorations, at least in Elmer's opinion. He loved how everywhere he looked he could see a single point of light cascading into a string of blue icicles. Then as if dancing to a silent tune, the lights would swirl across the floor and ceiling to become tiny beads of red and gold. His absolute favorite moment of the light show was when all the lights joined together to form a single bright white star, which then magically separated and transformed into the image of the Milky Way overhead. Even his underground web of tunnels was transformed into a labyrinth of sparkling surprises; no longer secret or closed to the public, it was now part of a ticketed experience that became extremely popular over the past year.

Of course, it did take him some getting used to—no longer hiding out in such living arrangements. He loved where he lived now; Pastor Max set him up in his own apartment. He never would have predicted in a million years that he'd be surrounded by so many people who cared about him. No longer was he isolated and lonely. Instead, he was Uncle Elmer to Harry and Emily's beautiful babies. For the first time in his life, Elmer could finally say he felt seen and was part of a real family.

Inside the mall, in the newly renovated Games & Gadgets Galore store, Mr. Abdullah greeted his staff as he proudly walked through the store and to his expanded back office. Opening the door and entering into the room, he beamed at the little family inside that he had helped to bring into this world. Staying silent, he watched undetected.

"Peek-a-boo!" Harry puckered his lips as he pulled his hands away from his eyes. The sound of giggling made him laugh out loud. He cupped both his hands, covering them again. Seconds later, he jazz-handed them away and, in the baby-talk-voice he had perfected over the last twelve months, once again sung out his high-pitched, "Peek-a-boo!"

His twins sat in their identical carriers on the coffee table in front of the very same couch where they were born and where Harry now sat facing them. As they squealed in delight, their entire little bodies shook with pure joy.

"I could do this with you all day," Harry lovingly gazed in awe at his one-year-old little miracles. He reached out both his hands—one to caress the peach-fuzzy head of his youngest child, his son Mack, and the other to tussle the jet-black curls of his eldest—by a full 17 minutes—his daughter, Elle. "The sound of you two giggling will never get old."

"Harry, keep peek-a-booing; Don't stop," said Emily as she walked over to where they sat. Sounding like an encyclopedia reference, she recited a passage from memory: "The *What to Expect* book said that 'Peekaboo stimulates baby's senses, builds gross motor skills, strengthens visual tracking, encourages social development and, best of all, tickles their sense of humor. It's not just a game. It's teaching your babies about object permanence: The idea that even though they can't see something,'" Emily paused to adlib: "Like your husband's handsome smiling face," She winked at Harry. "'...it still exists.' AND I'm getting this all on video."

Harry looked up at his wife and her oversized eye gear that practically covered her entire face. The sound of what was also now familiar to him—the buzz of his drone that seemed to mimic a lawnmower-on-helium—grew in volume. Out of the corner of his eye, he could see it making its descent from up above. The babies saw it too, as their laughter gave way to grunts and growls. The white little aircraft hovered just off to Harry's side, its camera documenting the babies' every move.

"Emily, I think it's going to make them cry again," Harry shook his head with a knowing look of what was surely coming.

"Almost done, Sweetie." Emily, her eyes hidden behind the drone's FPV goggles, tip-toed closer to her little family, accidentally bumping her hip into the sofa's armrest. "Ouch!"

The babies' eyebrows rose as their eyes grew wide. Their little faces sported skewed expressions that made Harry laugh even louder at what he assumed was the reason—his wife's bug-eyes.

"I take it back; the drone is not going to make them cry again." Harry rose to his feet and wrapped Emily in his arms. He then pulled back just enough to gently remove the goggles from her face. He looked into the eyes he loved so much. "You and these freaky-looking glasses are."

Emily's hazel eyes carried an ever-present look of childlike wonder—a trait that both Mack and Elle inherited from her. "Freaky-looking glasses?" She feigned offense. "I'll have you know that these are cockpit glasses with full immersion monitoring." She grew completely serious. "You must have one phenomenal wife if this is the gift she gave you for Christmas last year."

Harry kissed her. He could do that all day, too. Then he grabbed her by her shoulders with both hands, looked into her eyes, and said, "You're right. I do have one phenomenal wife. But not because she gave me the Parrot Bebop 2 Quadcopter with Skycontroller 2 and Cockpit FPV Glasses for Christmas last year." He paused a moment, cocked one eyebrow and whispered, "Let's set aside the fact that I rarely get to play with it because she is always flying it around."

"I'm sorry, did you say something?" Emily cupped her ear in jest.

Harry tossed back his head, laughing. "I have a phenomenal wife because the real gifts she gave me were these two adorable munchkins... and her heart"

Both Harry and Emily looked over at their beautiful babies bouncing away in their chairs staring back at their parents as if, somehow, they understood the conversation about the love they all shared.

Suddenly, the whirl of the still-hovering drone began to sputter and cough; before Emily could work the controls, it crash-landed, right into the Baby Trend Sit N' Stand Tandem Stroller that Mr. Abdullah and his wife gave to them as a gift.

Mr. Abdullah tee-heed, and only then did Harry and Emily notice he was in the room.

"Oh, Mr. Abdullah," Emily walked over and gave him a hug.

Harry followed, first shaking his hand and then grabbing him in a bear hug.

Just then, the office door swung open and shoved Mr. Abdullah and Harry mid-hug, almost toppling over. In walked Randy, dressed from head-to-toe in what had become his signature jolly green elf costume, carrying a tray of batteries.

"Oh, hey, sorry, boss," Randy set down the tray to help steady Mr. Abdullah, who then stabilized Harry.

"Randy, how many times have I told you, son, to not go charging into places?"

"I know," the adult-sized elf responded. "Hey, it's the babies," he added lumbering over to where the twins played.

Mr. Abdullah smiled, joining him, stopping in front of Mack and Elle. He leaned over until he was eye-to-eye with the babies and began making funny faces at them. "When my missus insisted on buying you this Baby Trend Sit N' Stand Tandem Stroller, I didn't argue." "After all, with six of these little ones under her belt, she is the expert." He then straightened his frame, turned to the stroller itself and retrieved the fallen drone. "And while it is designed with cup holders and a tray to keep mom and dad's phone, keys, and drinks from getting lost, it is not intended to double as a landing strip for unmanned aerial vehicles."

Harry poked his head outside the still-open office door, motioning to the cherry red golf cart with the giant glittery bow perched on top parked in the corner of the store. Mr. Abdullah turned to follow his gaze just in time to see his own wife—his own very pregnant wife—break up a scuffle between their six children, all of whom were jockeying for a seat in his vehicle. "I don't think your new toy is intended to seat nine!"

"Oh!" Mr. Abdullah shrieked at the sight. "Children!" he shouted, as his wife giggled—something that only served to make him laugh as well.

"Hey…" Harry said to Mr. Abdullah in a low voice. "It's my missus who's hooked on that baby stroller you gave her. But next year, I'm expecting one of those…" He pointed to the golf cart. "…under my tree. So do your wife-whispering, Christmas gift-giving thing, ya hear?"

Mr. Abdullah exaggerated a wink.

"Oh, poo. What are you two conspiring about?" Emily caught a glimpse of the new toy she figured was part of their little conspiracy. "Wow!" She said, her eyes taking in the entire store. "I just love how you two renovated this place."

"Your Harry did all the work and such a marvelous job! So smart for you to start your own firm. Gives you more time to spend with your family and look after the other things that matter."

A younger, more tentative voice cut through. "Excuse me, speaking of poo," Randy said. He balanced the tray with one hand and fanned the store's sales flyer under his nose with the other. "I think one of your babies needs an oil change or something. Pew!"

"I got it!" Emily moved toward the stroller and pulled out diapers and wet wipes and a changing mat from the bag resting in the bottom compartment. "Which one of you is it?" She asked her cherub-faced little ones who squealed in response. She knelt down until her nose was at just the right level to give each of her children a proper sniff test. She saw Randy cover his nose and mouth with his hand, holding back from tossing his cookies. While she wanted to laugh and jokingly torture the boy who she had come to know well, Emily herself got a whiff of the foul odor and gagged. "Okay, Mack, you're it!" She began unbuckling her son and lifting him from his seat.

"What's with the tray of batteries?" Harry asked, turning to Randy.

"Mr. Abdullah has me practicing thinking ahead," Randy shrugged his shoulders. "When he said that you all were coming today for Pastor Max's party, I figured it was a smart move to plan ahead with alternative power sources. You know, just in case, 'cause of what happened last year."

Mr. Abdullah rolled his eyes. "Randy's working his way up the ladder here. Lots of opportunities to grow." He then leaned over to Harry and whispered, "Hopefully mentally and not physically." He patted Randy on the back. "Consider these batteries to be this year's Games & Gadgets Galore giveaway. Free with every purchase."

Harry nodded and grabbed one of the gifts. "Great idea, Elf! Now help me find one of those baby-cams to sit on the nursery shelf. Get it? Elf? Shelf?" Harry slapped his own knee, clearly amused with his humor.

Randy rolled his eyes.

With a wink, and a chuckle, Mr. Abdullah put one arm around Harry and the other arm around Randy. "Lots of opportunities to grow. For us all."

In another part of the mall, not far from Games & Gadgets Galore, music pulsed throughout the Burn Baby Burn Bootcamp Fitness Studio. The 1970's disco tune of the same name boomed through the speakers, vibrating the walls and fitness flooring of the wide-open space.

Dr. Haywood, dressed appropriately for the season in his baby blue medical scrubs featuring dancing snowflakes and snowmen, couldn't help but move his body to the music. As he mouthed the words "burn baby burn," he clapped his hands and spun around, working the room of senior citizens and disabled participants, each one dressed in their own exercise suit, and all of whom stood shoulder-to-shoulder, row-after-row, waiting for class to officially begin. Showing off his best *Saturday Night Fever* moves, Dr. Haywood focused his attention mostly on Vi, Vern, and Vincent; all three were in the front row bopping along to the music.

Damian and Isabelle stood together off to the side, just under the announcement banner that read: Grand Opening! Maplefield Mall Burn Baby Burn Bootcamp Fitness Studio.

"You know this is all because of you and your bad influence on me, right?" Damian asked her.

"I'm just shepherding black sheep," Isabelle lowered her head and narrowed her eyes seductively. "I consider it part of my corporate social responsibility."

The two kissed but separated a moment later when they heard a somewhat embarrassed voice chastising them, "Shoot! You both be needin' to get a room."

They opened their eyes to see a fly, yet professional, Karina at their side. Her signature hoop earrings and Mexican-inspired clothing now gave way to a black and white ensemble. She wore an oversized black sweatshirt with white lettering that read, *"Cool Story, Bro. Now Go Make Me A Sandwich,"* and a chunky beanie with the words *"You Wish"* written across its folded brim. Her bright-red fingernails, trimmed to work-friendly lengths, clashed with the neon-orange, 50-foot, heavy-duty extension cord coiled over her shoulder. Clicking her tongue, she used her free hand to pull the walkie-talkie off of her belt loop, press the side button, and speak quietly into it. "Karina for Holly, I got them both."

A moment later, Holly's voice came over the walkie-talkie's speaker. "We're ready when they are."

Karina looked Damian and Isabelle up and down, then broke into a smile. Her confidence and excitement were contagious. "You ready?"

"Yup. Lead the way," Damian nodded.

Karina spun on her heel, hugging the wall to stay out of the camera's view. She directed the two across the room where Holly was hunched over her video camera, watching Ian's interview with Dr. Grey through her viewfinder. Holly looked over at Karina, and waved her, Damian, and Isabelle to her side. She placed an index finger over her lips, letting them all know to stay silent.

Ian held the microphone up towards Dr. Grey, as she continued speaking.

"As an OB/GYN, I love helping to bring babies into this world," she said. "They bring such promise and possibilities! I think that should be true for everyone from cradle to grave. For older adults and people with disabilities, the number-one priority must be maintaining their quality of life. Movement has such a positive impact on both the body and mind. I'm very encouraged by the programs being put in place here." Dr. Grey gestured toward the dance fest with Vi, Vern, Vincent, Dr. Haywood, and so many others appearing in the background. "Helping people find their fountain of youth, so to speak, starts with keeping the body and mind at play. Workouts designed to help build strength, retain mobility, and improve balance and stability are great for everyone regardless of age. I'm thrilled to be putting my skills to work here as a new mall board member, and it's exciting being part of the team bringing together so many people from all walks of life for so many good reasons."

"Thank you, Dr. Grey." Ian addressed the viewing audience on camera, gesturing behind him to the exercise class in progress, "This time last year, none of this was here. So much is different this Christmas Eve, from our unseasonably warm weather outside today, to the restructuring and renovations that have been made here at the mall, to the new programs and experiences that are responsible for Maplefield Mall's unprecedented growth—all under the direction of newly appointed mall manager, Darci Timbers. We'll be talking to her later on this evening when we broadcast live from the annual Christmas Eve Kids Cheer Fest."

Ian motioned to Damian and Isabelle to join him. The two moved to stand beside Ian.

Suddenly, the youthful voices of two very excited girls called out, "Aunt Izzy!"

Isabelle turned toward the sound just in time to see her nieces, Lauren and Maddie, along with her sister Ivy, waving from just outside the entryway. Isabelle beamed and waved back. She then exchanged a happy smile with Damian. Ian, addressing the crowd, returned their attention back to the interview at hand.

"We're here with two well-known figures—the founder of the 'Burn Baby Burn Bootcamps' and a nationally recognized expert in corporate social responsibility. These two have partnered together to start a movement that goes beyond exercise classes and end-of-year corporate giving programs. Damian and Isabelle, what news have you to share with our WACK-TV fans?"

In the WACK-TV newsroom, Carter sported a cheery Santa hat and munched on his beloved candy canes while sitting at a large, round table in the center of the room. Surrounded by his entire team, Carter had taken it upon himself to host the scrumptious Christmas Eve feast spread out before them. The monitors overhead projected Ian's interview with Damian and Isabelle at the mall. More monitors hung in full view showing other local news station feeds, each one broadcasting Ian at the mall with a banner underneath that read: Courtesy of WACK-TV.

"It's about time Ian actually mentioned our call letters!" Carter barked.

Back at the fitness center, Isabelle and Damian continued to share their vision with Ian, the media, the TV viewers, and the audience in attendance.

"That's right, Ian," Isabelle confirmed. "We realized we had to do something, given the growth of our aging population and our adults in need of behavioral health services. WE needed to be the solution that promotes sustainability of senior citizen housing and behavioral health care centers, our providers and health care systems, and ultimately the broader communities around them."

Damian chimed in, "Which is how we ended up here, developing what we like to call 'the mall on a mission.'"

Isabelle continued, "So we've evolved the concept of corporate social responsibility to enter into strategic partnerships with all sorts of organizations nationwide to create health care networks, infrastructures, and environments that deliver better quality care, promote health and wellness, and offer innovative approaches to living with physical or mental disabilities and conditions—especially those associated with aging. Companies who invest in our programs not only contribute significantly to the betterment of society, but they are also likely to save on costs and generate more revenue due to the health and productivity benefits of a workforce that's more healthy overall—both in body and mind—AND a local community that's much more active, engaged, and inclusive."

Damian nodded, "Right. It matters less and less about our differences because we are aiming to focus more and more on our commonalities, no matter our gender or what we look like, what age we might be, what physical condition we find ourselves, or what socioeconomic status we hold…"

There was an eruption of excitement and awe from the crowd that interrupted Damian's speech when Pickpocket yelped out a throaty WOOF! and Rainbow joined in with her equally loud SCREECH! Everyone in the Burn Baby Burn studio gawked at the giant-sized American Staffordshire Terrier and the all-white Moluccan Cockatoo that entered the facility together. Playfully teasing one another as they flew and bounded among the exercising bodies and camera equipment, the mismatched woman and man who were following them seemed to also be playing a similar game.

"Your big, strong dog is such a naughty boy," Andrea batted her eyelashes at Hank.

"How can he resist the beauty and grace of his fine-feathered friend," Hank responded taking Andrea's hand and walking with her right in front of Holly's camera frame. They both paused for a moment, oblivious to all that was going on around them, and kissed.

The entire room came alive, cheering and applauding the unknown couple.

"Oh, my!" a shy and embarrassed Andrea ducked behind Hank who broadened his shoulders and puffed out his chest in a gallant, yet comical, effort to help her hide.

"We," Hank began, without a clue what he was going to say. "Well… our bird and dog…" He then focused on the camera and on Ian. "Oh, crap! Are we on TV?" He readjusted himself and gently moved Andrea out from behind him and to his side. With one big inhale, he blurted out, "Hi, I'm Hank. This is Andrea, pronounced *On-Drey-A*. We just opened up the Fur and Feathers rescue pet store here in Maplefield Mall. Come on in and visit us. We'll match you up with your perfect pet."

"Thank you," Ian grinned but gently shuffled them along.

Rainbow and Pickpocket circled their caregivers, tangling everyone up in wires and threatening to pull down the lights and camera equipment.

Even Holly had somehow gotten twisted up in the mess of it all, and almost lost her footing. But Vi and Vern stepped in just in the nick of time, saving her from a fall. Whether they were or weren't related, the trio were just fine not knowing for sure. Spending time together over the past year helped them both heal past wounds and forge new relationships. Now, they were a family, for better or for worse.

Leo and Pastor Max stood just outside all the commotion in the fitness studio, alternating between wide-eyed wonder and shoulder scrunching winces.

"I suppose I should step in and do something," Leo remarked to his friend, unable to take his eyes off of the scene unfolding in front of them, which was looking more and more like an episode of some reality TV Christmas caper starring the Keystone Cops. He took one step forward, saying, "The more things change…"

Pastor Max extended his arm out sideways in front of his friend, blocking his way. Placing his hand on Leo's chest, he held him gently back. In the most serious of tones, he finished his sentence for him: "…the more they're exactly as they should be."

The two howled in laughter. Leo wiped at his moist eyes, accidentally noticing the time on his wristwatch. "Oh, jeepers. Look at the time. If I don't change into my Santa suit and head over to the party, Mrs. Claus is going to demote me to elf status."

Max erupted again in a belly laugh that had him doubling over. "You… Right…That suit…"

"Ha. Ha." Leo shook his head and uttered as he walked away, "Keep laughing, buddy." Which was exactly what Max did.

"Just remember," Leo called out over his shoulder. "He who laughs last…"

"…didn't get the joke!" Max could barely spit out the words he was laughing so hard.

Backstage, Darci sang out, hugging her iPad to her chest, and twirling around like a toddler on Christmas morning. "They're ALL coming!"

"Who's all coming, dear?" Betty tapped her black, patent leather boots, the pointy tips of which peeked out from underneath her white petticoats and brilliant red skirt. With both her hands, she impatiently smoothed down her bodice and picked at the furry edges of wispy white fur, swirls of gold filigree, and sprinkles of glitter that made her feel as if she really was Mrs. Claus. "Oh, where *is* he?!" She exhaled in a bit of frustration.

"He who?" Darci stopped her twirling to ask.

"Leo. I doubt he's even dressed yet. We're supposed to be the first thing guests see when they enter. And where are our elves?"

Darci laughed at how much their roles had reversed. Betty used to be the calm, cool, collected one while she was the one who was more prone to fret. What a difference a year had made. "Don't worry, Betty. Santa will not be a no-show this year. Everyone is going to be a…" She trailed off and then pondered out loud, "A show-show? A show-up? Showstopper? Show-man?"

Betty chuckled. "Okay, okay, Darci. Ms. Show-off."

"Oh, except for Elf Karina. She's with the TV crew now."

"Can we manage with just Elf Randy?" Betty propped up the familiar wire-rimmed glasses onto the bridge of her nose.

Darci pulled the Elf on the Shelf out from where he was hiding just underneath the leaves of the Christmas cactus sitting on the little table nearby. He seemed to like hiding in that spot on Christmas Eve. "Look what I found? Does this elf count?"

Betty reached out to take the little green guy. It was then that she noticed. "Darci, look!" She pointed to the red flower beginning to bloom on her plant.

The two leaned over to examine it more closely.

"How does it do that?" Darci wondered. "How does it know it's time for it to magically bloom at Christmas?"

"I guess it's just one of life's little miracles," Betty whispered. "Some, we may never know or fully understand." She paused, thinking. "Do we still not know who keeps positioning that Elf on the Shelf each year?"

Darci shook her head. "I think it's got to be Elmer, but he still says no."

Betty straightened up. "Well, maybe we're not meant to know. You know, that's okay with me."

Darci joined her stating decisively, "Me, too."

Betty fondly looked over at Darci. "Your father *did* love you. He just didn't know how to both love *and* lose someone he loved—*and* be okay with all the other emotions that come with being human."

"I know," Darci said quietly. "It was his choice. He said as much on that last voicemail he left me." Darci paused. "He must have known he wasn't going to make it out alive. He started out saying, 'Darci, this is your father!'" She fought to hold back tears.

"That was very Darth Vader of him!" Betty joked, trying to ease her friend's grief.

"Ya, think?" Darci rolled her eyes. "He said that he knew I wasn't picking up my phone intentionally and that he totally understood why. He said most people didn't want to talk to him, and he understood why that was, too. He wanted me to make the kinds of choices he said he didn't have it in him to make without my mom at his side. He said he thanked God every day that I was just like her."

Betty brushed back Darci's hair. "That's why he left everything to you, dear," she said. "He knew you'd have the courage to make choices from your huge heart."

Darci swallowed back tears. "I wish I had answered his phone call."

Betty shook her head. "No, Darci, dear. You weren't meant to, and I think you know that deep down inside. He was supposed to leave you that message. It is his gift—that you now have with you forever and ever to play back and hear his words of love for you whenever you wish."

Darci nodded. "That's the last thing he did say. 'I love you, Darci.'"

Betty took the girl in her arms and comforted her, just as a mother would do. "Love comes in all shapes and sizes and seasons and styles..."

Just then, Leo, fully dressed in his Santa Claus suit finery, came racing into the room, startling both Betty and Darci. In one hand, he carried his own coffee cup while, with the other, he juggled a cardboard tray holding two more Venti cups from Starbucks. He took a sip out of his own cup, swallowed, and let out an exaggerated, "Ahhhhhh!" He then looked at the two women huddled together and sang out, "I'm on time. Here I am all dressed and ready to go! AND I bring gifts! They were out of your peppermint mocha, Betty, but Mmmmmm! Mmmmmm! This gingerbread latte is so worth the calories." He then rubbed his Poly-fil-stuffed bowl-full-of-jelly-like belly. "Swimsuit season is a long ways away."

Betty and Darci looked at Leo, then at one another and roared with laughter.

Later on, a massive crowd gathered at the entrance of Maplefield Mall's food court. Positioned high on a riser at the front, Betty again stood doubling as Mrs. Claus. Seated in a giant-sized, red-velvet throne, Leo was putting on his best imitation of Santa. The pair were playing their parts perfectly, smiling and waving to the adoring crowd surrounding them—one that seemed to keep growing with its numbers already totaling at least a few hundred.

"This is what I wished for," Betty leaned over and whispered into Leo's ear. Her left hand, its ring finger sparkling with a diamond engagement ring, rested on Leo's shoulder.

Leo turned his head to look up at her. Smiling, he reached for her hand and kissed it. Indicating her ring finger, he nodded at it, responding, "I'm glad you finally said 'yes.'"

"I'm glad you finally asked," Betty beamed as she surveyed the crowd, looking for the people she now called her family.

Down below, Ian and Holly stood front and center with their camera crew that now included Karina. When her school schedule permitted, Karina eagerly joined Ian and Holly on location, learning what she could about journalism and reporting the news. Vincent, too, was allowed to help on the weekends and was doing a fine job of keeping passersby out of the camera's view. While Holly videotaped, Ian spoke into the microphone, capturing their B-roll footage before the actual ceremony began.

Betty beamed with pride at Darci who had seamlessly stepped into her role as mall manager. She watched as the young woman, her iPad always in hand, made the rounds, greeting guests and multitasking with directives she periodically gave to staff who approached her with last-minute questions and updates.

Vi and Vern were off to the side, chatting with Damian and Isabelle. Betty saw the group as two sides of the same coin: One couple at the start of their lives together and the other with years of experience in life and love. She also watched Hank and Andrea and reflected on how two people

271

so very different from one another seemed just as perfectly matched as the now-inseparable Rainbow and Pickpocket. The two were on their best behavior for once, curled up together underneath one of the banquet tables.

Betty was also glad to have finally met Mr. Abdullah's wife and six children—oops, correction—seven children. No, wait. She noted the one on the way. Eight children! She was elated to hear the news that they adopted Randy, whom she could now see towering above them all. He was the very favorite elf among all of the little children present.

Harry, Emily, and their twins, Elle and Mack, had become somewhat of permanent fixtures at the mall. Ever since Harry took over new construction plans for mall's expansion, every single storefront was leased. Dozens of businesses were currently on the waiting list to take up shop at the refreshed mall.

And what could she say about Pastor Max? Any thoughts of abandoning the Open Kitchen evaporated over the past year due to the donations and volunteers partnering with him to do good works within his community. Other people's generosity finally allowed him to have a life all his own. This year, Betty couldn't believe it when he told her they had enough financial support to invite 200 children to participate in the Christmas Eve Kids Cheer Fest.

But, in Betty's opinion, the shining surprise of them all had to be Elmer. She watched him shyly stick to the shadows of the room. For so many years, that young man lived so very much alone, homeless, in the belly of this mall. Now, he was really starting to come out of his shell. How she wished she had known earlier what he was going through; maybe she could have helped. But he was too ashamed to share his secret with anyone. Oh, how much had changed for him this past year! She would always think of him as her own Secret Santa, whether or not he was responsible for her annual reappearing Elf on the Shelf.

Betty took the little green elf out of her pocket and sat him back onto the Christmas cactus flower, patting him on the head.

When Betty turned back to face the crowd, Darci looked up at Betty and nodded, saying, "It's time!"

Betty walked up to the microphone and spoke into it. "Can you all hear me?" Her voice echoed throughout the room.

The crowd began to quiet down. She could see Pastor Max, surrounded by the 200 foster kids, his finger to his lips, shushing them.

"Welcome, everyone!" Betty turned to gesture to Leo who was now standing beside her. "Santa and I are so blessed to be here this Christmas Eve with you. As you know, this time last year, we weren't so sure where we'd be. And while this, indeed, is the end to my time serving as the Maplefield Mall Manager, it's only the start of even greater things to come with Darci Timbers taking over. Darci, how about you come up here and join me?"

Leo started the applause that rippled through the crowd and rose to a thunderous beat.

Darci purposefully climbed the steps up onto the stage to stand at Betty's side. She waved at the crowd and, when she reached Betty, she gave her a spontaneous hug.

Betty addressed the audience: "One of the highlights of our year at Maplefield Mall is Pastor Max's Christmas Eve Kids Cheer Fest. Hundreds of children in the foster care system apply to participate and if they keep their grades up, if they stay out of trouble, if they pay it forward with acts of community service, then they may be selected by a team that includes their teachers and counselors to be among the lucky children to attend this event tonight."

The crowd again applauded.

"This year, we have been blessed by several factors that made it possible to host so many kids. There are too many to run through now, but these generous contributors are listed in your program books. And we sincerely thank each and every one of them for their continued support—especially at the holiday season."

Betty paused to allow for the applause. She then continued, "I do want to acknowledge one benefactor in particular, though and, while he is no longer with us, his legacy lives on through his daughter, Maplefield Mall's new manager, Darci Timbers."

Betty whispered, "Darci, would you like to say something about your father?" Betty had no qualms asking Darci to speak publicly about her dad because she could see from her entire demeanor that Darci was at peace with what had happened last year.

"Thank you, Betty." Darci stepped up to the microphone. "My father, Malcolm Wiggins, and I didn't always have the best relationship. If I'm honest, we didn't have much of one at all, due in great part to us losing my mom when I was born. When I was old enough, I changed my last name to her maiden name, partly to remember her, but partly out of spite for him. Hindsight is 20/20, and I wish we both would have handled things differently. But, it's never too late to make things right, something my dad taught me, even in his final hours. He entrusted his life's work to me and challenged me to do with it what best serves the people of this community. I'm very grateful to him for his generosity and faith in me. To that end, we'll be further renovating and expanding here at the mall. In the coming months, not only will you be seeing new shops and eateries but also more programs to foster community engagement and provide neighbor-to-neighbor support."

Betty led the applause. Darci gestured for her to join her at the microphone. Betty was a little unsure of why Darci called her over and when she approached the mic, she simply said what she felt in her heart: "Thank you, Darci. We are so grateful for your father and for you!"

Darci embraced Betty again and then continued addressing the crowd, "Actually, Betty, this mall wouldn't even still be here if not for you and your hard work over the past forty years. You've helped to make this magical mall not just a place to shop but also a place to hold unique experiences that bring people closer together. I, personally, wouldn't be who I am today without your mentorship. My father saw that in you as well."

Betty's face began to take on a reddish hue. She turned to face Leo and mouthed the words, "What's going on?"

He shrugged his shoulders and feigned ignorance, mouthing back, "No clue." But the huge grin on his face put the validity of his response into question.

Pastor Max maneuvered through the crowd and joined them on stage.

Darci continued: "Betty, you have always gone out of your way to champion others, often setting aside your own wants and needs. So, we wanted to give you something to remember us by." Darci nodded over to Randy and waved him forward.

Randy skipped, as any giant elf would do, to the very front of the stage. He then pulled out a dolly hidden behind one of the plush red curtains. Leo covered Betty's eyes with his two hands. Randy wheeled the surprise out, causing the crowd to say, "Oooohhhh! Aaaaaahhhhh!" Positioning the dolly directly in front of Betty, he skipped away, watching excitedly by Karina's side as she and Holly were primed to videotape Betty's reaction to her gifts.

Darci prompted the crowd. "On the count of three." They all counted down with her to the reveal. "One, two, three!"

Leo removed his hands, and Betty looked down at not one, not two, not three or four or five, but an entire seven-piece set of her beloved red leather, vintage Dooney & Bourke bags.

Betty threw her hands up in the air, then brought them back down to rest on her cheeks. "My Dooney & Bourke bag!" She cried out. "This style's been discontinued since…Oh, my! How did you ever find these?"

As the audience clapped, Darci announced even more surprises. "We did a little digging," she said into the microphone. "That bag of yours has quite its own reputation around here. A jolly old Santa told us that it was the first thing you bought yourself with your very first paycheck as mall manager…and that it very well may have been the only splurge you have ever given yourself since."

Betty turned to give Leo a scolding look. He pretended to cower. Noticing the happy tears now falling freely from Betty's eyes, he couldn't keep himself from her any longer. Leo came to her side and wrapped her up in his arms.

"Why?" Betty choked on the word, whispering it into his ear. "That was a secret."

He whispered back, "Some secrets need to be shared."

Darci continued into the microphone. "Betty, we're sending you and Leo on a bon voyage trip to Italy, in celebration of your upcoming wedding and honeymoon!"

Shock registered on Betty's face as she frantically shook her head. "Darci, I can't. I couldn't possibly…"

Darci whispered to her, "Sure you can! Consider it back pay. Dad would have wanted you to have this!"

"This is too, too much! Thank you, everyone!" Betty could barely get the words out as Randy wheeled her new possessions off the stage.

Pastor Max took center stage then. "Oh but wait! There's more! Ginsu knives!" he joked.

Most of the crowd laughed right along with him except the younger members who did not get the reference to the classic TV commercial.

"Betty, over the years, you have made sure to feed our families during the Christmas Eve Kids Cheer Fest," Pastor Max explained. "Last year, for the first year in a long time, that didn't happen. We all know why. However, something else happened instead."

Darci called out over the microphone. "Elmer?" She scanned the room until she spotted him entertaining the twins with Harry and Emily. "Elmer, come up here. This involves you, too!"

Surprised to hear his name, Elmer stood upright, clearly a bit disoriented.

Betty, Leo, Darci, and Pastor Max all pointed to him, waving him to come over. Harry and Emily encouraged him forward. The crowd began stomping their feet and clapping their hands in a wave of celebration, chanting "El-mer, El-mer, El-mer, El-mer, El-mer…!"

As he weaved his way to the stage, Pastor Max continued. "Elmer helped rescue some of us who were trapped in the mall last Christmas Eve. On top of that, he also helped to create a new youth program at the Open Kitchen. He is a real hero in our eyes. So tonight, we're going to continue what he started. We've got those same 50 kids from last year here with us tonight. Let's have them come out."

A parade of familiar foster kids entered the room. Divided into their respective cooking teams, each teen held their team's Christmas culinary creation.

Darci added, "The yummy dishes you'll be eating tonight—and voting on—were created by these impromptu chefs. And, in the first annual

Christmas Eve Kids Fest Cooking Competition, there is, indeed, a prize. Each member of the winning team will receive a $1,000 shopping spree in this mall!"

The crowd applauded. A jubilant Betty beamed at Darci and nodded as she took her place for what would be her last time serving as official mall manager event chair.

"And now," Betty said, reading from a rolled-up holiday scroll, "without further ado, with the release of these balloons, the quest portion of this Christmas Eve Kids Cheer Fest begins. Kids: Catch one balloon, pop it, and inside you'll find your vouchers to exchange for gifts offered to you by participating stores throughout the mall. When you're done shopping, come back here for free gift wrapping, live entertainment, more good eats, and to take your photo with Santa and yours truly. Are you all ready?"

The crowd roared with anticipation. Ian and Holly continued videotaping the fanfare and festivities.

"Release the balloons!"

Darci nodded to the team, and from above, hundreds of balloons and festive-colored confetti floated down to the waiting guests below. Christmas tunes played over the speakers, and Dr. Haywood kicked off the dancing by grabbing Dr. Grey by the hand and twirling her about. Harry and Emily, each with a babe in arms, followed suit.

Ian and Holly, who captured on tape every joyful moment of the day, gathered at Betty's side. As Holly focused her video camera on her, Ian raised the microphone, "Betty, this has to make you so happy, as much as it must be bittersweet."

Not taking her eyes off of the people who were there from all walks of life—at her magical mall—joining together to celebrate, Betty responded, "You know, for so long, all I kept hearing was that malls were mourning their last Christmas's, but I know that Christmas will never end. And, as long as malls like ours continue to be places where people can come together and experience the true meaning of the season all year round, there'll always be cause for celebration. It's like the Christmas cactus that blooms on Christmas Day, or my Elf on the Shelf that mysteriously shows up each year. They're all little miracles and, no matter where they happen, or how or why they do, they just *are*. And I'm so grateful for that. So, I'm leaving my first love—this mall and all of you—in capable hands, for my true love—Mr. Kris Kringle! But I plan to be back at this mall every Christmas. What happens here when we're all together as a family is a miracle, and I wouldn't miss this for the world!"

ABOUT THE AUTHOR

Published author, speaker, podcaster, content producer, and Founder of Madness To Magic, Paolina Milana's mission is to share stories that celebrate the triumph of the human spirit and the power that lies within each of us to bring about change for the better. Her professional background includes telling other people's stories, both as a journalist and a PR and digital media marketing executive. She currently serves as a Court Appointed Special Advocate (CASA) for children in foster care, as well as an empowerment writing coach using storytelling to help people reimagine their lives, write their next chapters, and become the heroes of their own journeys.

Paolina's first book, *The S Word* (She Writes Press, May 2015), earned the National Indie Excellence Award, and soon to be released is its sequel, *Committed: A Memoir of Madness in the Family* (She Writes Press, May

2021). Another title, *Seriously! Are We THERE Yet?!* (October 2020), is the first in her "children's book for adults" self-help series, and *Miracle on Mall Drive* (November 2020) is her first fiction novel. Her free podcast, *I'm with Crazy: A Love Story,* is available on Apple Podcasts.

A proud, first-generation Sicilian, Paolina is married and lives on the edge of the Angeles National Forest in Southern California. She welcomes readers to contact her at powerlina@madnesstomagic.com.